D0818659

THE HEBREW TUTOR OF BEL AIR

THE HEBREW TUTOR OF BEL AIR

ALLAN APPEL

COFFEE HOUSE PRESS • MINNEAPOLIS • 2009

Coffee House Press books are available to the trade through our primary distributor, Consortium Book Sales & Distribution, www.cbsd.com. For personal orders, catalogs, or other information, write to: Coffee House Press, 79 Thirteenth Avenue NE, Suite 110, Minneapolis, MN 55413.

Coffee House Press is a nonprofit literary publishing house. Support from private foundations, corporate giving programs, government programs, and generous individuals helps make the publication of our books possible. We gratefully acknowledge their support in detail in the back of this book.

Good books are brewing at coffeehousepress.org

LIBRARY OF CONGRESS CATALOGING-IN-PUBLICATION DATA
Appel, Allan.
The Hebrew tutor of Bel Air / by Allan Appel.
p. cm.
ISBN-13: 978-1-56689-224-7 (alk. paper)
1. Tutors and tutoring—Fiction.
2. Motorcycles—Fiction.
3. Bel Air (Los Angeles, Calif.)—Fiction.
4. Los Angeles (Calif.)—History—20th century—Fiction.
I. Title.
PS3551.P55H43 2009
813'.54—DC22

ACKNOWLEDGMENTS
I am indebted, as always, to my wonderful wife, Suzanne Boorsch, and to my beloved children, Sophie and Nathaniel. Many thanks also to my friend Rabbi Jim Ponet, who appreciates offbeat Jews; to Allan Kornblum and Coffee House Press for their loyalty through the years; and to Paul Bass, my editor at the *New Haven Independent,* who appreciates novelists as journalists, and therefore lets the novelist flourish.

This book was made possible, in part, through the invaluable support of fellowships in fiction from the Connecticut Commission on Culture & Tourism in 2005 and 2007. An excerpt appeared in the *New Haven Review of Books,* summer 2007.

To the memory of my parents, Morris and Pearl Appel,
and my teacher Dr. David Lieber

THE HEBREW TUTOR OF BEL AIR

CHAPTER ONE

Gentlemen and Ladies: My name is Norman Plummer. You've asked me to describe for you something of my religious background by way of how I see the connection between motorcycling and Judaism in my life. Naturally you want to know some of my autobiography, if I'm a card-carrying rabbi—I'm not—and where I've taught, and what I think of God, and if I'll be the spiritual leader you're seeking for the King Solomon Bikers Club.

Well, the short answer is I haven't been into a synagogue in years, although once, when I was very young, I could recite the entire morning service by heart and get not a vowel of it wrong. Once I knew Amos and Judges so well, I could perform that ancient trick where if you stuck a pin through the pages of those texts, I would tell you all the words it punctured, on all the pages. I kid you not.

As I say, that was a long time ago, and since then I've ridden many miles. In addition to the faith of our own fathers, I've come to appreciate the Buddha and the perfect cheeseburger and everything in between because they, like all that exists in the world, are an expression of the divine.

If you want a traditional rabbi, it's obvious I'm not your guy. However, I've been riding for four decades now, long before the Jewish bike clubs got going, and for me Hebrew prayer and the murmur of the motorcycle engine are almost one and the same sound. I'm going to tell you how this came to be in the story that follows. These pages I'm submitting are my application for the job, no more, no less.

It all began with a box of skullcaps.

There were three types of skullcaps I offered back then: cotton-thin black ones or white ones, and then your third option were these folded paper contraptions that opened up into a box like a fez that the old men wore in the main sanctuary. Few kids selected these, so there was always a good supply, and I rather fancied them myself. When I rubbed the paper ones together, which I did as I awaited customers, they made a *susurrus,* a word I had recently looked up in the dictionary—a low, whispering insect sound.

Much time has passed since that spring and summer of 1963, when handsome young JFK had recently saved us from annihilation, and we said a special prayer at Passover that year too for Martin Luther King, who sounded like one of our own prophets, only black. All in all, we were breathing easier in L.A. that summer because the Russian nuclear warheads would now not land on the interchange where the Harbor, Hollywood, and Pasadena freeways intersected, and melt it like an ice cream cake left in the sun.

Many peoples' lives changed that summer of 1963, and I'm fairly certain mine did also, but it was not because of brave sit-ins or the new Peace Corps or even the prospect of discovering a new world through space travel. No, it seems to me that long-ago assignment, my skullcap distributorship at the temple's Junior Congregation, likely had set the course for my life. Even today, whenever someone walks into a room where I am seated, my impulse is to rise and offer, if not a skullcap, then at least something—in some fashion to serve.

In those days in Los Angeles, when Sandy Koufax kept tossing miraculous no-hitter after no-hitter and Frank Howard's home runs neared five hundred feet, and the Dodgers as a result won game after game all the way through the World Series too, still, I sat or stood just inside the door to the little linoleum-floored room off the main sanctuary, our Junior Congregation, and handed the skullcaps out to latecomers who arrived for the services without the proper headgear.

Dr. Levin, my revered teacher, as well as the rabbi, the cantor, and the other dark-suited men who prowled the halls and classrooms of my religious school, had designated this role for me. They were always looking for ways to set me up as an example for my less studious peers.

Since I could neither sing nor chant, nor read from the Torah, and since my arms were so painfully skinny, and no amount of Weight-On or other products I consumed could reshape them or give me strength enough to hoist the holy scrolls aloft and parade them around our Junior Cong room, I was a problem to honor. And this business of honoring, in my case for being the school's most promising scholar of the L.A. Jewish Diaspora, was not to be taken lightly.

At first they had asked me to give my own little explanation of the section of the Bible we read in the synagogue each week, a kind of mini sermon. I probably could have done that, but it felt more than wrong. For here I was, in my view, hardly more than a pipsqueak of a Hebrew student who merely came on time each day and happened to like decoding the Hebrew words and who loved Dr. Levin's sly smile and his English Leather cologne, and they were asking me, as a result, to interpret the word of God? No, I preferred to stick with my skullcap distributorship.

The girls, entering in their rustling Sabbath dresses, often requested the white cotton variety, which I kept in a pile, neat as a stack of tortillas, in the corner of my box just for them. I especially liked holding them out, with a nod of welcome to Cong, and with a formal but, I hoped, cool gesture of my hand. Then I watched as everyone found seats and Biff Waterman, our Cong president, gave me that special look reserved for us officers, that services were about to begin. We had two sections of seats, all wooden and uncomfortable, although they did recline slightly. Ed, my dad, thought Biff's father had made a mistake picking them up for Junior Cong. It was in a salvage sale, Biff said, from a movie theater going out of business because the streetcar service bringing customers nearby had ended in L.A. that March of '63, after nearly a hundred years. Ed knew that theater and often went there, he said, between calling on his mysterious customers. Once he even threatened to return the seats.

Like much else in his life that he promised, however, Ed didn't follow through, and the seats, creaky and hard-backed, but with burgundy-colored velour cushions on which a pressed finger could make interesting patterns, all remained, as did I.

I remember vividly how the others prayed in that particular way of young teens—glancing up fitfully and often to see what people were wearing or who was mimicking the intense devotional praying style of Dr. Levin. My imagination conjured them fidgeting a herky-jerky mixture of traditional waist-bending *davening* with the dance moves of a new English singer, Mick Jagger. Biff often worked up quite a sweat, while the girls, now rustling rather noisily, watched him and occasionally giggled. All the while I kept my watch by the box. Praying made me uncomfortable, as did making fun of Dr. Levin, and the skullcap box and the responsibilities it entailed offered me exemption.

My other job, a more familial role of honor, happened at home each Friday evening. There, with my back propped against our elephant-foot sofa, polka-dotted green, within earshot of my mother, Esther, so that she could appreciate the incredibly mature and ingratiating phone manner I was developing, I left messages for my friends to show up, please, at Junior Cong services the following morning.

The mothers seemed to have all the time in the world to chat with me, such a well-spoken young man they were happy to think their child was friends with. It was my fate, I suppose, to get to know many of the mothers better than I knew the kids themselves. Every time someone stood before me to receive a skullcap, I looked at him and heard his mother's voice.

Ed called my checklist my hit list and would regularly do a commentary that included, Got another sucker? and that was when, as if on schedule, Esther would tell him to shut up with that stuff. Despite the razzing, which I also received and dished back at Junior Cong, I somehow felt Ed and Esther needed me to keep calling and distributing. Yes, Ed and Esther—from as far back as I could remember I was more comfortable calling my parents by their first names. A psychologist I once met riding in the Rockies said it was just a strategy to make believe Ed and Esther were not really my parents; he may well have been right.

When Dr. Levin set me up in the back of the room during the quarter-hour break he took Tuesday and Thursday afternoons, I had what amounted to my *third* unpaid job for the Jewish people, tutoring my classmates who just weren't fathoming the intricacies of Hebrew. I certainly did not think that Levin was going out to the payphone in the hall to call his bookie or broker, as some alleged. He was the saintly and always pleasantly cologned Michael Levin, with an alabaster complexion and three slightly curling nose hairs, in a face that reminded me of a fluffy Jewish cat. Was he not simply going outside to pray the afternoon service because he sensed, and rightly so, that turning his back on us (as he had done before) to pray in an East-facing corner of the classroom, bending rapidly up and down from the waist while reciting his mile-a-minute prayers, was mildly distracting? I had not yet become Ed's cynical son and was certain Levin was clean as the driven snow. Proof was the white stuff began to fall once while I was covering as he *davened* away in the hall. Clearly Levin had summoned this meteorological miracle to L.A. entirely through the fervor of his prayer.

The bar mitzvahs of Biff Waterman and most of my Junior Cong pals that soon followed—a long season of these Jewish confirmations that launched several catering businesses of the mothers whom I'd gotten to know—were incredibly lavish affairs, as they were universally referred to. They were caricatures of American Jewish life that will therefore go undescribed here, except to say this: that while the expenditure of thousands per bar mitzvah marked the boys' formal entrance into the adult Jewish community, the almost immediate reaction from my friends was a total termination, with glee, of their formal Jewish education and regular attendance at Cong. However, many still came, on occasion, to hang out with me by the box of skullcaps.

I took a different path. By this I don't mean to imply a kind of pride or that I sat down one day and formally chose, because sometimes—actually more often than not—we just drift to our destiny. My own coming-of-age ceremony was in every aspect, and especially as compared with friends', precisely the old-fashioned discount end of the bar mitzvah party market, the genuine non-affair that I had expected from Ed and Esther—as well as, religiously, a completely bland and unremarkable event occasioned by my inability to sing or chant. Still, the bar mitzvah launched me into a next phase of serious Jewish education, which I absorbed with a kind of delirious, guilty joy.

Offered a full scholarship, I enrolled in the local Hebrew high school, which met on two weekday afternoons at the temple and then on Sunday mornings—Sunday mornings, when, Biff told me, anyone in his right mind should be sleeping groggily after the parties, then roll out of bed no earlier than noon, and then go up to Dodger Stadium early to get the autographs of Junior Gilliam, Don Drysdale, and Maury Wills.

On such bright and promising Sundays, Hebrew High convened up in Hollywood. Still too young to drive, I traveled on the bus with the Talmudic tractate *Baba Metzia* under one arm, an encyclopedia of baseball statistics under the other, my nose bearing my cool, new black glasses practically touching the sports page photo of Koufax, which I somehow also managed to hold. Koufax, our living Jewish god, who having struck out ten batters—ten!—at last night's game against the Giants, smiled at me in that bond of the Jewish sports star with the uncoordinated Jewish scholar-child that never ruptures through all time and eternity. Amen.

Feeling in a kind of perfect balance back then, I read in the quiet, bumpy thrall of a force I am not sure I understand even today.

After twenty minutes or so on the bus up Fairfax, we turned right just beyond Paramahansa Yogananda's Self-Realization Fellowship, passed in front of Tiny Naylor's drive-in restaurant, with the succulent aroma of its profoundly non-kosher curly fries calling to me like an olfactory siren, and then onto Sunset. Seven stops later on Sunset—I counted—I pulled on the bell cord, then hoisted my briefcase and myself out at Wilcox, and beheld the nine-floor, white stuccoed tower of the Hollywood Health Club. The seventh floor was rented by the University of Judaism, in whose lower division, as it were, L.A.'s Hebrew High convened, and there I spent the morning and early afternoon studying Hebrew language and history, the Bible, and the Talmud.

The murmuring of my Talmud study partners—I remember an Israeli who kept lifting up his T-shirt to show me on his belly his scars from the 1948 war and also an unhappy Orthodox boy from Venice named Sandor, who frequently brought me a cold stuffed sweet cabbage to nibble on during our break. Then there were the thuds, flops, and occasional grunting expletives of the weightlifters penetrating our classrooms from the health club above. Yet somehow all this seemed an appropriate acoustic mix, the soundtrack for my introduction to Jewish law, and I was flourishing.

Inspired, I wrote a muscular poem about the heroic founding of the State of Israel, which I more or less plagiarized from Tennyson's "Charge of the Light Brigade." My teachers didn't seem to notice or care about my adaptation; my guess is that there were not too many entrants in the contest. For it I won a prize, a large framed map of Israel and an apron with the same map on it that I proudly presented to Esther. Bible became my favorite subject, and in the Book of Amos I found a haunting voice that seemed somehow to sound like my own, only three thousand years older.

I memorized large sections of Amos. He experienced an earth-quake that he described in the first lines, and shortly after we stud-ied it, we experienced our own, a whopper on the Richter scale that threw all the toys off the high shelf, caused a crack in the L.A. River aqueduct, and tilted me out of bed. A "great noise" meant God was angry and I sensed I just might be too, but, unlike God, I didn't quite know it and certainly didn't have a tectonic outlet.

Amos knew that leopards could not change their spots or Negroes their skin—Amos called them Cushites—and, were we ever learning that too. After Bull Connor turned dogs on kids my age in Birmingham, with Ed pulling me along proudly to the rally and saying, This way to the future, kid, we demonstrated with the Congress of Racial Equality out in Westwood. The essay I wrote about it, said my English teacher, was the best she'd ever read.

The following Sunday I gobbled up Micah and Hosea and Joel. I read and re-read them all that April, May, and June of '63, and even signed up for one of those summer enrichment programs at both my schools, Hebrew and English. Books, books, books, and I was nice to every Negro I met, the way Ed was. The world, at least for a brief moment, all made sense then, my place in it along-side King and Kennedy and Dr. Levin and the Minor Prophets of Israel, whom I loved then and still do.

The prophets were like short, ancient, paperback books writ-ten by very pissed-off authors, always outraged, even scared, looking over their shoulder, with no time to linger, and had there been bikes then, theirs would have been waiting nearby, I have no doubt, engine on and purring, for a quick getaway into those Judean hills. The Minors, with not a word or breath to spare, especially got to their righteous points quickly, were easy to read, and you also could make silly rhymes out of some of their names: Habbakuk.

So it was a red-letter day for me, though hardly surprising, when as school was just beginning to wind down, in late April, I announced to my proud parents the news that finally I had been offered my first paying job with the Jewish people. Twelve bucks a session, it was agreed upon by me and Levin, who made the arrangements on my behalf. Twelve dollars sounded like a fortune, and in cash no less. Unlike any of the kids, he knew how poor my parents really were, how sketchy Ed's gambling livelihood was, or as he diplomatically put it, how "modest" we were compared to most people in our very upwardly mobile community.

Dr. Levin also knew our 1956 Plymouth was more often than not broken down, the mechanic refusing to release it to Ed until the entire repair bill was paid. This made carlessness a semi-regular condition for us, no small matter in farflung L.A., because Ed often insisted on paying only half until he test-drove the vehicle after every repair. When I assured Dr. Levin I could provide my own transportation—I was sixteen by then and could drive, both the surface roads and the freeways, in a used car of my own that an uncle had helped me buy—the deal was sealed.

All I had to do was one afternoon a week drive up to Bel Air to work with one Bayla Adler, daughter of a family that was making a killing in nursing homes. It was very much a growth industry, Ed explained to me after I had summarized the offer. My father thoughtfully put down the pages of his *Los Angeles Times,* which usually curtained his face from his arrival home to dinner time, and scrutinized me oddly, as if the two of us had suddenly become business partners.

The country's entire elderly population, Ed elaborated with an impressive expertise I didn't know he possessed, was now slipping down toward us in the L.A. basin, where life was easy, the ocean was a bus ride away, and there was rarely any snow to shovel. I'd invest in the business myself, he said, if I had any money.

As Ed went on enthusiastically about the rights of the elderly and infirm, and his latest scheme to invest in a pneumatic device to raise and lower the entry steps of buses—this, mind you, in a town where nobody but Ed and the cleaning people rode them— he began to gesticulate so infectiously, pointing beyond our living room and me and out our dusty picture window. It was as if he were, for the briefest instant, transformed into some living-room minor prophet himself.

And I too began to imagine all America, from Nevada east to the Atlantic, somehow arrayed on one three-thousand-mile chaise longue, of the kind we had on our patio. It tipped directly toward L.A., so that people were rolling, night and day, directly into the receiving docks of the Adlers' nursing homes. There they were scooped up by Bayla, whom I imagined to be a huge cartoon sort of girl, in overalls, and with immense muscles, like a female version of the wrestler Haystack Calhoun. After she caught the elderly, she would tuck them into freshly made white-sheeted beds at her parents' nursing homes. There they would live in a kind of L.A.-happy-ever-after, just like Charlie's grandparents in *Charlie and the Chocolate Factory*, thus forever financing this fantastic money-making Hebrew tutoring job that was about to begin for me.

Ed said I should have held out for fifteen an hour. I was just too nice a guy, he went on, a tendency I would have to be careful not to indulge seeing that I was now in business.

I'm not in business. I'm just a Hebrew tutor, Dad.

You're Norman Plummer. My kid. Don't put yourself down. Money is money. After a month, ask for a raise.

I haven't even met them yet.

Don't sell yourself short. After two weeks is o.k. too.

Dad.

And polish your shoes. A first impression is very important.

CHAPTER TWO

My car was a 1954 Hudson, a white two-door tank that I bought
despite Ed's objections. I thought it was exceptionally cool except
that it leaked oil a bit—actually about a pint every twenty-five
miles. Embarrassed that his far more well-to-do brother had
financed it, Ed always provided me with a dozen cans of motor oil
in the trunk, just in case. Unlike my friends and their fathers, Ed
and I really knew nothing about cars except that like water to a
throat, oil was good for them. The Hudson's impressive leak gave
us a manly conversation topic and me regular opportunity to pull
to the side of the road, carefully roll my sleeves up, taking much
more time than necessary (just in case any kids from school were
driving by then), and, finally, stick my head and arms beneath the
Hudson's hood, appearing, should anyone happen to see me, a
regular guy with mechanical know-how.

I also kept my books, pencils, and worksheets with Hebrew exer-
cises in a red milk crate next to the box of cheap 10-40, the jack,
and the spare tire. I should have moved them to the back seat out
of respect because some of the books had blessings and other texts
with God's name in them. But I liked how they were either stained
a little by the motor oil or smelled of how the world worked.

If you run into any other Hebrew tutors in Bel Air, he said to
me that first morning of my work, unionize.

I believed my parents were, you see, just about the only poor
Jews in Los Angeles, except for the man on the corner who sold us

the daily newspaper. This extraordinarily short and rumpled man was named Benjy, and I remember deliberately stretching myself to tower over him, which I could do by the time I was ten, then feeling bad about it. I sensed there was something wrong that a grown man was called by a diminutive kid's name, but everyone called him Benjy, and I followed along.

He always wore the same clothes, even in the hot weather: a slightly too-roomy brown tweed suit, dingy white shirt, and broad brown tie so loosely and badly knotted that even I, a novice at the complexities of the Windsor, was at times tempted to redo it for him. Benjy also had a strange, out-of-focus way of looking at people. It scared me, and I was glad he had a habit of keeping his cap pulled low over his forehead, obscuring his rolling left eye. When you put the coins in his hand, his *thank you, thank you* and brief comments about the weather or how the Dodgers really had a chance for a pennant that year were an odd string of crumpled syllables that sounded neither English, nor Yiddish, but a kind of international gibberish, the secret language, I thought, of spies or madmen.

I avoided the newsstand as much as possible. It was especially disturbing to me how friendly my father was with Benjy, hailing him heartily each time we walked by, urging him to come out from behind his piles of newspapers and magazines, and slapping him on the back, after every transaction, Benjy, my old buddy.

I often had tried suggesting to my father that Benjy was really from Venus, the evidence being not only his rolling eye, but also a third eye, likely to be found in his forehead. That was why he was always pulling his hat low over his brow, the way I had seen it done in a *Twilight Zone* episode. He was just concealing his interplanetary identity until it was time to do his Benjy part to take over the earth.

Are you nuts?

Listen, Ed, I said to my father, as I summarized the episode that had gripped me as much as the prophecies of Amos: There's this roomful of passengers at a roadside diner. They're there because their bus broke down at the same time that a flying saucer may have landed in a field nearby. The cops think the aliens are trying to avoid detection by mingling with the bus passengers. So you begin to wonder who the alien in the room is. Well, it turns out not to be one of the passengers but the soda jerk, who, at the very end of the program slowly pulls the white cap up over his forehead revealing his third eye, just like Benjy.

He's Jewish, said my father. Believe me.

He's from Venus.

Then there are Jews on Venus.

Forget Benjy.

You see where scholarship leads? said my mother.

To nursing homes, said Ed.

Bel Air, my mother replied, with an almost girlish lilt in her voice I had never heard before. Bel Air.

Then she went to look in one of her magazines, which she carefully collected in order to follow the lives of the movie stars, some of whom, according to her sources, lived near where I was soon about to be gainfully employed.

Never mind that the family of Bayla Adler was Hollywood star caliber only in location and probably their wealth. Esther pored over her map, coordinated the address I had on the sheet of paper I'd been handed by Dr. Levin, and, after considerable study, determined that the Adlers lived right there, right where the mansion of Paulette Goddard, the great star of the early cinema, had stood. It was likely the very place!

They own nursing homes, Mom.

Bel Air, my mother kept repeating. Bel Air. Beautiful Air. Bel Air, as if the words were magical, like from an opera, or, better yet, a movie. You're the Hebrew tutor of Bel Air, they both kept saying to me. Don't knock it.

So I was not surprised on my way to that first session with Bayla that I allowed some of Ed and Esther's excitement to seep in. I still remember the date, April 23, just a week or so after we'd relived our liberation from slavery in Egypt, and I was on my way to Bel Air.

Come on, come on, I whispered to the engine. I'll give you a big drink of oil later, but now, come on! I hadn't allowed enough time, I was hurrying, and I coaxed the Hudson as fast as I could, west toward the beach. I visored my eyes with one hand and eased my foot up and down on the accelerator, understanding, finally, how Sunset Boulevard got its name: because it actually took you directly out, it seemed, to exactly where the sun set itself down in the sea like a great melting orange.

Who wouldn't want to hurry to see that! People in bright quick cars heading for the beaches, some with boards strapped on top to catch a wave or two before dark, zipped by me in lanes on either side. With so much oil leaking, I couldn't safely make much more than thirty-five miles an hour, and the normally noisy engine was really grinding.

Still, I didn't mind. Just a few miles to go, there in the distance was Bel Air, and beyond that the Pacific Ocean where you could launch yourself all the way to China and Japan, and, in the meantime, I was going to my first real job. The tight-jawed feeling I often had in the lower part of my face, which made my mother scold me not to grind my teeth but to show my smile more often, eased up. Ten minutes later, full of enthusiasm and purpose, despite oil and traffic, I arrived quite nearly on time.

As I parked, I noticed a curved driveway, lined by small saguaros. I opened the trunk and tucked my tutoring materials under my arm for the first Hebrew lesson with Bayla Adler. I felt like a real worker: a guy who did his job not just with his brain, but also with his hands, the kind of guy my father admired, a real working man.

CHAPTER THREE

It was a large house, pinkish in the light of the setting sun, with palms gently waving like hula skirts. The far wings rose up into a turreted second floor, not unlike the medieval castles, surrounded by robber-infested forests, that I used to build. Here the whole magical place was plunked down in a desert by the sea.

Two longer wings ran off farther, toward a green-hedged garden on the left, and, on the right, the flickering blue light of what had to be a pool. Over the central section of the house rose a tower, looking neither municipal nor ecclesiastical, but more like a mix of the two, as if created on a movie set by someone who hadn't seen either in a long time.

As I formulated how I should introduce myself—Hi, I'm the Hebrew tutor. Or, with more formality: Good afternoon, I'm a student of Dr. Levin. Is this is the home of Miss Bayla Adler? I extended my finger and leaned on the bell. It didn't ring, it chimed. Then, before I could compose myself to deliver my lines, even before the reverberating notes had receded into the house's interior, the door swung open, as if a person might have been waiting there all along.

You must be Norman, the answerer said.

Right.

Here was a woman, tall and stately, and whose features I could at first barely make out because she was standing in the shadows of her vestibule. Here, if my mother were right, Paulette Goddard and other stars had elegantly leaned on door jambs, just as this woman was now, in the glamorous decades of yore. The woman was now asking me my Hebrew name.

Before I could reply, she said, No! Let me guess: Nehemiah?

Right again.

Well do come in. Nehemiah who led the Jews back from exile in Babylon.

I think so. Yes.

You're not certain?

The very one.

Well, your task, young man, will be to bring my daughter back from *her* exile. Do you think you can do it?

I'll certainly try.

I'm referring to the exile of ignorance of our traditions.

Oh *that,* I said. Sure. I surprised myself with a self-confidence that seemed to speak with a voice of its own, without having consulted me. I can do that.

Good, then. Bayla's all set. She's just a little younger than you, I'd guess, almost sixteen, you know. I'm sure Michael Levin told you all that.

Yes, he did.

She's been fighting bat mitzvah as if it were a painful operation. You're going to change all that.

Right. If you say so.

I do say so, Nehemiah. Now, she's waiting for you at the dining room table, with pencils I sharpened myself. Would you like a cold drink before you begin?

No, thank you.

Perhaps some milk and cookies? Oreos? Fig Newtons? Or my personal favorite, Mallomars? They're kosher now, you know.

No, it's all right.

You'll need all your strength. Are you sure?

When I hesitated, she said, The dining room's that way. Why don't you go and introduce yourself to Bayla, and I'll bring the cookies in shortly after. You might find you're hungry later or need some energy. How's that?

Great . . . Mrs. Adler?

Well, of course. Who else could you possibly think I was?

Mrs. Adler was not only tall but thin, model thin, with a clear and oval face that I by then could make out, and with a nose and cheeks that appeared—to the eyes of someone who had gotten an A minus in his first art history course at Los Angeles High School—downright classical. She also had very white skin, like John Singer Sargent's *Madame X,* and large, haunting dark eyes. What I remember most after all these years was how she exuded a perfume, green and slightly tangy, like the jasmine at day's end that sometimes drifted into my bedroom from the garden of our neighbors, the Nefussis, Greek Jews, whose house was just beyond the hedge that lined our driveway.

Nursing homes or not, Mrs. Adler had the looks and scent of a star.

Go on now, Mrs. Adler was saying to me. What are you staring at?

And now it registered with me for the first time that she also had a trace of an accent, a European accent.

Don't just stand there, Nehemiah. By the waters of Babylon the exile awaits you. Then she added with a fetching smile on her pretty face, which, like everything else here, seemed perfectly organized: I've heard superb things about you from Michael Levin, and I've left your money right there on the table, as an inspiration. Believe me, you'll need it. See you in a minute.

How to describe my first sighting of Bayla? She sat at the far end of a sleek wooden expanse, a table with three or maybe four leaves, whose deep shine seemed to go on and on. It struck me that this was not a table, such as we sat at, but The Table, an important gathering place, where captains of the expanding nursing-home industry or, before them, movie producers might have met to discuss matters of utmost importance, which most certainly did not include Hebrew tutoring. I thought that after this first session maybe I would ask for a more intimate space to work.

Although she remained seated, I guessed Bayla was not tall—maybe five feet two at most. Yet as I neared where she sat statue-still at the far end of The Table, she somehow grew, or enlarged her presence for me. Her hair was dark and cut in perfect bangs, framing a very white face, the color of flour. She possessed solid shoulders too, and appeared, except perhaps for the alabaster complexion, nothing at all like her tall, svelte mother. Here was a compact young athlete in resigned repose but also, I sensed, wanting to be elsewhere, in action, perhaps on a running track, or dashing across a green field with a hockey stick in her hand, anywhere but at a boardroom table fiddling with a sharp yellow pencil and awaiting a Hebrew tutor.

Only her eyes seemed to follow me as I neared. I thought I could hear Bayla Adler's heart resounding in that space, or maybe it was the beating of my own. I don't think I would have been surprised if she had thrown the pencil at me for target practice, or suddenly flung the chair out behind her, and lunged forward to tackle me. However, she remained seated and silent as I nervously unpacked my stuff, and the whole vast place radiated with her antagonism. It was otherwise exceptionally quiet in that room, like the huge refectory hall of a castle, but empty of all knights and ladies and servants, except for Bayla and me. Finally:

Hiya.

Bayla said nothing.

My name's Norman.

Nothing.

You're Bayla. Happy to meet you, Bayla. I'm going to work with you on your Hebrew language skills. It should be fun.

Liar. She spoke.

No, it really will. I extended my hand. She didn't even look at it. I'm happy to meet you.

No you're not. You're doing it for the money.

That's . . . not true.

No? It's always about money, you liar. Twice a liar.

There was a pattering of high heels beyond the dining room, and I was suddenly grateful for Oreos, or whatever Mrs. Adler was about to bring our way.

Just remember, Bayla said, dropping her voice into a low, hushed new octave, confidential and threatening, whatever I say when she can hear it is coerced. You know what *coerced* means, Hebrew tutor?

I nodded.

How do you say *coerced* in Hebrew?

I don't know.

How do you say *prisoner* in Hebrew?

I don't know that one either.

Then what can you teach me?

CHAPTER FOUR

When we concluded that first session, in which Bayla refused to utter even one Hebrew word, I felt, from my waist up, filmed in sweat. My shirt was drenched. I thought both Bayla and Mrs. Adler would hear me as I rose from the chair sounding as if a strip of adhesive tape were being removed from my back.

Although Mrs. Adler had re-entered precisely an hour after she had delivered the tray of cookies and milk, which was mostly still untouched, it felt as if she'd been away half the day. Now she interposed her perfumed self between us. She draped one of her long arms over my shoulder, leaned in, and peered at the notebook where I had printed out the Hebrew letters in block and in script. Bayla, instead of copying them, had spent the time writing beside each letter, in elegant but mock-Hebrew script, a single word in English for each of the letters of the Hebrew alphabet I had been intending to teach her: *bullshit, bullshit, bullshit. Aleph, bet, gimmel bullshit.* I was certain my career as a Hebrew tutor was over before it had begun.

I'm really sorry.

Please, Nehemiah, Mrs. Adler said. You've done very well.

I have?

Bayla is still here, isn't she? And you too. Progress comes one step at a time, Nehemiah. Many of the others didn't even last this first hour.

I'm sorry?

Bayla didn't tell you?

Bayla folded her hands neatly on the table and looked away from her mother with a triumphant gaze out toward the pool.

One we sent screaming back to Poland, Bayla finally said.

Lithuania, Mrs. Adler corrected.

Who cares where he came from! His beard turned white and his artificial leg, where he had carved the Hebrew alphabet, suddenly snapped and broke and he nearly had to crawl back to his car. I refused even to help him.

Bayla's got a vivid imagination.

So now they're trying young ones. I bet you couldn't grow a beard if you wanted to.

All right, dear.

It's all true, *Mother*, and you know it.

There was something about the ridicule that Bayla loaded onto the word *mother*. She seemed to take a long, delicious time for it to be fully pronounced. It was like mustard on a hot dog.

She didn't tell you, did she, Hebrew tutor? But you are in a long line of my failed instructors. I'm thinking of sending a letter to the Guinness Book of World Records. World's most incorrigible Hebrew pupil. Your moment will come too, and you'll be part of the evidence on my application.

Oh, Nehemiah, don't trouble yourself, Mrs. Adler said. You've done a good job. Bayla is being positively charming, chatting away like a genuinely civilized member of the species. Anyway, I'm sure some of the basics have sunk in, even if she hasn't done her written work properly. She'll admit to that.

No, she won't, Bayla said.

Good then.

May I go now, Mother?

Say goodbye to Nehemiah. And tell him you're looking forward to seeing him next week.

Goodbye, Nehemiah. That's all I'm going to say. And by the way, what the hell is with this Nehemiah stuff! That's so stupid. His name is Norman.

I don't care what you call me.

No, as long as we pay you.

That will be quite enough, Bayla.

I'm the child of gamblers—a card and horse player on the pater-nal side—and Esther, while she put down Ed's gambling habits, herself played bingo several nights a week and on Sundays, but always, she added, only with the sisterhood in the basement of the temple, directly under Junior Cong's room. Why do I tell you this? Until I learned better as an adult, I considered the game of bingo, like the dietary laws, practically a formal part of Judaism.

I was therefore not in the habit of refusing cash that was laid on the table before me. Still, at the end of that first hour working with Bayla, a qualm arose and seized me: I told Mrs. Adler I couldn't accept the money.

No, please take it, she said, and she moved the four crisp bills—two fives and two ones—near to where my hand dangled at the edge of the table. Not that I didn't want the money, and not that I thought I hadn't earned it, because I had really ransacked my ingenuity to overcome Bayla's resistance. I had tried to use my sev-enteen-year-old charm, such as it was, fashioning the Hebrew let-ters into little animals, like the camel on bent knee from which the third letter, *gimel,* derives. I had turned the *bet* into a house and suggested that Bayla add the final wall. To teach the vocalization of the vowel sounds, I had made bird noises, turning myself into some absurd Hebrew cuckoo to amuse her.

Still, I hadn't broken through and felt I couldn't take the twelve dollars.

We'll just keep it for you, if you insist, said Mrs. Adler. These very bills, until next time.

Yet Bayla, who glanced quickly my way, was trying to tell me something. Her eyes were the same poker eyes I recognized in Ed some nights when he came home happy with the tale of a few win-ning hands. And I knew that Bayla knew what I was doing was only a strategy. Refusing the twelve dollars was my way to restore a little esteem, for myself and, yes, to firm up an impression with her mother. But it was obvious it would not work with Bayla. Refusing to utter a single Hebrew sound, making me squirm by revealing my mercenary heart, she had won the whole first round. And yet, as I drove slowly toward home, returning along Sunset, I felt oddly happy.

As soon as I entered, I sensed my parents' eagerness. They had to know how it had gone with Bayla Adler. My father sat behind his paper perusing the race results and the stocks, and Esther busied herself in the kitchen dicing onions for salmon croquettes. The little orange patties speckled with pimento, onion, and celery were one of the few things she cooked that I really liked and looked forward to. It was to be my reward dinner.

As I settled in, Ed lowered his paper several times, allowing me more than the usual furtive audience as I sat nearby and began doing my homework. They weren't going to be the first to ask, and I wasn't going to divulge voluntarily.

The silence, which was often the consequence of these you-go-first standoffs, filled up our small house with a crackling gray atmosphere. Ed finally folded his paper and lay down on the sofa with an oh-my-aching-bones groan. He reached up and clicked on the oversized radio that sat like a shiny, rectangular mound of Jell-O on the adjacent table. With its magenta tuning dials beneath a display that read *Berlin, Warsaw, London, Paris, Vienna*, the radio always amazed me when current news emerged from it, and in English: It seemed Krushchev had announced the Russians had a hundred-megaton nuclear bomb, but Kennedy, who'd taken care of those nuclear missiles in Cuba, would surely protect us again. They were playing chicken with each other and everyone knew it. Kennedy wouldn't allow us to be vaporized. No way, José. I liked Kennedy, and I was tremendously proud of how everyone had cheered for him in Berlin. He was my kind of guy. We both had cowlicks that were hard to tame. He was young and I was young, and we both wanted to live and play more touch football and not be fried or crushed in a thermal pulse. Sure, it was scary. The nuclear clock was ticking loudly, but still the parents wanted to know about the tutoring.

Our dining room table suddenly came into a dismal focus I had not experienced before: Suddenly I was at a meager square, a mere nothing of a table by comparison to Bayla Adler's, and, moreover, it was littered with all kinds of junk strewn across a really cheesy, stained oilcloth covering. Worse, directly in front of my cleared homework area was an enormous, cut-glass punch bowl where Ed had a habit of tossing all the unpaid bills, circulars, and scratch sheets. This bowl, which had been one of their wedding gifts, could have provided beverage for fifty. Yet I don't think we ever had, all totaled, a half dozen friends, that is, non-relatives, who visited us in our little house to drink from it, never enough for a real party. What wonderful punch we could have made, if the bowl were not so deeply misused. I suddenly hated the bowl, and a lot more; it represented everything wrong in my life. It was nothing but a crystal wastebasket sitting there before me, a centerpiece telling me how *everything* was so shabby and sad.

Next to the bowl, and positioned with a thoughtless asymmetry that also began to irritate me, was a lazy Susan that had once been made of attractive blond wood but that now was cast in sudden, severe light. Its adhesive label said it had been made in Ceylon. I loved the irony of lazy Susan's name, and Ceylon was a faraway place from which I had collected several heavily cancelled stamps and that I was one day determined to visit. But the lazy Susan's neat compartments, which should have held coconut pudding mix, onion dip, and exotic Ceylonese condiments for the parties we never had, were, alas, crammed with packets of poker chips and decks of cards unusable because maybe they had six tens or maybe only three kings. This was the overflow parking for more of Ed's junk mail and for his old horseracing forms.

I decided to pick up my books and finish my homework in my bedroom.

What's wrong? Esther asked. Not enough light?

The light was fine.

Turn off the radio, Ed. Our professional tutor can't concentrate.

I clicked the door behind me, sat down at the desk, and tried to continue to work. Yet I kept thinking of that strange girl. Then, feeling guilty, as if my parents would really interpret my leaving badly, I got up. As I opened the door, I was surprised to hear the rustle of the *L.A. Times.* I followed Ed, who was now retreating into the dining room. I had no intention of letting him get away with it.

What's with the surveillance, Dad?

It's a small house, son. A person has to pass by on the way to the can.

I see. So you're not spying on me?

The Russians are spying on us. We're spying on them. I'm not spying on you.

You can tell us or not tell us, Esther called from the kitchen.

No matter what room in the house she stood in, she was right beside you. Always.

I leaned in the doorway, assessing my next move. I was dressed in shorts and the long tube-style athletic socks I then favored. They rose nearly up to my knees; still I reached down and yanked one up even higher. I crossed my right foot over my left, casual as a shoeless tennis player who had just won a match and now stood relaxing and bantering in the clubhouse.

There's nothing much to report. It went well. It went O.K.

O.K. then, Ed said. He says O.K. That's all we need to know.

Fine, Esther said. We'll eat soon. You'll tell us everything over dinner. The both of you, don't forget to wash your hands.

Maybe it was all the TV coverage of Birmingham that distracted— or inspired—her, but at our next session, and definitely by early

May, Bayla's resistance had spread and deepened. She said that she had no interest in learning Hebrew because she did not have a bat mitzvah at age thirteen, and she had no intention of doing it now. No matter how often her parents guilt-tripped her about the million boys and girls in Europe who were killed before they even had a chance to have a bar or bat mitzvah, she was determined to resist.

It's not my fault what happened to them. Sure, I feel really sorry, O.K. So I'll dedicate my *non*-bat mitzvah to them.

I listened to her in a state of astonishment, or awe, or disgusted disbelief, or some other emotion I could not yet identify.

That's what you told your parents?

Yes.

And what did they do?

They walked out of the room.

This was a moment for a different tack: If you don't go through with a bat mitzvah this time, you'll put me out of business before I begin.

She continued to make my hour with her grudging, difficult, and awkward, but I began to have a certain respect for Bayla's resistance. Being the Hebrew tutor, I of course could not say this in so many words, yet I allowed it to be seen. I continued to teach, and she watched me or scribbled or drew caricatures of my face. I complimented her on her art and encouraged her to use her obvious talent and intelligence to master the relatively easy task at hand, and to put us both out of our misery. I tutored and she ignored me, but, still, some kind of accommodation was reached.

However, the basic groundwork for Hebrew literacy, which was my assigned task, was certainly not being laid, and I began to worry that if Bayla didn't make at least a little progress, I would really be let go. Yet her mother, attentive as ever with the cookies, and keeping our schedule, apparently never quizzed her or checked up on us, as I was certain she was going to do, and she never once criticized my primitive pedagogy. A handsome young

Nehemiah, as she once put it, was tutoring Bayla, and she seemed content enough with that, for now.

We soon began to spend a good part of our hour together talking about school and teachers and eventually about our parents. I learned that Lucille, that is, Mrs. Adler, was Bayla's stepmother.

I think she's good in bed with my father. A real trophy wife, if you know what that means, Hebrew tutor.

I did, I guess, or I thought I did at the time. Actually I wasn't sure how much Bayla herself understood of what she was saying. I thought she might simply be out to shock me.

You're supposed to honor your parents, I responded or—since memory of that stage of life usually makes us look better to ourselves—what I actually might have uttered then was more likely some pathetic riff I concocted on the spot, a medley of clichés and nervous stammering: You're supposed to honor your father and your mother, Bayla. I don't think the Ten Commandments make a distinction between fathers and mothers and stepfathers and stepmothers.

I might even have written out the commandment to honor your father and your mother in Hebrew block letters running up and down an outline of an ornate tablet. After all, Bayla liked drawing.

Bayla leaned toward me, quickly took in my handiwork, and then studied me. It was as if my face were now her text. I'm sure only seconds went by, but it felt a lot longer.

What a load of crap, she finally said.

I did not argue the point.

CHAPTER FIVE

When I arrived for the fourth session—I believe it was the second week in May—Mrs. Adler was not there. Bayla herself greeted me in the darkened vestibule, wearing a tight suede skirt and white blouse. She was barefoot too. Late afternoon light poured down in shafts from a set of triangular skylights I had not noticed before. They filled the vestibule with a kind of golden crisscross that slanted over Bayla's breasts. Adolescent though they were, they formed enough of a valley where I saw a delicate chain with a piece of jewelry lying in glistening repose. It was no Star of David.

You can close your mouth, Hebrew tutor. It's a whale's tooth.

I thought it was a cross.

Oh, don't you start policing me too. What do you want to drink?

Without waiting for my answer, she turned, and I followed. I thought she would turn right, toward the kitchen, from which our refreshments usually emerged. Although I had described the layout for my mother in considerable made-up detail in response to her insistent questions about "Paulette Goddard's house," now my true uncertainty about where Bayla was taking me filled me up and seized me with a kind of exciting ignorance.

She turned left. Then she went back down the steps into the dining room, our Hebrew study hall. She moved slowly and confidently, pausing to allow me plenty of time to follow and catch up. She didn't have to glance back at me even once beneath the swinging bob of her hair to know I had seen the new flick she seemed to have inserted into the curve of her little hip as she walked.

I sat down in my accustomed place at the side of the table and waited. My back was to the large oak credenza, flush against the wall that ran parallel to our table, and this time I didn't have to turn my head to know, from the sound of the clinking glassware, that Bayla was opening liquor decanters.

One ice cube or two?

Excuse me?

In your whiskey.

I don't drink whiskey, Bayla.

Oh, come on. A little won't hurt you. There's other stuff here too. Vodka? Gin? Cognac. What would you like?

We should sit and do our work.

What do you do for fun, Hebrew tutor?

Before I could answer, if I had had an answer, I felt her standing behind me. Then there was the cold thrill of a glass filled with ice cubes on the back of my neck.

How does that feel?

This time I opened my mouth, but no words came out.

I'm wearing my mother's perfume. I know how much you like it. Are you surprised I notice such things, tutor?

Everything you do surprises me.

And we're drinking her bourbon.

I'm not drinking.

You should.

She won't mind?

She won't ever know. Will she, Hebrew tutor?

Sit down, Bayla, and stop saying *Hebrew tutor.* We should get to work.

All right, she said, but it's so boring.

Then she promptly dropped herself onto my lap, sidewise. I don't weigh too much, do I? She took a sip of her whiskey. O.K. Teach away. I'm ready. Are you?

She put her arm around my neck as she drank the amber liquor. Our faces were very close. I felt as if I were now a page of the newspaper, and she was staring at me the way Ed scrutinized the *Times's* crossword puzzle. I liked being studied by her. I liked it all too much.

Wanna sip? Bayla said, pressing the glass against my shut lips. Isn't baby hungry? Isn't baby thirsty for some nice whiskey?

I said I wasn't.

I bet you've never gotten drunk. Not even once.

Please don't.

You're such a bore. You don't know what you're missing.

You're missing your Hebrew lesson.

Don't worry, Hebrew tutor. You can do no wrong around here. You're a real hit with Mother, you know. Look, she even gave you a tip.

I followed Bayla's eyes—heavily mascaraed today—to the end of the table and the shining tray that usually held our Oreos. Bayla stood up but instead of walking around she leaned her whole body across the table to reach the tray. Finding herself not long enough, she lifted herself up and slid on her belly across the table top—ooh, this is fun, she said. You ought to try this too— and her arms made the motion of the Australian crawl. She was being ridiculous, but her skirt scrunched up and her flutter-kicking bare legs glistened.

When she retrieved the tray, she retraced her slide and propped herself once again on my lap, declaring, For you, sir. Special delivery.

I opened the white envelope: Dear Nehemiah, the brief note read, You are a wonderful tutor for our Bayla. Had a business appointment. Sorry. Couldn't see you today. *Shalom.* And many thanks.

Besides my customary twelve dollars were two crisp twenties.

That's Mother. Well, we have the whole house to ourselves. Carlos is cleaning the pool, but he's really nice. He's no problem at all. So what do you want to do now?

I eased her off my lap and stood, and she stumbled, but regained her balance, all the while holding her glass, and with barely a drop of whiskey spilled onto the gleaming floor. She repeated the question: So, what do you want to do?

What a teacher and a student are supposed to do, I said.

Bayla smiled, took another long sip, and slowly tilted her head in careful, deliberate profile toward me, elongating her beautiful neck as she swallowed. It was a gesture I was certain she had seen in a Lauren Bacall and Humphrey Bogart movie. She smoothed down her skirt and moved back to the credenza on silent bare feet. I stood at the edge of the table, my arms at a disciplinary horizontal across my chest like someone in a different movie. I felt like Glenn Ford, that too-good high school teacher in *Blackboard Jungle.* I watched Bayla, and I listened to her too, as she noisily added more ice and more whiskey. She also had begun to hum, and I was drawn to the sound and fearful of it at the same time.

Oh, Hebrew tutor. Oh, Hebrew tutor, she kept repeating, because she now knew I did not like the phrase. Oh, Hebrew tutor, she said as she promenaded with her refilled glass up and down the room. Her humming also shifted in tone as if she were sharpening a knife with her voice.

Oh, Hebrew tutor.

I forced myself not to look at her, and to let her get the siren act out of her system. Finally she approached, and in such deliberate stages that it was like a dance. When she arrived, she nestled against me at once so composed and so still that it was all I could do not to take my hand and stroke her beautiful black hair as if she were an affectionate pet sniffing at me.

Suddenly she moved and placed her whiskey glass on top of my Hebrew reader.

There now. We don't want to stain Mother's table, do we?

She slowly undid the button of her blouse beneath the whale's tooth.

I thought our study hall would be the perfect place to do it, she said.

If I moved, if I allowed myself to stare at her now, especially in her eyes, something important in me would alter, and badly. She somehow knew I was frozen, and she placed my chin in her hand and turned me slowly toward her, as if she were resetting the time on the face of a large clock.

I did not push or fling her away, although I imagined myself doing precisely that. The ideal Hebrew tutor within would have, but I was not as good or as moral as he was. I knew it and Bayla knew it. And we just leaned against the side of the table pressing against each other in a swoon of silence, perfume, whiskey, and a pressure of flesh, and I don't think I had ever felt so alive with every possibility the world had to offer as I did then. Or have since.

Oh, Hebrew tutor, she murmured after some minutes in her most mature whisper yet. Oh Hebrew tutor.

CHAPTER SIX

What would another boy have said or done? How would Biff Waterman have responded? I don't know how long she cuddled there waiting for a gesture or a word from me. I thought of a photograph I had been looking at the night before in my American history book: colonists on some green and desolate shore wanly waving goodbye to their supply ship as it moved out of the harbor; waving as it left them on that threatening coast to get through the winter alone; maybe the ship would return with supplies in the spring, and maybe it would not. I was waving on some shore, and Bayla was slipping away from me.

This package may never be delivered again.

They always deliver three times.

Are you certain?

When I did not budge, she walked slowly to the end of the room. I averted my eyes but sensed she had stepped up to the vestibule, because what she said echoed through me as if I were an empty container.

What happened to you, Hebrew tutor? What happened? How did you get this way?

What do you mean?

I mean, how did you get this way?

That night at home I went straight to my bed, lay down, and stared at the patterns of dots in the stucco ceiling. I had rushed right through the living room, barely able to say hello to my mother as she sat turning the pages of her *B'nai B'rith Messenger* in her accustomed seat on the sofa. I couldn't linger there even for a second of small talk as she always wanted me to; it was as if Bayla's question had followed me home, and it was now sitting there, shaped like a kind of human question mark, its legs crossed in my father's chair, staring at me and echoing, as she had: *how did you get this way?*

Ed was not around, which meant he was probably out at Santa Anita for the night races. I heard Esther clatter in the closet and begin to vacuum and sing along with the radio. I listened with the intensity of a crewman on a sub in one of the World War II movies I watched over and over again. I broke open my books, found there was plenty of homework to do for my classes; I was bored with the texts but also glad for the distraction they provided. I studied slowly for an hour and a half, prolonging each assignment because I knew Bayla's question waited in the wings for when I would be done.

I finished American history and English and made sure I knew the bylaws of the British East India Company. Then I picked up a book of Hebrew short stories Dr. Levin had given me and started reading one.

The style and vocabulary of the author, I. L. Peretz, were nineteenth-century Hebrew. It was tough, but I stuck with it with a patience that surprised me. Using the dictionary, I finally figured out the story was about a strange character, a young, athletic sort of rabbi, a type I had never before encountered in Hebrew lit. He was new, still unproven, to his little village in Poland, and in his first year he shocked his congregants because they saw him hoisting his axe early on the morning of the Day of Atonement, and going out to the forest. He was gone for hours, apparently working on the holiest day of the year. It was unheard of, and the scandalized congregation was about to run him out of town for his sins when it was discovered that he was bringing firewood to a sick woman who lived deep among the trees. She had recently lost her husband and son; a blast of cold winter had come early; she was too weak to cut the wood herself but too proud and too alone to ask someone else.

This rabbi put keeping the old woman warm and alive above obeying the law. He was a hero. I too wanted to be one, but in my life I was very far from a hero's path, except in my dreams. And yet I wondered, had I this very day been presented with an opportunity to prove myself? Was I being tested? Wasn't it heroic to be resisting the seductions of Bayla Adler? By doing the obviously right thing, despite the hot temptation of it all. This held real possibilities, or so I needed to convince myself, and I turned the idea in my mind. I felt ridiculous and noble and deeply ashamed all at once, and I could not sort out which was which. In the midst of this there was an unwanted tapping at my door.

I don't mean to disturb, darling, my mother's voice reached me. But you seem out of sorts tonight.

Not really.

The tutoring went well?

Yes.

You don't want to open up?

No.

You're getting along with the whole family, right?

Yes.

That's good, because I've been meaning to ask: one of these days, if you didn't mind, could I visit their house with you? Are you there?

Where else could I be, Mom?

Because you know how it is with me, and it is definitely Paulette Goddard's place. I just want to get in there and look around while you and the girl are studying. I promise I won't get in the way. Norman?

Have you seen me pass through the door?

It wouldn't be a problem, would it?

I'll have to ask Mrs. Adler.

I wouldn't want it any other way.

I have to get back to my homework now.

Of course.

An instant later, I sensed my mother outside again. She cleared her throat, and waited. When I did not respond and instead burrowed even deeper into my book, hoping that she would simply go away, to my great surprise, after some time, she did.

Despite my fear—or hope—that Bayla might greet me next time spectacularly naked in the vestibule, our tutoring resumed the following week, May 15, as usual, as if little of significance had occurred between us. I remember it fell just after the holiday, Lag B'Omer, marking thirty-three days since Passover, with the Hebrew letters *lamed* and *gimmel* having a combined numerical value of thirty-three. This fact was going to be my teaching warm-up for her because Bayla liked numbers, but I never got around to using it.

She was a tiny bit more serious and perhaps a bit less sultry. There were no carelessly buttoned blouses or tank tops and no mini skirts, even though mid-May had grown suddenly hot.

Lucille, Mrs. Adler, also needed the dining room for afternoon meetings that she was conducting at the house. There were a number of men whom I took for lawyers or partners in the nursing-home business who were there, and the house was filled with a sense of business urgency. There were bulging briefcases and long legal pads on the great table, and Cadillacs and other fancy cars had bumped my Hudson out of its accustomed berth. The good part was that, as a result, this week marked Bayla and I beginning to have our lessons outside.

We sat at one of the several tables arranged around the pool deck, beneath a white umbrella, Bayla in a bathing suit with a terrycloth robe over it. She remained in her chair throughout the lesson and paid attention, more or less. It was all unexpected, this newfound non-defiant behavior, as if she were under a kind of invisible order, but I saw no reason to jeopardize my good luck by questioning her.

A specific bat mitzvah date had even been set for about four months hence—Friday, September 13. It would be the week after school resumed and a week before the high holidays for that fine Jewish New Year, 5724. I also soon found out that I was no longer alone in my labors. Bayla was receiving lessons from other tutors, people referred to the family by Michael Levin, who also turned out to be Lucille's uncle. One was a music tutor, a cantorial student whom Dr. Levin had somehow found, who was teaching Bayla how to chant her section of the Torah. It was a full court press for the Bayla bat mitzvah. Most of these people must have come at night or when I wasn't there, and I began to imagine Bayla being ministered to by a legion of servants, just as Paulette Goddard must have been. They also asked me, good English student that I was, to help her with her formal bat mitzvah speech.

That Sunday morning up at the University of Judaism, Dr. Levin asked me how the tutoring was going. He listened thoughtfully and seemed amused by my description:

There I am in my short-sleeved white shirt with a tiny portable blackboard, really not much bigger than a kid's toy; a Hebrew dictionary; and Bayla by the pool, asking me for a break, taking a dip between studying the present and past tense, shouting the auxiliary of the verb at one end of the pool, swimming a length, and then emerging, streaming water, and shouting out the accompanying verb at the other end.

At least you are keeping her interested. Levin sighed, his face growing a little pained and melancholy, and he said in that question-answer way of his: Jews often live and learn by the water. Why? The easier to take off when they have to.

Carlos, the muscled pool guy who had been a competitive swimmer in Mexico, was also now coaching Bayla through the spring and summer, so she could make the swim team at her school in the fall. The hour with him was right before mine. If I arrived early, I watched them practice. I didn't want to watch them, but I couldn't help myself.

She has a good butterfly, no? Check out her body, man. Beautiful, no? Problem is she does not have enough length; she's too short to win.

Bayla came to a stop mid-stroke and whipped herself around. I am not too short! she snapped and splashed water all over his face.

We'll have to stretch her, eh? Maybe you take one end, Hebrew tutor, and I'll take the other.

Just shut up, Carlos. And don't call me short or him Hebrew tutor ever again. That's an order. Then she gave me a look that seemed to arise out of an understanding we somehow were supposed to be sharing. But what was it? I returned to my chair beneath the umbrella.

Although our tutoring time was now at hand, she was still swimming away and Carlos was still coaching, and, as the minutes passed, clearly she was choosing the pool over me yet again. And who could blame her? I continued to stare at them.

Carlos lifted himself out onto the deck and lay on his belly, his head propped on his hands to observe how Bayla, as she swam by, raised her chest and torso out of the water. He talked to her encouragingly at every third or fourth stroke, urging her to have more arch, to kick more, to kick, arch, kick, arch, kick and arch, girl!

As I sat there, my fingers clutching several sharpened pencils, I realized how ridiculous, and jealous, I was becoming. How could I possibly compete with this? Let me hear that *Baruch atah adonai* again, Bayla. Nice guttural. Nice pronunciation. Nice coordinated movement there at the back of the throat. Let me hear that again *cha, cha, cha. Baruch, uch, uch.* Way to go, Bayla! In that moment I wished I were anyone but myself.

I watched for twenty-five more minutes and realized that there was going to be no Hebrew lesson that day. I took my money; it

was always there: the fee, the overly generous tip, the frequent notes
from Mrs. Adler—I was to call her Lucille—and I went home.

The following session—our first in June—the housekeeper let me
in. Bayla was outside but not in the pool; rather, she was waiting
at the table when I arrived. I saw Carlos at the far end of the deck
kneeling over a sack of some chemical. He looked up briefly when
I arrived and hailed me: Hello, Hebrew tutor.

I did not respond. I made a point of ignoring Carlos and
wanted Bayla to notice. She smiled at me and looked more beautiful than I had ever seen her. She placed her hand across my arm
as I sat down. Although I didn't know what her gesture meant, I
loved it, and the feel of her hand was light and warm and elegant.
I stared at her fingers. She had become so tanned already. I let her
hand linger there as if it were a symbol or evidence of something.
But of what?

Don't let him get your goat.

No way.

You're the best tutor I've ever had. I want you to know that.

What's going on, Bayla?

Hey, thanks to you I'm bat mitzvah bound like all the other little princesses.

I mean with him. With Carlos.

Oh, forget him. He's a big jerk and you're not.

O.K., fine. But, look, what gives, really?

I told you. It's a testimony to the skill of my Hebrew tutor.

I'm going to sit right here until you stop putting me on.

Bayla moved forward on her chair and looked intently at me.
Then she folded her hands, the way I remembered from our first
session, a gesture that signaled a revelation to come—or that she
wasn't going to speak another word.

I waited.

All right, they're paying me. I don't know if they will tell you,
but you should know. It just seems fair.

Paying you?

For the bat mitzvah. I get twenty thousand if I go through with it without gagging. Amazing, huh! They're putting it in an account for me, starting today, five thousand a month and then maybe even a bonus in September, when the dreaded deed occurs. I have it in writing from my father and from Lucille. She wasn't happy about it, but, hey, they've got the money. I get access to the account when I'm eighteen, and I don't have to go to college either, if I don't want to. I have it all in writing. They threw Carlos in too. My personal swimming trainer for as long as I want. Twenty thousand, no dumb college, and Carlos. What do you think?

I told her I didn't know what to think.

I asked for a whole lot more, but my father wouldn't go for it.

No?

He's very tough on me, which I don't even understand. Lucille made him that way. He wouldn't care if it weren't for her. I don't know what my father sees in her. Do you?

Your mother?

My stepmother.

I don't know what to say.

You don't understand attraction, Hebrew tutor.

That's not what I'm here for.

You're making me laugh.

Tell me about your negotiations with your father.

He said he didn't want to spoil me. I said o.k., and then we bargained. You know how it goes: At first, I told him I wanted fifty. He offered fifteen, and we settled for twenty. I think he was proud of the way I negotiated. What did you get for your bar mitzvah?

I got a three-hundred-dollar u.s. savings bond from my uncle and tickets to a baseball game.

You poor boy.

Mine were gifts, not bribes to go through with it.

I require bribes.

Bayla, please.

It's true. Still I wouldn't have done it, even for a million, without you, Hebrew tutor. Should I give you a cut of the gross?

It's not about money.

No? Then why is she slipping you a hundred or two hundred every week? I know what's in the envelopes.

Your family is very generous, but I'm not doing it for the money.

Oh? You feel bad, don't you? I used to like making you feel bad but no more.

I'm grateful for that.

But I could change my mind. I could change it any time. Why do you like talking to Lucille? She's ugly. Don't you find her ugly?

Bayla, she comes up to me and she talks to me. She's interested in what I'm doing. That's more than I can say for some people. That's not ugly.

Oh, I'm interested in you all right, but you work for me.

I do? I smiled then. I felt like reaching out and caressing the side of her cheek, as I'd seen Carlos do. Or the top of her head.

You work for me, Hebrew tutor.

Of course I do, so let's get to work.

She remained immobile, staring at me.

When I decided that I might just try matching her stillness with my own, she said: I'll give you a cut of my twenty thousand if you don't tutor me. You can sit there and read. Just hang around. Do your own school work. I know you can't live without it. I can't believe you're going to summer school too! Hey, I'll pay you twice as much as she's paying you.

Stop it.

I mean what I say.

For a change, I felt quite good sitting there opposite Bayla. The vast house, the servant or two working away deep in the interior rooms folding the towels and napkins along a profound crease, the palm trees I could reach out and touch from beneath the umbrella, Bayla. . . . All of this somehow felt less like a strange island I had washed up on, as it had before, and more a place I might well grow accustomed to. I liked being fought over.

Bayla looked about, saw no stepmother and no other potentially disapproving eyes, and reached into her mesh bag by the foot of the chair. She withdrew a pack of cigarettes, lit up, and blew a large ring my way. When it had floated past my ear, she said: She's after you, you know.

I looked at her, a long, slow, Bayla-type look.

She responded by blowing more rings, which became elongated ropes, then ribbons, then yokes, over my shoulder and went on: That's o.k. with me, you know. No, it's really not, Hebrew tutor. I can't stand Lucille, but I suppose I can't expect you to bite the hand that feeds you.

Now came another smoky interval of silence and then a sound of perhaps screeching tires on a distant road or freeway that drifted over to us on the wind in Bel Air.

Why don't we change the subject? I said.

I was surprised at the alacrity with which she agreed: o.k., have you ever ridden a motorcycle, Hebrew tutor?

She knew I hadn't.

Carlos has a big bike. On weekends, if I can sneak away, he takes me riding, up in the hills over L.A. On the dirt roads. Have you ever been up there, off the road, in the real hills, I mean? Hair blowing in your face, your eyes closed, speeding along so fast that your heart is in your stomach?

Why are you telling me this?

I'm going to travel around the world, she went on, stretching out her legs and looking beyond the pool, the house, and all of Bel Air. After I set a new butterfly record at school, I'm outta here. I'm going to buy a cycle like his and ride it through Europe. I'll take pictures of all the old synagogues we pass and mail them to you, if you like. Oh, I'm sorry, she said, moving her hand down my arm. I swear I won't hurt your feelings, and then I do. But you're not going to go and sleep with Lucille while I'm gone, are you?

For God's sake, I murmured. We?

I thought for some reason of Michael Levin and wished he had been there, in his dark blue suit despite the heat, to hear every single word of this.

Some niece you have! What have you gotten me into? I wanted to say to him.

When I raised my eyes from the table on whose cloudy glass my gaze had fallen to escape Bayla's taunting, I saw her waving. I turned, and over my shoulder Carlos was saluting us. Presumably he was finished with his work or taking a break—who knew what he did around the place!—and then he dived into the pool. I watched, nervous and a little awestruck as he swam with extraordinary ease and power two lengths in four or five strokes each. Then he appeared to beckon Bayla to join him.

Yet it was time for our lesson to begin, and so I began: Today we are studying the future tense of the verb *to be,* I said.

To be or not to be? That's for you to decide, Hebrew tutor. I've already made my decision, but frankly I'm not so sure about you. Think on it while you join us for a little swim.

Although Mrs. Adler had given me permission to use the pool, I had not once brought my suit. It simply didn't seem right. I was working. There was my responsibility to teach, and then, of course, there were my skinny arms to conceal as well.

Come on in, Hebrew tutor, Carlos shouted.

Bayla rolled her head in exasperation, looked over at Carlos and then back at me. You want to use one of my father's suits? He's about your size.

Absolutely not interested in swimming.

Yet I suddenly didn't want her to leave me alone there again by the table, with the pages of our Hebrew reader and papers fluttering. Despite her constant teasing, I didn't want to relinquish her to Carlos.

Tell me everything about your plans.

She crossed her legs and moved forward in her chair as if pleased with the challenge. Well, first is to see northern Mexico, the

Yucatán, Mexico City, and then all the way down through Central America. After that, all of South America. I think I'd like to learn Portuguese. It's such a beautiful-sounding language. Then Chile and Argentina—we avoid Paraguay because my father says it's full of Nazis—and then around Tierra del Fuego. We'll have sex at least once in each country, and by then maybe I'll be with him and maybe I won't.

With Carlos?

Yeah, the big jerk. Who else is going to *habla* the *espagñol* until I learn it? But I could learn. I could travel alone too. Do you think I could?

I think you could do anything, Bayla.

After I'm done traveling, I return to the United States. Not to this dump, but to a faraway place, a fancy place, a huge hotel. I'm going to make a party for all the people I've met during my trip. I'll take their addresses and invite them. I guess I'll invite him— she nodded at Carlos—and whatever other lovers have joined the party. How about a place like the Plaza Hotel in New York, where that girl Eloise hangs out? Or maybe a hotel close to the United Nations. Do you know any hotels in New York?

I told her I didn't.

Well, we'll find just the right place, and then we'll all go to the window at midnight and sing, *Heenay Matovu Ma-Naim,* the very words you taught me. *How great it is to pray together!* Then she began to hum them. You'll be in New York by then, studying to be a rabbi, and you can help lead us.

I told her I didn't think so.

You'll be invited, don't worry. You'll probably be wearing one of those little black suits like Michael Levin; you'll be hunched over and praying all day long.

I don't pray.

You could have fooled me.

I pray for you to cooperate.

Norman, you're such a wimp. Why don't you ever hold your ground? Why don't you say to me, Bayla, I pray because I believe in God? So what if it's not cool to say that, but if you do, you do. You don't have to conceal your religious feelings from me.

What religious feelings?

There's nothing to be embarrassed about just because most kids in the world find it totally dumb. So what! Lucille loves all your prayers and the way you're letting your sideburns grow long. I notice the way she wound her index finger around your ear the other day.

You noticed that?

There's nothing I don't notice about you, Hebrew tutor.

Thank you, Bayla.

Thank me for nothing, please. Just remember that you are invited to drop by and lead us in the song, so we get the words right. How good and pleasant it is for people to sit and to screw each other. It will be my contribution to world peace.

Bayla, you're talking such nonsense. I hope you're putting me on like you always do. And such stupid, risky nonsense.

Really? Sex? What do you know about it? Read a book on the subject? Do you think sex in Afghanistan is different, say, from what it is in Mexico or Brazil? I bet the Nazis are all into leather in Paraguay. But then you wouldn't be the one to ask, would you?

I couldn't say anything.

Don't you at least have an opinion?

I think it would be colder in Afghanistan.

Do you think about having sex with me?

After your bat mitzvah. When you've become a woman, and I no longer work for the Adler family.

You don't mean that.

No, I don't.

Then why'd you say it? You know I can't stand liars.

Everything you've just said is untrue, a lie, an exaggeration.

Is it? I exaggerate, but for the sake of telling the truth. Carlos is a shit sometimes, but Carlos does not lie. He knows exactly what he wants. Girls like that, Norman. At least I do. Carlos is not afraid to put his arm around me and pull me toward him until I can feel his whatchamacallit against my belly. Now do you or do you not want to have sex with me, Rabbi Norman?

Don't do this, Bayla.

You must be completely truthful. Let's play that game. A true game.

I stared at her.

I think you'd be terrible to have sex with, Norman. I know boys don't like to hear this. But you'd probably murmur *Baruch atah adonai*s and you'd whisper Hebrew vowel sounds, instead of the real stuff.

She undid the belt of her robe and walked away from me toward the deck. Carlos was swimming now, on his back, lap after effortless lap. I saw only the yellow sun, the blue sky, and Bayla. Slowly, the robe slid off of her, dropping in a white pile by the deep end, and Bayla, in a yellow bikini, climbed onto the three-foot board. Without hesitation, she did a beautiful swan dive, entering the pool like an arrow with the smallest disturbance of the water when her feet fluttered in.

She deliberately, I believe, stayed under for a long time. When she surfaced, Carlos reached for her, but she evaded him and scampered up the ladder. She pushed her hair back and shook it out in a spray. Then she walked back over to the table where I sat; I believe by then I had broken a pencil into three pieces.

Dry me, would you, Norman.

Bayla lay down and stretched out her legs. Her bikini, drenched in water, had achieved the impossible; it seemed to have become even smaller. I shuffled my notebooks. Then I took the towel that she had thrown over the arm of my chair and addressed her beautiful form as if it were a kind of text: her glistening torso the main section, her arms and legs, the first level of the commentaries; then the swale of her little breasts the entryway to the mystical meanings, and I dried every glistening drop.

After I had finished, I couldn't think of anything to say. It wasn't as if I felt empty of response. She was the most beautiful creature

THE HEBREW TUTOR OF BEL AIR

I had ever gotten so close to in my life. But she was so out of control, so cross, so unpredictable, so challenging, so absolutely unlike anyone I had ever met in high school or Hebrew school, as if she had stepped out of a movie about bikers or renegades, and that's the reason she belonged in this luxurious Bel Air bower, as if she were materialized from some life more celluloid than real, as if she were Marlon Brando's girlfriend, or had been James Dean's, but then what was she doing studying Hebrew grammar with me?

But I couldn't say any of this to her. I couldn't say a thing.

She frequently had this aphasic effect on me, and I wished I could have explained why. I wished I could have said to her what I've learned since about God or spirit or whatever you want to call it—that when the world comes at you in its most amazing forms, silence is the greatest praise of all. But all I could do then must have looked like ugly gawking to her: unpoetic glances, with my fuzzy, adolescent chin on my hands.

She peered back at me then in that way of hers, alluring and disdainful all at once, a glance that pulled me toward her like a spell.

There's water left in my belly button.

All right.

Dry it, silly. Or lap it out with your tongue. I wouldn't mind that.

Stop it, Bayla.

Stop it, stop it, she mocked me. Oh, I know, you want to talk about Hebrew, or another subject, right? Any subject. O.K., I'll have mercy on you. What subject? News of the day? You remember all those ships lining up, the blockade of Cuba?

What about it?

Wasn't that exciting? The missile crisis? I think Castro was cool, playing chicken that way. Shows a lot of guts. Very cool.

Cool, I said to her, like about four zillion degrees cool and we all melt.

You always look on the negative side, Norman. Your mother is right.

So what is the positive side of nuclear war?

I don't know, but there's something beautiful about it. You tell me.

Such as?

The way it will happen again, when you're least expecting it. The power of it and the surprise. That's what's beautiful, Norman. My father thinks it will happen, and he knows things. We came close. Boom! He talks to people in Washington who know things. I'm not interested in getting old and dying in a nursing home. Are you? I don't think JFK is either. *He's* really beautiful. I don't think he wants to get old and die in a nursing home.

Lucille says he has lots of girlfriends that you don't read about in the paper. I don't blame him. That wife of his has a pointy chin like a witch. We could die any time, Norman. We could get blown up in a second. In less than a second.

In less than that even. But it won't happen. They just signed a treaty. They're stopping testing. Don't you read the papers?

I know what I need to know.

They're banning testing anywhere above ground.

So they nuke all the people who are already dead?

No, Bayla.

I hate when you get that tone with me.

I apologize.

So you want to die, Norman, without seeing a woman naked?

What makes you think I haven't?

You're lying to me again. I know.

Maybe I am and maybe I'm not.

O.K., what's a naked girl look like?

For God's sake, Bayla.

And I'm not talking about what one looks like in one of those magazines boys read. My father has a whole pile of them. I see them all the time. And it's really ridiculous. I'm talking about this, this, and this, the real thing.

Jesus, Bayla.

I'm pretty much naked now, aren't I?

I don't know what to say.

Don't say. *Do.*

Here? Now? This is crazy. With Carlos skimming bugs over there, in the shallow water?

You want me to ask him to move over to the deep end? I could send him home too. Should I?

Jesus.

Jesus is something I do not expect to hear from my Hebrew tutor. Carlos works here. I can order him to do anything I want. Absolutely anything.

She began to shout something at him, but I stopped her.

O.K. It's up to you, Norman.

As I sat there, my fingers folding the corners of my papers, rolling up over the lines of Hebrew letters, Bayla gave me the most piteous look, as if I were some wounded creature she had found on the side of the road and taken in.

Oh, say something, then.

What?

How should I know! Recite something in Hebrew, I guess, Hebrew tutor.

And, to my everlasting embarrassment, I did.

CHAPTER SEVEN

Sometimes when I'm out riding alone on one of my bikes (there are three), especially when I'm cruising in the early morning light, or when my job takes me driving past the Basketball Hall of Fame or, my favorite, the Scholar-Athlete Hall of Fame in Kingston, Rhode Island, I sometimes think that if there were a Hebrew Tutor Hall of Fame, I'd have a good chance of being inducted. My main stats would include how long I was able to resist Bayla Adler.

Then again, maybe when all the facts are in—especially about the money—the Hall of Fame judges well might place an asterisk by my name.

I would offer to make my case, however, that we really needed the cash. Right around the middle of June, when Lucille began placing the hundred-dollar bills in my envelope, Ed had entered into some sort of betting arrangement with Benjy and, as all of Ed's schemes did, it had worked out badly. My father rarely got in so deep that the guys with bats came searching for him, but being a bookie, even part time, was nothing any self-respecting father of a Hebrew school genius should be up to. I had no details and I didn't want them; only Esther let me know, repeatedly, that I should not follow in his footsteps.

What are his footsteps?

I was so weary of warnings, and also exasperated by the clichés that conveyed Esther's warnings. But how many traits can you criticize in your parents at the same time? Hadn't I reached the temporary limit?

Where will the footsteps lead, Esther? To hell? To Santa Anita? To Vegas? Where will those mysterious footsteps lead?

Don't make fun of me. Don't mock me. It's for your own good. All I know, smart guy, is where you shouldn't follow.

She spent that whole night away from me, avoiding the dining room table and my other homework locations; I knew she was crying. I had made her cry. I had done it before and now I had done it again. In addition to Hebrew and my other studies, this was one of my callings.

I couldn't sleep and instead sat in bed reading by flashlight. After midnight, with Ed still not home, I went to Esther's door and knocked. I said that I was sorry, and I promised her I'd get her in to see Paulette Goddard's mansion. She didn't answer, but I knew she had heard.

One evening, not long afterwards, as I was driving home from an enrichment class at the University of Judaism, I stopped at the red light half a dozen car lengths from Benjy's newsstand. I had the baseball game on the Hudson's scratchy radio, and there was a full count against Junior Gilliam, with Don Zimmer and Wally Moon in scoring position. Last of the ninth. I was focused on Gilliam—my baseball hero at that moment both because he was a Negro and because he was a terrific player, a utility infielder and all-around talent underappreciated, I thought, by everyone in L.A. except me. I was listening hard to the count against him, when I thought what I saw at the newsstand had to be a dream.

Loping out to deliver a newspaper to a car stopped three in front of me was a man whose profile and shambling walk were familiar, but he was not Benjy. I felt my grip on the steering wheel grow tighter. It was not dark yet, just a little shadowy, and in the waning light I was certain the figure was my father. I heard the cheering of the crowd over the radio, but I still don't know if Gilliam got a hit, because, almost without thinking or looking further, before the light turned green, in a kind of panic that blinded me to the danger, I made a sudden U-turn across traffic and away from the newsstand, and took the long way around toward home.

I guess I was not surprised that Ed did not come home that evening. I didn't want to turn my back on Esther by going into my room, so we turned on the TV and watched whatever was on.

They had begun to argue more and more, almost always about money. Yet I was still surprised when she said during a commercial: I never thought I would tell this to you. I have always done my best. Maybe you don't see it or know it. Not until you have your own kids probably will you understand it. But there you have it.

I have what? What is *it*?

Don't go criticizing me again.

I just asked, what, Ma? You haven't told me anything. What do you want to tell me?

Only that sometimes it happens between people, she went on. Sometimes it happens. Your father is becoming impossible to live with.

But the rest I knew by heart already. How he had squandered the savings, how he had blown the small profit from the sale of the house they had had when I was born. Horses, poker. Running bets for other people for pennies. And how the forty dollars a week that Ed gave her for groceries was not enough. Never enough. He had no idea of the price of a quart of milk, or what it cost to put bread on the table.

While they had argued often, there had usually also been a jokiness to it, exaggerated threats and counter-threats; Ed indulged her ultimately. Yes, I knew there was something wrong, but he had never belted or threatened her, or if he did, it was like on the *Honeymooners*. Ralph loved Alice and Ed loved Esther. And Ed could always carry it off with that familiar put-down humor of Milton Berle and the other Jewish comedians we watched regularly on TV, so that my mother, though drowning in exasperation and defeat, could still laugh, which made her seem pretty to me. She would throw up her hands as she stood in front of the dining room bowl, reach her arms deep into it, lift up all the scratch sheets and unopened bills, scattering them into the air like confetti, and declare, Hallelujah, now everything's paid!

Late one night, a couple of days after Esther had shared with me what I thought were just repeated complaints, they went at it with an anger and a humorlessness I had never experienced before.

This was like CinemaScope, and I knew I couldn't miss it, so down the purple-carpeted hallway in my bare feet I walked. Peering around the corner at the end of the hall, I thought I was seeing my second apparition of the week: my mother for an instant airborne, or rather, being suddenly flung out of the closet, fluttering in her housecoat past the night table, arms extended like a twisting figure from mythology. It was breathtaking to see my mother fly. When she hit the bed, she seemed to disappear into the dark blue coverlet. For an instant I imagined her covered over by waves until in one, two, three springy bounces she rose like a person on a trampoline and gathered herself on the edge of the bed.

Don't you ever go through my wallet! Ever!

You're hiding money from me. You take it and give it to the horses instead.

I never bet the rent. Don't I always keep a roof over your head?

The other women have money to have a girl come in once a week.

Since when are you so finicky? Do I ever complain about the place?

It's a mess. You have no eyes.

So clean it up. You don't work.

Neither do you. And it's not enough for food. You have a growing son.

What's he got to do with it?

You understand nothing.

CHAPTER EIGHT

Although I had kept from them both just how much Lucille Adler had been tipping me, on a night in mid-June just after I'd marveled at how Warren Spahn and Juan Marichal dueled each other for sixteen straight innings and I ached again to be a hero in somebody's life, I began to place serious money in Esther's old leather purse, which she kept a secret from Ed in the bottom dresser drawer. She had shown it to me once long ago, the wad of ones and fives that was the private stash she had proudly wrested from her budget; she had wanted me, and me alone, to know.

It's my *knippel,* she had said, using one of those memorable, funny-sounding Yiddish words that had all the aura of her childhood, and of the childhood of all the Jews who kept secret hiding places way back for hundreds and thousands of years.

It was not the first time I'd had a sighting of this *knippel,* a mottled blue leather purse in the shape of a small shoe box, with a mirror speckled and scented by face powder beneath the top cover.

I had been getting dressed for school on that long-ago morning when the phone rang. No one ever called that early, and there had beeen other signs of an unusual red-letter day to come. I was perhaps four years old, and, it seems from this long distance that every few hours then delivered up an important new discovery. Esther was wearing the green skirt that I liked; it had long pleats, with loose, fuzzy threads, like the ferns that grew in the forests. I liked to hide inside this skirt. As she listened intently to whoever was speaking at the other end, she sat slowly down onto the sofa and I leaned into the skirt. I sensed Esther grow tense. She raised her free hand from the small of my back to her face, and I saw her fingers spread out and press into her cheek. She replaced her arm on me and drew me toward her.

Canada. Winnipeg. Oh no! My God! When? No, no, no, no, she said, fumbling with the phone. She couldn't replace it in its cradle properly, but I was there to help her, and I did.

Then she looked at me, her eyes wide as quarters. I did not understand except that they contained fear. She leaned forward. She began to rock back and forth, wailing, and she wouldn't relinquish me.

I don't have a mommy, she began to whimper. I don't have a mommy any more.

That's all right, I whispered back lamely. That's all right.

I remember how she stood and walked into the dining room and down the short hall to her bedroom, and I helplessly followed. She knelt in front of the dresser drawer, removed the *knippel* and from it a few bills, which she placed on the top of the dresser. Then from the bottom of the purse she carefully withdrew a picture of the grandmother I'd never seen and showed it to me: a large, severe-looking woman in a flowing black dress with a white apron and tall, ruffled lace collar. My mother brought the photograph to her lips.

"Now *I* don't have a mommy," she repeated, and she began to sob again. This time she did not merely cry, as she had a moment before, but she shivered, like Dr. Levin in prayer, only her arms were holding her sides as if to keep them from separating from the rest of her, and her back heaved.

It's O.K., it's O.K.

Yet I also wondered what she had meant by emphasizing *I. I don't have a mommy.* Was I supposed to feel guilty that I still did?

All I could think to do was to summon more reassurances in my little kid's whisper, primitive compassion doing a feeble job of keeping grief at bay: It's O.K. I'll take care of you. It's O.K. It's O.K.

With the clock ticking down until two and a half months before the dreaded B-Day, as Bayla called it, my tutoring had increased to twice a week, even though Bayla often spent my additional time not studying but swimming. Still, I was paid for both sessions, and I began to be able to deposit twenty and then forty dollars, once or twice a week in Esther's secret purse. Once I put in fifty. It was not about keeping food on the table. I certainly could have gotten away with putting in less or nothing at all, especially since we never really went without food, and because my mother had never asked for any of it outright, never for even a dollar. Ed was spending more and more nights away from the house. "Working late downtown," was the euphemism Esther still used, but we both knew where he really was. All those bills were my magical payments both to keep him away and to lure him home.

On one of those nights, as I studied among the papers overflowing from the bowl on the dining room table, she turned off the TV and said to me in a voice inquisitorial but without accusation:

Darling, is it all from the tutoring?

Where else could it be from?

You must be very good.

Apparently.

But they pay you only twelve, and you've put tens and twenties in there. So much money. How do you do it?

Don't interrogate me, Mom. They added hours, you know. I'm glad to help.

But you're not spending anything on yourself.

What do I need? I'm fine.

Not even a pair of pants?

I look O.K.

You always look neat and handsome. But how do you do it?

Let's say they gave me a raise.

They did? It must have been a big one.

It's a raise.

You must tell your father.

Why should I do that?

She dignified my off-hand question with far more consideration than it deserved. She surprised me. After a long pause, she said: You should tell him because he's your father.

Oh.

And he'll be proud of you.

If I tell him, he'll hit me up for some, and then you won't have it, will you? You want to risk that?

He's not like that.

Come on.

There's an awful lot of money there.

Do you want more? Do you need more?

Of course not.

Then, just let it be.

The evening wore on, and as she sat and read I noticed she was also talking to herself, just slightly, in a whisper, a low thrumming I hadn't noticed before. If headlights washed by the front window or if there were a sound from the driveway or a noise on the porch, both of us looked slowly up. We didn't really expect Ed to be back any time soon, but we searched for him anyway, startling at a car door slamming out on the street, and noticing, far more than usual, the creaking and breathing sounds of the house.

We wanted him to come through the door, because he made us laugh and, frankly, it was dull there without him. But we also wanted him to stay away; he'd return when he was done following up on whatever mysterious angle he was pursuing; whatever odd job he had come up with; maybe he wasn't really gambling, maybe he was working hard with Benjy. I tried not to think about it.

I finished with my essay on onomatopoeia in *Silas Marner* and was well advanced now in my Hebrew, and I was moving quickly through the Book of Judges. It was like a great war movie, spears and ambushes and heroes like Gideon cutting off the thumbs and big toes of the enemies of Israel. I imagined the blood spurting out on the chopping block, and I wondered how they cauterized wounds in biblical times, but those weren't the kinds of questions I could ask Dr. Levin and the rabbis. Still, I let myself get as lost in Gideon, Ehud, and Deborah, and in the battles, sieges, and executions of Judges as I had with Audie Murphy in *To Hell and Back*. I would return to the text in front of me as if waking up from an absorbing dream.

In this manner, I could raise and lower my intensity of study even as my mother thought I was constantly hard at work. I was a kind of human household appliance whose temperature I, and only I, could control. I used all my knobs and switches to keep Esther's confessional approaches at bay. I did not want to hear more about Ed: if she loved him, how she loved him then, how he got the way he did, how thrilled he used to be playing catch with me in the park, how proud he was of me even if he didn't or couldn't show it because that was the way he was, what happened to the first business, how the fire really wasn't his fault.

I was giving her money, and the money was buying me release from such confidences whenever I chose to shut them down. Bayla was right. Sometimes, with money, it's like that.

CHAPTER NINE

My sessions at the Adlers' mansion became the best two hours of my week, and nothing—not the brutal heat of July and August, or my mother's seemingly never-ending need for a ride to temple—kept me from tutoring. There was the money of course, but there was also Bayla, and I felt I had to keep it going at all costs. After and before each session I played and replayed each detail of what had happened, and worried about what was to come. I felt as if I were an actor in a play that changed every Monday and Wednesday afternoon in Bel Air. I never was certain if the lines that emerged from me were right, or would wreck everything. So much was unsaid.

Yet it was, oddly, neither Bayla nor Lucille that I began to worry about most, but Carlos. At first my concerns took the form of simply hoping he'd be away, or occupied with some chore far away from the pool and patio, or running an errand for Lucille. She treated him badly, I noticed, which perhaps was why Bayla, in her inimitable way, was turning Carlos into her boyfriend, or her show-boyfriend, right before my eyes, and her stepmother's. And was it because Lucille seemed to like me so that Bayla was trying to hate me? The anti-Carlos.

But Carlos was rarely away. Even if I couldn't see him around the pool, I knew he had to be nearby pruning the bushes, sweeping the long curving driveway, or painting the little pump house. And I suspected that even if he had other things to do, it may have

been arranged so that whenever I was there, he was too. Bayla
arranged it so on my account, or maybe it was Lucille. I'd heard
all about "the help " mixing improperly with their employers, as
framed by the stories in my mother's magazines, so how fortunate
to have a stand-up Hebrew tutor nearby, just in case. Bayla and
Lucille were in some sort of duel or hunt or both. But who was the
prey and who was the bait?

I watched and I endured poolside, quietly, because I suspected
that beneath the taunting, Bayla had begun to admire me, if only
a little, for my ability to decode a foreign language, or for my
school smarts. Who knew why. If I went on about Khrushchev
and Castro, Bayla thought I was some kind of genius of current
events. All I had to do was read the newspaper and bluff the rest.

Tell me about Vietnam, she would say.

Let's study. There's no time. Your bat mitzvah is a month away.

No, tell me again, Hebrew tutor, about North and South
Vietnam and why a boy your age, that Buddhist monk, would
burn himself. Would you?

Please, Bayla.

Which side is Diem on? Which side are you on?

I sensed she yearned to know things, but either she couldn't seem
to apply herself or for whatever reason facts wouldn't stick. I noticed
this when we did have an opportunity to work. I felt that she was
watching my eyes, or my face, or my fingers writing out the letters,
words, and Hebrew sentences. Her concentration was in her body,
not her mind. She was being tutored not just in Hebrew and in the
butterfly, but also in several school subjects she had almost failed out.

Did Lucille tell you that?

Yes. But there's nothing to be ashamed of. People learn in different ways.

I absolutely hate her.

Why should she keep it a secret?

I hate her from her tight little scalp all the way down to her
ostrich legs and wedgies.

Don't think of me as a tutor, I told her, but as a friend.

You're being paid. Big time.

Then I'm your paid friend.

Fine.

After that, I began to notice that she tried a little harder with me, but we both knew what was unsaid: that above all she was an athlete, and I began to think for that reason, for that nonsensical reason alone, that all the tutors in the world would never avail Bayla Adler and she would remain as far from being ready for a bat mitzvah as Pluto is from the sun. And that's why my jealousy of Carlos cut so deep. What came to him naturally, she liked and might attain. What I did, she never could.

The small things about Carlos began to irritate me next—for example his habit of wearing brightly colored socks that went just over his ankles. And he wore neither sneakers nor sandals, but tassled loafers. Was that footgear in which to work at a pool?

He was also shirtless too often, he was a show-off, his muscles bulged all over his body like sacks of nuts; it was gross, and the garish socks, my God how the mind latches its jaws onto something and doesn't let go. Yellow socks, blue socks, periwinkle ones, and socks as orange as the setting sun were always on that young man's feet. They drove me nuts. How could he wear such things!

I should have arrived at 4:30, on the dot, tutoring starting time, but nevertheless, and against my better judgment, I continued to arrive early. If Carlos were going to hold her in the water on my time, I could poach on his time with Bayla as well.

However, after arranging our notebooks and our study area under the umbrella, and thinking about walking over to the pool like a peeved teacher, I always gave in, and stood poolside not to harass but to watch them in pure envy, and maybe even a jot of joy. How could I not, she was so beautiful. She was growing smoother and stronger, covering more and more territory with each stroke. When she dedicated herself to something—it surely was not Hebrew grammar—she could be fierce.

After a few minutes, having announced myself, I returned and positioned myself under my umbrella at our tutoring table and tried to read until she was ready. One afternoon I actually succeeded in letting myself be drawn into Judges and its chronicle of the invasion of Canaan, a text I had decided to revisit at Michael Levin's suggestion. It was a military story, a story of scouting, siege, and war, of revenge and conquest. Exactly the kind of action I rarely had in my life. Judges contained my kind of stories, martial vignettes that took perhaps six of Bayla's breaststroke or butterfly laps—I had counted—to complete one.

This afternoon Mrs. Adler, with a pencil stuck in the bun of her hair, which was severely pulled back from her head, suddenly appeared beside the table as I was reading. I heard a pause in Bayla's swimming as I looked up at Lucille, but then as Carlos shouted out, Kick, glide, kick, Bayla resumed, and Lucille, in a tight red dress, sat herself down in Bayla's chair beside me.

The conversation was the usual thing, but I became mindful and even a little troubled as I heard myself—no, more than heard, as I somehow began to *observe* myself—responding in my practiced Junior Cong fashion.

I noticed that Lucille seemed to be speaking in a voice loud enough for Bayla to hear, and we both knew she was. And yet Bayla and the bat mitzvah that was taking forever to happen were not today's topics.

Lucille wanted to know what I thought of Peter, Paul, and Mary's new song "Puff the Magic Dragon." I told her that I thought it was a little stupid but I couldn't get it out of my mind either.

What else can't you get out of your mind? she asked.

But Bayla had inspired me not to answer a question like that from Lucille. She also wanted to know what my college plans were, a bright young scholar like me. I was going to ask her not to call me a scholar, a word that made me feel like one of those pictures, in my history book, of Erasmus or bent-over little monks in robes, who had saved the knowledge of Greece from the Dark Ages. She had my number all right: study, study, study. Still, I was distracted by the perfume she exuded and by the glamorous leaning way that she sat.

And there was enough bright sunlight beneath the white umbrella, where we were practically shoulder to shoulder, for me to notice, also, that her face was exceptionally smooth and unlined. During one of Bayla's endless little games with me, when she had asked me what part of Lucille's body I liked best, and I had answered her nose, Bayla told me the nose was not Lucille's own, not a curve and not a cell of it original. Still, that nose, small and sculpted, seemed to lead her face this afternoon very close to mine, like that of a beautiful, hairless feline, in a kind of eagerness to hear whatever I answered, no matter how stupid, jejune, or banal.

Oh, what can I say to make you smile that way again, Nehemiah? The way you used to.

We had Michael Levin in common and, it seemed, much else. And with Bayla and Carlos splashing away near us, all my previous nervousness in talking to Lucille did drop away. I relaxed. I laughed, and when I did, Lucille leaned forward and said, Oh, Nehemiah, you have such a bright, warm smile.

My mother says the same thing.

There, that proves I'm right. You never speak about your parents. They must be wonderful people to have created you.

I suppose then was a chance, the best chance yet, to ask her if my mother could visit the house, but I didn't ask.

My parents, I lied, or told the truth because I'm not sure I knew the difference any more when it came to them, they're all right.

Oh, I bet they're more than all right. Is your father a scholar like you?

Not really.

And your mother—is she a woman of valor?

Well, she puts up with the both of us. So I guess so.

That's so charming. You'll go far, young man. Very far. A child like you is no accident. Give them my compliments.

To my shame, I let it go and said only, Thank you, Mrs. Adler.

Lucille. Lucille. Lucille. You must always call me Lucille, she said. You must not be afraid of me. For a scholar you sometimes forget things. But only now and then. Otherwise . . .

Otherwise what? Bayla's insistent voice pierced our intimate talk. She was still in the water but must have heard everything.

Otherwise, he's perfect.

I'm far from perfect, Mrs. Adler.

She looked at her watch, then up toward the house; she seemed to have just remembered that she left people waiting.

Isn't that enough swimming? The Hebrew books are turning yellow in the sun.

Carlos lifted himself out and sat dripping on the far side of the pool, and then stood up. Almost done, Mrs. A.

Bayla extended her arms to him, crossed them, and he pulled, lifting her up onto the deck.

She's looking very, very good.

Everyone knew a half hour of the tutoring time had already been squandered with Bayla in the pool, and Mrs. Adler, Lucille, still lingered with me.

All right, Lucille said, *I'll* study if you won't. It's a mitzvah, you know, a commandment fulfilled, to study. Isn't it, Nehemiah?

While Bayla and Carlos toweled off, my student's stepmother and I read some lines of Hebrew together in Judges and discussed them. Lucille's Hebrew wasn't bad at all. She'd gone to a school in Germany, she said, when she was very young. We got into the text, and, God help me, I found it exciting to study with her. I forgot, temporarily, that Bayla and Carlos were ten yards away toweling, preening, and stretching like a Greek god and goddess.

Fifteen, twenty minutes perhaps of ancient military history passed in a swoon of perfume. The part of this book I always liked best, she said, was how Jael cuts off the head of Sisera, king of the Midianites.

Did she sleep with him first? asked Bayla as she finally came over, forty minutes and fifty laps late and stood between her stepmother and me.

Well, someone's got to study some Hebrew around here, Lucille said as she rose, turned, and walked quickly in her high heels toward the house.

Halfway there, as I watched her, with her hourglass figure in that elegant dress, she pivoted on Bayla: You are the most insolent creature I have ever, ever known. You take Nehemiah far too much for granted, but he won't always be able to take it the way you are treating him.

I thought he was perfect, Bayla shouted back.

He's also human, which is more than I can say for you.

Witch.

I'm going to speak to your father about this tonight.

Go right ahead, witch.

Carlos and I exchanged a glance, suddenly extras on the set.

I'm so sorry, Nehemiah, Lucille then said, and her narrow shoulders seemed to drop two inches away from her neck. I'm doing all I can, but everyone reaches a breaking point.

CHAPTER TEN

I should have quit on July 4th or shortly thereafter, declared my independence from these people—ever so responsibly so, leaving them enough time to find another tutor for September's B-Day—but I did not. I was a very confused young man, enjoying being fought over as I never had been before, and it was lucky my car could not speed or I might have totaled it, trying to find a balance as I drove back and forth between exciting Bel Air and my other life.

When I neared the door to our house one night, a new sound from inside made me pause and listen. I was certain something bad, some new rupture had occurred. They were reading, and from the porch I heard the loud rustling of pages. I put my hand on the latch and I thought to myself, Now where else can I go and what else can I do besides entering this place? But my mother had heard me and called my name with such hopefulness that I would have felt awful sneaking away.

Ed was sitting in his chair. His old high-school poetry book was open in his right hand, his left on his knee, fingers outspread. I remember thinking that I always liked his hands, the size big enough to be masculine but not so big as to be clumsy, and the fingers well formed.

Hey, Ed.

The boast of heraldry, he began to recite in that bombastic way of his, *and the pomp of power, And all that beauty and wealth e'er gave, All await the inevitable hour, The paths of glory—*

I finished the quotation: *Lead but to the grave?*

Bingo! So how's that car holding up?

Good, I answered.

How'd the tutoring go?

Great.

It's always great, isn't it? Esther said without looking at me.

When he says it's great, it's great. Leave it alone, Ed said. You mind if I borrow your car?

I guess, but I'm the kid. You're the dad. I'm supposed to borrow your car.

Mine's a clunker. In the garage again.

I told your father about your raise, how well you're doing.

That's terrific, kid. What about the keys?

Where are you going, dad?

Ask your mother.

Ed left and didn't return that night, nor did he telephone, and she didn't know where he was going, or wouldn't say. We didn't know if he was going to come back at all, but we assumed that he would. Ed had disappeared for periods many times before. Esther had confided to me that his father had also, and an uncle. Some families produce rabbis, was the way she tried to have me look at it. Some produce doctors. Your father's produced *luftmensch*. It was a family tradition. Men did that, she tried to explain, during the Depression. Out of embarrassment at not supporting their families, they just disappeared. But then, they would always return, days or weeks later with a wad of money in their pocket and feeling better, feeling like men again. The current episode would be no different, it had only been a few days, we both now told ourselves, and it would be all right.

What did he mean, *Ask your mother?*

I don't know, she said.

What's happening here? You must know something.

What I know, she said, you could fit in a thimble.

Does he have . . . another woman, a girlfriend, somewhere?

Go ask your father.

He's not here, so I'm asking you.

Which was when she turned and ran faster than I had ever seen her move, and entered her bedroom, the door slamming behind her.

The following day I got a friend to drive me all the way out to Santa Anita. Finally I located the boxes where I remembered he used to hang out, but he wasn't there. I went to the newsstand several times, but Benjy had not seen him either. After two days, I was out on the porch picking up the paper and I noticed the Hudson had been returned to the driveway, but there was no sign of Ed. In the living room I noticed the depression in his chair was deep. Maybe he had brought the car back in the middle of the night, entered, sat down, and thought about staying but decided against it.

I'm very sorry, my mother said as she walked into the living room, her hands wrapped around a mug of tea. You shouldn't have to go through this. Your father is like a kid sometimes, just as you said.

That's all right.

You think I should get a job?

If you want.

A lot of women are getting jobs.

You don't have to get a job.

What would I do?

CHAPTER ELEVEN

The next days, the second week in July, while my father was gone, a heat wave seized L.A. I remember the heat pouring down my face as I sat in Ed's vacant chair and read his *L.A. Times:* Madame Nhu, first lady of South Vietnam, said that if another Buddhist monk wanted to immolate himself, she would offer to light the match. Amazing, and the monks doing these things were not much older than I was.

It was so hot that they were thinking of closing down public buildings but decided against it. We all broiled, and up at the University of Judaism, in rooms with faulty or no air conditioning, and with even the thought of how much the health club members upstairs were sweating making us also miserable, we felt as if we should be far away from this place. I was hardly studying. Michael Levin wanted to know what was wrong, and I told him, nothing, the weather was all. Nothing at all but the heat. My books, which also had sustained me, seemed suddenly stupid. I kept hearing *Study, study, study, you bore,* which was how Bayla described me. I did not protest.

With Ed not around to give my mother any allowance, I regularly handed bills to her—I was up to sixty or eighty bucks at a time. I had been thinking of looking for a second job, maybe counseling at the temple's day camp, but now there was no need at all. Frankly, there were so many twenties, sometimes I just didn't count. And Esther just took the money from me with a kind of dumbfounded gratitude. My expression told her to let it be. When she finally summoned the courage once again to ask me where it was all coming from, I told her I had plenty of money, that I was doing extra stuff for the Adlers, and they had given me another bonus.

Bayla must be doing very well, she said.

I didn't answer.

You'll make a wonderful provider one day.

At the Adlers, on my usual Wednesday, Lucille greeted me in the cool, air-conditioned vestibule. This time she presented me a book-sized box wrapped in green and with a white ribbon.

Go on. Open it.

A present?

Good guess.

But why?

Put your briefcase down, and open it, Nehemiah.

It's not my birthday.

No, she said, and it's not Purim either. It's just hot. Open it.

As she watched, I untied the ribbon, peeled off the tape, and slowly raised from its confines in yards of white tissue a skimpy green bathing suit.

It's from May Company. You never bring one yourself, and in this weather. . . . Put it on and get in that water.

Where's Bayla?

She's out with her father.

You didn't call me.

No. I hope you don't mind. It's so hot and I thought you could just enjoy the pool yourself. Today it's just you and me. Don't look so nervous.

I'm not nervous.

You don't have a pool at your home, do you?

No.

I know you don't like the water. I've noticed that men who like books often are shy of the water. Why is that, Nehemiah?

I don't have any idea.

Nor do I, she said. I don't much like swimming either. That's why, I think, Bayla does so much. To set her apart. She knows that if she's in the water, she'll pretty definitely be away from me.

Why don't you like the water, Mrs. Adler?

Lucille.

Lucille.

Oh, let's not have a discussion about it, Nehemiah, she said, rising slowly from her seat, so that her robe opened and I saw that she was already in her suit, a small red bikini. We should both go in if only for health reasons. You go on and change, and then I'll join you.

No, Mrs. Adler. I just don't feel like swimming.

Would you mind if I gave you a little kiss, dear?

She pulled me into her arms then, and I smelled her scent and bath powder all around the base of her neck and her chest. She kissed me, not on the lips, but near. Then she kissed me again, once on each cheek. Her face was so refreshing, like the touch of marble. I stood there feeling like a fool, with a bathing suit wrapped in tissue paper in my hand.

You're such a wonderful young man, Nehemiah. The pride of Israel should not be so morose. I know you have your needs and your family is not wealthy. You don't have to swim, dear, if you don't want.

I think I'll go home, Mrs. Adler.

You don't have to do anything you don't want to do. Just know that you're doing a terrific job with Bayla. You deserve this, and more. Here.

She placed a large envelope in the box, and on top of it the bathing suit, which Lucille rewrapped with her long, slow fingers.

It was all I could do to keep myself from running back to my car. I turned on the ignition as Lucille neared the house. As I passed her, she waved.

Come out any time. The heat's not going to lift until next week.

The envelope rested on the shotgun seat of the Hudson for the entire length of the drive down Sunset. My windows were wide open and the air blowing through was riffling some unfolded maps and old mail in the back seat. I half wished that the wind would lift the envelope Lucille had given me and carry it out the window. I would not have braked. I would have driven right on. Maybe it would have been better that way.

But the envelope stayed put as if it were made not of paper but lead. Stopped, finally, at the light not far from Benjy's newsstand, I could resist no longer. I tore it open and beheld hundred dollar bills arrayed inside. There were lots of them, spread out fanlike, so that I counted at least ten, a thousand dollars. And they were held by a silver money clip. When the light changed, I was still counting, and the car behind had to honk me out of my reverie. I caught the next light at La Cienega, and finally pulled over near the park. This time, I looked down and studied the money clip: it had Hebrew letters engraved on it. I didn't have to study that text very carefully to see that she had had it engraved with my name.

Two days later the heat broke, and my father returned. Nobody explained why the heat had come and gone, and my mother and I didn't speculate why Ed had either. It had happened in the past, it would likely happen again. With his return, my mother stopped asking me what kind of job she might get, and she stopped asking me about where the money I was placing in her *knippel* was coming from. Ed didn't ask her either how she had gotten along. He knew whatever he knew, and that was it. That was the way we lived.

When the studying resumed with Bayla after the weekend, it was like always, except once Lucille asked me if the suit fit, and she asked so Bayla heard.

Green is not your color, Bayla said.

Lucille turned away quickly and got busy with the family's business, as she did periodically.

On Wednesday there was only Bayla. Bayla—and Carlos. Doing their demonstrations of the crawl and the butterfly and all their touching in front of me as I sat with my books. Maybe Bayla knew what her stepmother had been up to and was taunting me all the more. Would she and Carlos do everything short of having sex right there on the deck? Maybe that would be my next task— like a referee in some love match, where all I wanted to do was change roles but could not, to separate them right there, arm and leg on the patch of soft grass by the deep end. I didn't know what to do.

When Bayla noticed my painful staring at her, she relented: Oh, Carlos is a big jerk. You're the tutor. Don't be jealous of him. Anyway, it's worth it to you to suffer, isn't it? My family pays very well for the service.

Very well.

She's not a nice woman, you know, Hebrew tutor. It might seem that way to you because I can be such a bitch. But don't be fooled by Lucille. Don't let yourself be pushed around.

I'm just the Hebrew tutor, I said to her.

It had become enough of a joke that I could even make it. Please, let's study a little.

She worked with me for five unfocused minutes and then went back to the pool.

You said a little, and a little it was and will be, Hebrew tutor.

Occasionally, Bayla lay, balanced on Carlos's arms in the water as he watched her, held stationary, practice some technique. As she looked at me from this position, Carlos would raise the back of his hand and caress her face. I averted my gaze immediately to my books and read aloud in Hebrew. I really raced, as Michael Levin had taught me, attacking the Hebrew words as if speed fueled the power to make it all go away.

Help me be Bayla Adler's Hebrew tutor, I seemed to be praying. Help me not to focus on her incredible body. Strengthen me to be proper and upright and moral, and set an example for conduct with her, and with her stepmother. Do you hear me, God? Do you hear me, God, in whom I do not really believe, but in case that's a mistake (as Ed had explained Pascal's view of the odds) I address this to you anyway and to your people Israel.

I was getting very nervous about the bat mitzvah—how close it was, how little she was really learning—but not Bayla. The main change in her behavior was that she seemed to have more intense arguments with Carlos. She would lose patience quickly with his instruction, give him the finger, and stalk away from him and toward me. I would rise in my chair to welcome her, but she always halted as I stood stupidly there, and she turned away from me, and dived in, and began to swim laps. Five, ten, fifteen, perhaps twenty laps she swam, until Carlos said something angrily in Spanish, to which she did not respond, and then he stormed away.

One afternoon when she finally stopped and climbed the steps at the shallow end and swathed herself in white towels, she walked over and sat in the chair beside me.

O.K. O.K. Let's do it.

Let's do what, Bayla?

I, you, he, she, she said. *Ani, atah, at, hu, hee. We, you* plural male, *you* plural female, *they* plural male, *they* plural female. *Anachnu, atem, aten, haym, hayn.*

Very good, Bayla.

She stood, gathering the workbooks from the table, and arrayed the texts and the text of herself on the deck before me. Here were her lovely shoulders, here was a splashed-up rivulet of water slowly meandering toward the band of her bikini bottom. I forced myself to look at her eyes—mostly. I heard some clattering from the shed where the pool pump was kept and where Carlos often worked—when Bayla spent her precious few minutes with me, he often went there.

I, you, he, she, you plural, they plural.

I was the Hebrew tutor. If in Bayla's eyes I had made myself into an old man, so be it. She knew who I was and I knew it too: the non-Carlos in her life. She knew the Mosaic effort I was making. I was satisfied that she knew and understood this. She had to understand it. My effort was all in my restraint. The discipline of a Hebrew tutor. Those were my muscles, my strength, my talent, my principles, my laps.

At home, as I sat doing my work, Bayla grew in my imagination. Behind the shut door of my room she made many appearances, alone and just for me. The most moving of them, however, and the most enduring now that many years have passed, is by far also the most chaste: She arrives late for Junior Congregation, dressed in her bikini beneath a diaphanous white Sabbath dress. She startles me at my box by the door where I, having grown into an ancient old man, have fallen asleep. She is both modest and a siren, as only she can pull off. Here, my beautiful Bayla, I practically croak to her in my old voice, I have saved this, the most exquisite skullcap in the world, just for you. As I place it on her delicately, almost reverentially, like a crown, she smiles mysteriously at me, and I wake up.

CHAPTER TWELVE

Our next session, on July 30, coincided with the Tisha B'Av com-
memoration of destructions, expulsions, holocausts, and all things
bad that had happened to the Jewish people. We ended early
because Bayla was allegedly going shopping with Lucille. I was
bent over packing my books in the trunk of the Hudson. As
mother and daughter drove off, I felt a hand on my shoulder.
When I turned, there was Carlos. I tried to step aside, but suddenly I felt his fist land sharply on my chin. I had never been hit
in the mouth before. I fell back into the trunk and landed beside
my box of Hebrew exercise sheets. My glasses went flying. Inside
my cheek I tasted sourness and blood.

As I struggled out of the trunk, Carlos grabbed me by the shirt
and began dragging me as he would a sack of his chemicals,
toward the pool. I felt certain that he was going to throw me in or
try to drown me. We passed the diving board, with Carlos punching me a few more times but not nearly so hard as before as long
as I didn't struggle.

At the utility shed, which could not be seen from the house, he
dropped me.

I'm not a fool, you know. You think I don't see what's going
on? You think you're entitled to her?

My face dripped blood as I slowly stood up. I knew I couldn't
fight him. Who could I fight besides Ed and Esther? My main aim
was to preserve some shred of my image of myself by at least not

crying and whimpering, but that's when I felt a jab to the shoulder, then two fingers pressing against the middle of my forehead.

You think I'm nothing? One of the servants?

We're all servants here.

She's the best thing that has ever happened to me.

Good for you.

I love her, man, and you trash me in front of her. I can tell. I see it and I feel it. Over and over again. Every chance you get.

I don't talk about you. Carlos, please.

You don't have to talk; you don't have to *say* anything. What do you have against me, little man? You think because I take care of the pool I don't have a right, a feeling? You know what love is?

Of course I didn't know what love was, not in any of its forms, not even in the one I recited every day in the paragraph after the Shema: *And you shall love the Lord your God with all your heart, with all your soul, and with all your might.* Compared to Bayla, God seemed easy to love, but of course I didn't have a clue. However, I said I did. That was a very bad call.

My lie infuriated Carlos, and he rolled more of my shirt in his fist than I had left on my back. He kept drawing me toward him. We were nose to nose. His eyes were blue and intelligent in a wild, even poetic sort of way. I had not seen his face this close before. The hair falling over the sides of his ears was streaked blond. He had a sharp jawline and high cheekbones. He was handsome and strong, sleek and wiry, like those kids in surfing films. When he slapped me in the face, not hard, but slantingly across the nose, I felt myself begin to bleed from there, too. I tried to keep from weeping.

I hurt too, you know!

I don't have any power over her.

I could hear my heart beating. He was pushing his advantage even as I sensed that in a strange way he was also backing off.

Just state your weapon, man. Knives? Fists? You got them, don't you? Fists? Or, wait, maybe you want to try to whack me with your books? Let's fight for her.

I couldn't directly answer that demand. I was barely breathing, as if I were suddenly watching a gangster movie and living it at the same time. Only the blood I tasted was fully real.

You're hurting me. I don't say bad things about you, Carlos. I never do.

You think them, though. I feel what you think, man. And if I feel it, she does too. We've got plans.

I know you do.

Oh, she's told you?

Yes. You're going to go riding together. On the motorcycles. Mexico, South America.

Good, good that she said it. There's nobody like Bayla.

Nobody.

o.k., then. Love's a powerful thing, Hebrew tutor.

I wouldn't know.

You're learning. Good that the teacher learns a little something too.

Slowly he eased up on me. He brushed off my shoulders. He picked up my wallet that had fallen to the ground and gave it back to me. He took out a handkerchief from his pocket and offered it. When I did nothing but stare at it, he wiped my face for me. I was so touched by this gesture, I had to hold back tears again. Carlos said he was sorry if he had scared me. He offered to pay for the cleaning of my shirt, which had blotches and streaks of blood on it. I told him just to get the hell away from me.

This didn't happen, did it, I said, less for the sake of his job than for that of my pride.

No, it didn't.

Then he walked away, shaking his head derisively. That hurt as much as the pummeling.

That evening, fool that I was, I walked into our house without having taken off my shirt. I think it had oddly become some kind of badge of honor. God, had I lost, but at least I had struggled, if only a little, and I had certainly shed blood for Bayla, in a way.

My mother was fairly squeamish, and as I opened the screen door, she seemed to weaken. It was as if I could hear the air going out of her.

My God!

Just a bloody nose, Mom. While I was driving, so I couldn't stop it.

Here, she said, taking me by the arm. Let's get you into the bathroom. I'll warm up a washcloth for you. There's blood all over your teeth.

I'm fine. The air's dry. The capillaries in the nose get brittle. You know what happens to me.

Capillaries?

Yes.

A bloody nose. On the way home from the Adlers. I already told you.

A nosebleed, she repeated, leaving me to begin ministering to myself in the bathroom. A nosebleed! Everybody thinks I'm stupid.

An hour later, after I had rested with two washcloths, their warmth spreading over my forehead and beneath my nose, making me feel like a prize fighter after a bout, I rose to my mother's call for dinner. Just the two of us again that night.

I heard from Daddy. From your father, she said. He's earning some money for us. He'll be home soon.

Sure, he will.

I tried to smile at her, and told her that the bland food was good. As we were cleaning up, she asked, Have you talked to Mrs. Adler?

About what?

You know what. About visiting. Paulette Goddard.

I haven't found the . . . opportunity, yet. She's so busy over there. People are coming and going all the time. Their nursing home business and all, and the planning for Bayla's shindig. I don't think it's such a great idea right now. Maybe later.

When later?

I don't know. Later. But I won't forget.

You won't?

Later.

All right, she murmured, her voice dropping into a tone of disappointment that stabbed at me, but, I guess, not sharply enough. I knew that after what had happened between Bayla and me, and now between Carlos and me, there was no way I could tell Bayla that I was bringing my mother by. I couldn't risk her ridicule.

CHAPTER THIRTEEN

I had never seen so much cash in my life as I did that summer. The envelopes Lucille Adler left for me contained by then eighty dollars a session, not including tip. With barely six weeks left to the bat mitzvah, I found an additional ten one-hundred dollar bills in the envelope placed beneath the Hudson's windshield wipers. With this incredible tip was a note of thanks from Lucille and her nursing-home husband, David, the nursing-home king, as Ed called him. *Looking forward to meeting you one day soon,* he wrote.

I felt more than a little guilty as the cash kept growing, but also I thought that perhaps this was just the way very rich people acted with their money. This was what they did in Bel Air.

Normally I didn't open an envelope right away but set it down on the seat beside me, like a passenger I was driving from Bel Air back to L.A. Sometimes there was still the scent of Lucille's perfume, or Bayla's, arising from it. Occasionally I leaned over and touched the envelope with my fingertips as I drove, just to prolong things.

After that first major bonus, it got to be a serious game for me to see if I could wait until I got home. When I was certain I wouldn't be disturbed, I placed the envelope at the center of the green ink blotter on my desk. It had become an important ritual, all this waiting, and now, for the reward of my work and all this patience, I peeled back the flap and gasped at the amount.

After he confronted me, Carlos disappeared. I wondered what had happened to him but didn't ask. Maybe he was fired. Maybe he had gotten some work in the movies doing stunts in the water, the way he had often talked about. Bayla never said.

Instead, she seemed to apply herself more to her Hebrew studies. It was as if a seriousness had taken hold of her, but not from a deep source. Maybe it was the rapidly approaching B-Day, but frankly I wasn't sure. On the first Wednesday in August, we remarkably started the lesson on time, because there was absolutely no one to disturb us, not Carlos, not Lucille, not Bayla's mystery dad, not the lawyers or other business friends. In fact, the whole mansion was eerily empty, and the grounds as well. The whole length of Arroyo del Toro Drive, I had noticed, was quiet. Bel Air seemed positively deserted, as if an evacuation had been carried out and everybody had been informed except the two of us.

God help me, I must have dozed, because I heard Bayla shouting, Wake up, Norman! Are you or are you not ready?

For what? I startled.

You know for what.

As if she were listening to a voice, but not mine, she said, very slowly: I think this is the moment. Then she looked at me, with her eyes slowly filming over, it seemed, with an even deeper brown of seriousness. Yup, this is the moment.

What moment?

To decide.

Oh, come on, I said. Decide to keep working—or you'll get up there and say what?

She took my chin in her hand then and turned me toward her. Now she was the tutor. Maybe she had always been.

Face it. The way you're living, the way I live in this place. This stupid speech. You hate your parents, Norman, and I hate mine. What else do we ever talk about? That's our true subject, not Hebrew, not some speech. Who cares about stupid speeches? So, what are we going to do? Kill them? Let's write a speech to give over their dead bodies. Norman?

Bayla, I repeated, with as much seventeen-year-old gravitas as I could muster, we should work on your speech. That's where you thank your parents for all they've done for you.

But I want to kill them. Well, only Lucille.

Let's work.

Norman, if I have to make a speech, let's include a lot about killing and violence. What do the Jews say about nuclear war and incinerating yourself?

I think we're against both. Get in stuff about your parents.

Hebrew tutor, you know anything about guns? Knives? Poison? I think poison is the way to go for Lucille.

As she sat there, saying these things and flipping casually through the pages of the Torah and her Hebrew workbook, as if they were the pages of *Seventeen* and those other magazines girls read, I sensed Bayla had somehow transported herself into the future, where the deed, whatever it was going to be, was already done. She was there already, in big sunglasses, in a new bikini, on a new beach with blindingly white sand, enjoying the first morning of a future after her crime, simply asking me to do the logical, exciting thing: step into the future with her.

CHAPTER FOURTEEN

Calm yourself, Bayla. In fact she was calm, very. That was the most alarming thing of all.

If you love me, Hebrew tutor, you'll help me get rid of Lucille. If you asked me to help you get rid of Ed, I would.

I don't want to get rid of him.

But you've said he's useless. You said you hate him for what he does to your mother, and I hate my stepmother for what she's doing to my father. So, why not? I hear pool chlorine will do the trick nicely. There's a twenty-five-pound bag over there right where I'm pointing. Twelve pounds of poison should cover it for Lucille. The rest left over for your family. Be my guest, no charge.

You don't kill your parents just because you don't like them. It's not the Jewish thing to do.

Let's start a new tradition.

You have a problem, then you talk to them. Talk to your father.

The way you talk to yours?

She of course had a point. A very good one.

Norman, that car of yours is useless for a getaway.

We are not killing parents, yours or mine.

Fine, fine, she said, you chickenshit. But at least let's get away from here. Think of it as a gift to them. The gift of life: on the occasion of my bat mitzvah you keep me from killing my parents. And I keep you from killing yours. There, we did it! Doesn't that count for a lot more than giving a dumb speech or chanting the Hebrew, which you know I'll never do?

I was too astonished to say anything.

Look, I've thought this through. We can't take my parents' cars; they'll be easy to track. So we take Carlos's bike and we're gone.

I thought you were going to run off with Carlos, not me.

Aren't I allowed to change my mind? Anyway, I'm saving him for international travel. You're domestic.

You're crazy.

You know I'm not. You know that what I propose is the sanest, most exciting, most brilliant offer you've ever had in your sad little Hebrew-school life. So come along. It's so god-awful hot here, we'll travel north. My father has a cousin with a cabin in the woods at Lake Gregory. We can get there easy the first day. We'll swim naked across the lake. No one will find us.

Please, Bayla.

I just hate when you use that paternal tone with me. Stop or I withdraw my offer and you can just spend your life growing your sideburns and twirling them around your ears. Norman. You're my friend, my paid friend. So now we take the next step together, you and me.

Back to work, Bayla. You don't have to thank your parents in your speech. You don't even have to mention them. Just go through with the ceremony.

No. No! You ever notice that Lucille never goes near the pool when I'm in it? She's afraid of me, and she should be. I'm going to kill the witch if you don't help me get out of here. Now you've got a real job, Hebrew tutor. Like you always say, he who saves one life, it's as if you save the whole world. So save the witch, and have a good time with me, and you'll do something you'll remember all your life.

I'm going to remember you all my life, Bayla Adler, regardless.

Look at me, Norman. Look up and don't bury your gaze any more in those pages. Imagine me on the bike. We ride for a few hours and take a break, take our clothes off. All of them. Can't you picture me lying naked on a huge rock in the Mojave Desert under the morning sun, a saguaro behind me, and you there, too. Then we find a motel. You and only you alone with me in bed. We'll see the bikes parked outside our window. The sun gleaming off the handlebars. That'll be my bat mitzvah, with you, my tutor and my rabbi, my only guest, my lover. Afterwards we'll go ride some more, another motel, another hot shower and night of sex, and then another ride.

I swear to you she said all this. I have not made it up.

You have ten seconds to decide.

I sensed my heart beat once, its lubdub slightly different, as if it already knew what it would decide, and I was not confident it would do it again. And then it did, the interval thick with fear and fantasy.

Oh, Bayla.

Oh, Hebrew tutor.

We'll fill the saddlebags, we'll plan crimes. Just tell me yes.

Crimes?

Yes. Decide. Decide, you old man, world's most ancient seventeen-year-old boy. Decide.

Who are you, Bayla? Who sent you here to do this to me?

Come with me, and you'll find out.

Bayla?

If you don't, I'll tell you this: I'm the future you'll never have because you're too timid. Maybe that's why you're so sad, Hebrew tutor. Not for your parents, or for the Jews, or for the Holocaust, or for all of Jewish history, but for yourself. You act like you're scared already and the future hasn't even begun for you. I see that.

All of that's on my face?

I have to know. Now, Norman. Speak.

I opened my mouth and I felt the future rush in and force itself down my throat. It felt like a gag, at first, but then I could breathe again, as a long ribbon of breath unfurled inside, and I said, Yes, Bayla. Yes, I'll go with you.

CHAPTER FIFTEEN

Bayla called. Her voice on our old black telephone seemed like my little L.A. version of the call of our prophets—inevitable yet still utterly surprising. Our departure, she said, was imminent, maybe as soon as Monday.

Sure, I said, sure. How long would we be gone?

Unclear, she said. Depends how much you love me.

Maybe I'd better ask what to pack?

One change of underwear, she said. We'll pick up whatever we need on the way. Traveling light and fast, Hebrew tutor.

Sure, I said to Bayla. Exactly.

I chose single words that wouldn't reveal anything. It was exciting to be a kind of spy in my own life. Let Ed and Esther think I was going over Hebrew questions Bayla was asking on the telephone.

I've decided I should bring a knife, Norman.

Good, Bayla.

The way I figure, we'll be sleeping outdoors, under the open sky. What if a bear comes sniffing around? Got to be able to defend ourselves. Stop worrying, Norman.

Yes, Bayla. Very good. That's excellent. Uh-huh.

I flattered myself with the notion that I was thinking through what I was about to do, but there was nothing linear or logical about it, just the same film I kept screening: We are riding on the highway, just as she had described it. I'm on the back of Carlos's Yamaha, little Bayla in front with her arms raised holding the handlebars, and we're cruising toward the horizon.

Maybe that's why I decided to cut the small rectangle of lawn, a chore I always delayed or ignored completely. If I was really leaving, which I was, I told myself, the least I could do for my parents was leave them a trim lawn. So I got behind that little two-cycle engine as if to prepare for the future, and maybe also to prepare for the hum and vibration of the Yamaha, our getaway bike.

I'll call you back, I said. I need to mow the lawn.

It was comforting to walk behind the mower and to smell the green of the grass, to bend down and to flick the snails out of the mower's path, to, in some manner, take care of the home that I was about to desert.

Late that night, my parents had another big fight. Ed had scraped enough money together to get his car fixed, and he wanted to go to Las Vegas, leaving early Sunday. My mother refused to go, even though his winnings from a previous jaunt, he said, had won him three nights free lodging at the Fontainebleau Hotel.

Esther wanted to stay home, she said, to be near her friends in the temple sisterhood. And to pray at temple. Ed always told her his gambling was the equivalent of her praying, only it required more skill. And, please, he really wanted to listen to the ball game. Then she accused him, as usual, of being some kind of Jewish heretic who compounded sins by acting as if he knew far more than he knew. The word *pray* almost always set Ed off, and it did this time too.

You don't care about praying, he said to her. Every time that rabbi says jump, you jump. If you think he knows anything more about God, or how to talk to God, than anyone else, you're crazy.

And who appointed you to sit in judgment on the rabbi?

Well, you should stop talking to him about things you shouldn't be talking about.

Such as?

Such as you know exactly. What I do is my business.

My business, my business. Mr. J. P. Morgan.

Let a man be in peace!

In Las Vegas you'll have peace? I don't need whatever you go there for, she said, turning suddenly and going past me into the kitchen.

Las Vegas is for single men and playboys, she shouted from behind the door, which was still swinging. Which are you?

As Ed tried to catch my eye in male understanding, I decided to deny him. My mother re-emerged, drying her hands on her State of Israel apron.

And maybe you should reconsider your plans for more than just me. Maybe once in a while do something with your son.

He can come to Vegas with me. He can come any time. He knows it.

Maybe do something he likes.

He's becoming a genius for all of us. What does he need me to study with? You want me to go to the library with you? Shlep your big pile of books for you? With pleasure.

No, thanks, Dad.

Everyone needs their fathers to give them some guidance, she said.

All right, let today be guidance day. It's my pleasure to inform you and your mother that we are having a special on our guidance items this entire week. Two guidances for the price of one. You want any?

Always with the jokes, the stupid jokes.

Then she turned to me, with an imploring tone. Do something with your father this weekend.

Maybe you'll like Las Vegas, Ed said. You've never been there. And if you get bored with gambling, I hear there's a growing synagogue. They have odds every week on whose side God will be taking.

What you do, Esther screamed, is not the way to spend your life. A man who can barely support his family shouldn't be so proud of how he spends his days. Sitting around the table with people whose last names you don't even know. You're best friends while you sit there, and then when the game is over, what are they good for?

They give me a loan when I need it. That's what they're good for. And the temple? It's good for asking for money over and over and over.

Some loans. With your blood you pay them back.

But I pay.

Big man. Very big. A life with strangers is what he prefers over home and family. What do they have, Ed, that we don't give you?

Stop it, I said. Just drop it.

Take him maybe to a baseball game, Ed. Instead of just listening to the radio, get up off the couch.

He's a big boy, he does what he does.

Always an excuse.

I don't need to go anywhere, I said. I'm fine. Anyway, I may be doing something with Bayla this weekend. Maybe later in the week.

My mother, who had been holding the kitchen door open with her foot, let it swing shut and came to stand beside me at the dining room table. What? she said. Doing what?

Something. A special assignment. Something.

That's it? Something?

With her, with Bayla. Maybe do something with the family, I went on.

Like units in a parade that hadn't ever marched together before, my little troop of lies began to form up.

You hear how this family, this *other* family, respects your son? He gives me money too, Ed. When I run out, when I don't have enough. When you don't, your son does. At least he earns.

Stop it, Mom.

Your father should know this when he sits down and loses in Las Vegas.

So I know, Ed said. Are you learning the Adlers' business? Are they going to take you into the business?

I'm still the tutor, Dad. Just the Hebrew tutor.

Other people know who you are, he said. Your abilities. That's good.

Ask him what he's doing this weekend, Ed.

No, you ask him. I don't pry. He's a man now. A man will tell you what he wants to tell you. A man isn't a can of stewed tomatoes that you should open him up with your mouth.

All right, folks.

So where are you going?

I told you. Somewhere, probably with Bayla.

And the parents?

I don't know, I said. I just don't know.

Another mystery man, she said. Between the both of you it's like I'm living with the FBI.

Look, I'm leaving for Vegas tonight, Ed said to me. If you change your mind, you can always drive out to join me. Take the Hudson, or the bus is cheap. I'll meet you in the lobby of the hotel. Name the time and I'll be there. You've got to see Vegas. A million light bulbs—it's never night there.

But I like the night, Dad. I like the night just fine.

Suit yourself.

That's the way it was then: That's the way it still is, isn't it? Everybody always leaving somebody, or returning. That's the great truth in the Hebrew world *shalom,* meaning both *hello* and *good-bye.* You never know which; when you're saying one, you're also saying the other. It also means *peace,* of course, which is just the wisdom that comes when you know every moment is both an arrival and a departure, and the present hardly exists at all. That's why today I have the word, in Hebrew and in English, on both sides of my bike.

I wonder always if I'll be the leaving one, or the one left, standing by the screen door staring as I go down the walk of Ed and Esther's old house, now long gone and made into apartments, pausing in the driveway in the dewy early morning air, as I mount the bike, as the hibiscus flowers and hedge of bougainvillea buzz with bees, as the jasmine drifts across the porch at sunset. Still there, always there, on the receiving end of a little wave, a flick of the wrist that could mean either see you soon, Mom, or this is how I bat away a fly.

Ah, we can't help but be the center of our own worlds, but— and this, by the way, is the prayer I intend to lead us in every day we ride—Lord, please allow our bikes and our egos to observe all speed limits!

Of course I understood early on that my leaving was not going to be like my father's. He was an absentee husband and dad. My mother used those words, absentee this and absentee that; she'd picked it up from her beloved rabbi, whose road she wanted me to follow, and here I am—am I not, brothers and sisters of the King Solomon Bikers Club—forty years of wandering later? Have I followed it? That will be for you to decide.

If only I could be like Rabbi Joel, somehow that would be a solution for Esther's woe. But Rabbi Joel was far too slick for me, too cool in his chauffeured Lincoln Town Car, and his inauthentic over-pomaded fake-Elvis hair. He needed the driver, Esther once said to us, quick to summon a defense that neither Ed nor I—riveted to our Dodger-Cardinal game, on the Sabbath no less —was even asking for. The chauffeur allowed the exceptionally devoted and extremely booked rabbi, she said, to refine his sermons in the back seat. No, rabbis should drive themselves, I've always felt ever since, and if you ride on the Sabbath, by the way, let your violation be worth it; let it be on a big beast of a bike, where, exceeding the speed of light, you'll be ultimately at rest, and therefore in no Jewish violation at all.

Where was your ax, Rabbi Joel? Were you facing police dogs and cattle prods in Birmingham that summer of 1963? Even in our time there were people cold and alone in the woods needing help. Were you leading the Jewish community of Saigon, pouring gasoline over your *yarmulkah* and *tallis* and lighting yourself up for God? If not, then why should I become someone like you?

Could I really leave my parents at all? Would Rabbi Joel console my mother in the back of the limo while Bayla and I were riding the motorcycle out of the Hollywood Hills? Would he read to her verses from Job, to demonstrate that her present suffering didn't even approach the biblical level, while Bayla and I cruised the freeway, heading north, my skullcap blowing off my head like a black leaf and flying away?

Flying away, that is, until decades later I caught it, and am presenting it now, to you. One of the fine things about riding is that there is no need for a *yarmulkah,* as a helmet will do. Ah, how many Jewish heads would have been saved over the millennia had we all been wearing helmets instead?

To play Bayla's game was to say to Ed and Esther, Sorry, folks, but I am not the child you take me for, nor the man you want me to become; no matter what happens from this weekend or week or month or year of joyriding or whatever we will do, nothing will ever be the same again. I will be crossing a line.

All right, please forgive me for exaggerating this as my little Alamo, but you don't have to stop breathing to feel that you're as good as dead.

CHAPTER SIXTEEN

If I left, wouldn't I become that most awful thing, an irresponsibly thankless child? One who turns his back, exactly like Ed, like the person in the world Esther was bringing me up most *not* to be? God and the People of Israel are like parent and child, Dr. Levin had taught us. One way to look at the awkwardly intimate I-Thou, divine-to-human relationship. What's the worst thing that one side can do to the other? Face away. Turn not thy face away from me, Israel!

And yet Bayla had promised that she would wear that little pink bikini top that I loved and her short jean skirt that drove me crazy, and after Lake Gregory we would travel, wind blowing through our hair, north and east to the central valley, and up toward San Francisco. She had friends there. She . . .

I went into my room—a space that somehow I had not really looked at honestly until I made the decision to leave it. You would think there would be books all over, shelves crammed with holy texts, but there were no bookcases, and few books, and the only complete set was neither Mishna nor Talmud but Readers Digest Abridged Classics. You would think my desk would be beautiful or at least orderly, like an altar, for it, after all, was the place where I sacrificed. However, it was a knock-off that Ed had picked up at Miller's Downtown Annex, serving the low end of the discount market, a desk with its dark, thin veneer peeling away at the drawer pulls even as we set it up.

I now saw peeling wallpaper above my bed, a strip of molding separated from the wall at nearly forty-five degrees, and above it a leak stain not ever correctly repainted. And then I had to stop my inspection and shut my eyes. If going into my room and slamming my door was already a form of leaving, then actually leaving might be nothing more than an anticlimax. I opened my eyes and took in the full scope of this cozy, so familiar threadbareness—what exactly was it I was gaining by entering into this little cell every night?

"How did you get this way, Hebrew tutor?" I wrote out Bayla's question in thick block letters, just as we had written out the alphabet and the commandments. I cut out the paper and taped it above my desk. If Bayla Adler were becoming my getaway girlfriend, this question would be her portrait.

I threw myself on the bed, gripping my ribs as if trying to keep everything within from flying apart. The mattress stopped bouncing and at least my body lay still. I stared up at the patterned dots on the stucco ceiling as if to find in them some revealed hint of direction or design that had been thus far hidden from me all my short life. Was I was going to continue to plant myself in the middle of my parents' sorrows forever? Be their witness and their windsock, blowing in her favor most of the time, occasionally in his, and by these deeds keep their marriage together? Through my strenuous efforts and achievements could I even do that?

That they might actually love each other, or at least have found in the other some thing that had been missing in themselves and that, as a consequence, there was a kind of bizarre working partnership here that made for an effective couple—all this marital wisdom entirely eluded me. So did the prospect that I was perhaps the *cause* of their fights, not the means for repair. I was so full of the *I* of myself. But Bayla, who had never even met Ed and Esther, saw, and Bayla knew.

The next day, a Monday morning, Esther got to the ringing phone in the hallway before I could get out of bed. It turned out to be a kind of gift for her. As she picked up and surmised, correctly, that it was Bayla, her mouth, thin and straight and all too expecting to dip into disappointment, magically began to curve up into a little smile of hopefulness.

When I took the instrument from her and trailed its wrinkled cord behind me toward my room, Esther called out, as my door was closing on her, Take all the time you need, dear.

Bayla said life at home was hell. She said Lucille and her dad were in the midst of a big real-estate deal to take over a dozen more nursing homes in the Valley. Maybe two dozen, maybe three. And the moment of no return was nearing—Lucille was forcing her to go shopping yet again for the bat mitzvah dress.

I told her I wanted one all in leather, Bayla said. Now she had to endure even more shopping—unless we cut out immediately.

Doesn't the fact that Lucille's whole family died in Europe, in the ovens, mean anything to you at all? I asked Bayla. I was shocked by my own question, as if someone I didn't recognize had asked for it.

It means, she answered in that clear, matter-of-fact way of hers, that she's angry all the time. It's not my fault what was done over there. How does having a bat mitzvah change any of that? How does that justify her being a bitch to me? She knew who I was when she married my father. She's into money and shopping, and she's got you, Hebrew tutor, wound around her many-ringed finger.

No, she doesn't.

Oh no?

No.

Then what's stopping you?

Certainly not your mother.

She's not my mother.

Lucille?

Don't even say the name.

Then how do I refer to her when I'm talking to you, Bayla?
Just say "the bitch." That'll do fine.
I don't like talk like that.
If you don't say it, Bayla went on, dropping into her ten-year-old childish mode, that'll prove to me you don't love me. Go on, say it. The bitch.
She didn't seem to care about my silence and quickly shifted back into her teenaged tone.
You know you and Lucille both have this love for the Jews thing, Norman. That's why she adores you.
She doesn't adore me.
Then why did you let her put her hands all over you and kiss you up? I'm not blind, you know. Maybe that should disqualify you from coming with me. Plus, even if I liked her, for a woman her age, there's only one word for it: disgusting.
You're exaggerating, Bayla. As always.
But that's what you love about me. Right?
Sometimes with Bayla, I felt as if we were in a play together, a kind of improvisation. She would act a part, and then I respond, and then she would adjust what she had planned, and compel me to say lines to revise my previous feelings if their expression hadn't quite suited her. I found this childishness charming, but only to a point.
Right? Right?
I didn't answer.
Right?
It irritates me when you do this pressure thing.
A girl has to know who she is running off with, Norman. So?
At such times my approach was often to try to get out of the verbal jam by consulting my dictionary, or the dog-eared paperback of *Bartlett's Familiar Quotations* that Ed had bought me for a Hanukkah present one year.
I'd flip to some quotation about friendship or love that might impress Bayla, or at least tame her anger about Lucille or her doubts about me, although she often wasn't appeased by my sententious

murmurings. I had always liked quotations—they were famous for a reason, being funny, true, and, yes, wise. I even fantasized that I somehow could absorb their wisdom without having to do much more living than letting my fingers graze the corners of the pages. Why did I have to reread *Hamlet* or any more Shakespeare, if I could commit "To be or not to be" to memory? "Tomorrow and tomorrow and tomorrow" had already been a big hit with Bayla when she told me how she had run away before. And once when the radio had been on beside the pool, and we'd heard Pete Seeger or maybe it was the Monkees, singing, For everything there is a season, turn, turn, turn, a time for everything under heaven. A time to reap and a time to sow, a time . . . I adroitly flipped to the page in *Ecclesiastes* from where the lyrics derived, and I had scored with Bayla Adler big time. Advantage Hebrew tutor.

I was in fact surprised and even troubled by how often deploying a little recycled erudition or yesterday's articles that I read in Ed's rumpled newspaper worked with Bayla, how if I explained the difference between North Vietnam and South Vietnam, she immediately thought I was an expert on all of Asia. No, she was not a reader of books, although I felt she could read through me and that in fact she already knew things that were written on the pages of my life that I didn't even know were there; pages that I had skipped, or ripped out, or had covered in thick black marker, Top Secret, to be withheld, especially from myself.

You're stalling me, Hebrew tutor, she said in a later, afternoon call. I still don't know if you love me and if you're going with me. I know I'm not perfect, but together we will be.

We admire people, Bayla, in spite of their faults. We love them because of their faults.

That's beautiful, Norman.

Like you.

Something really terrible happened the other day that I never told you about.

Tell me now.

When Lucille dragged me to that dress store the first time, and she was standing in front of it, and she was going on about how beautiful I would look in some ugly bat mitzvah getup, I said to her, Lucille, if you love the Jewish people so much, and bat mitzvahs are so important to you, then why did you get that nose job that cost my father twenty thousand dollars? Why do you want to hide who you are?

That's when Lucille slapped me. Right in front of the most expensive store on Rodeo Drive. I can still feel the sting, she whispered into the phone. I wish you were here and could kiss it away, Hebrew tutor.

I will be soon.

Will you? Are you sure, Norman? I couldn't sleep last night. I am worried you are going to chicken out. Are you?

No, Bayla.

Promise me, you chicken.

Again I was silent. I wasn't a gambler's child for nothing, and, yes, I always tried to avoid signing on the dotted line, even verbally. I reached across the bed and looked for another piece of canned wisdom, this time in Wit and Proverbs of Israel. I quickly looked up *chicken* and *chicken soup* in the index, but nothing fit.

Did I say the wrong thing to the bitch?

You said what you felt. How is that ever wrong? She was making me improvise again, change my perspective. Sometimes I chided her, sometimes I sided with her, against Lucille.

No matter what kind of nose she has, she's ugly, isn't she?

Please, Bayla.

You have a big nose too, Norman. I like your nose. Mine's very small. It's my mother's nose, my dad says. When I was born, he said he was worried it wouldn't be big enough to breathe through.

It seems to work fine, I said.

Carlos used to say that if it were bigger I could take in more air and swim faster. Poor Carlos.

I thought you're supposed to breathe through your mouth.

You do if your nose is too small. She breathed. I want to leave now.

No!

Why not?

I need a little more time.

Soon then? This week?

O.K., yes.

Good. You dither and I'll tell my parents you're sick. No tutoring this week, because, frankly, Norman, that's over between us. Right?

If you say so.

We're moving on, but together.

I didn't know what to say.

You can use the tutoring time to fret and to obsesss all you want, but remember that you promised.

Enough, Bayla.

I'll pay you too, for the time, and more. You'll see. Have you ever camped out, Hebrew tutor?

If there is a bear or deer who talks Hebrew, you are speaking to the person who has taught those creatures their *aleph-bet*.

You haven't ever slept out under the stars, have you? Oh, you're going to enjoy this. Hebrew tutor, I'm packed. I'm ready. You call me any time, day or night, and I'll be there. Just listen for my engine.

CHAPTER SEVENTEEN

Oh boy. I decided I had to talk to Michael Levin. Dr. Levin had brought me to Bayla Adler, he had set the tutoring up, and now he had to know. He was a holy, prayerful, religious man. If I presented it the right way, maybe he would keep it quiet, although that he was Lucille's uncle made me uncertain. Still, who else was there to go to? Hadn't Dr. Levin once prayed, and then the rains came? Maybe he could perform another more domestic miracle and get me out of this mess.

Forgetting saving my own skin, how could I tell Dr. Levin what was going on without risking the danger of blowing the whole thing for Bayla? Did I love Bayla Adler? If I did, shouldn't I show it by keeping my mouth shut? Yet, what did I really know about *love,* the word girls seemed to bandy about so easily? Love is what happens when someone speaks to you only with their eyes? Which means exactly what? Go to the eye doctor, Ed would have explained to me. Did girls have some secret knowledge, something inside them, inside their bellies, beside those fruit-shaped organs and tubes, that gave them an insight on love that boys simply didn't possess, and never would? Or were they just being silly? Love is not love that alters when it alteration finds?

While I wasn't ready to answer with love, I did feel, in addition to rampaging lust, of course, a real friendship that had at its heart a kind of loyalty. I was not only Bayla's Hebrew tutor, I was her Jewish confessor.

I think, incidentally, confession is something it would be good to work into Jewish practice not only on Yom Kippur, but every day as we ride. Don't you agree, my friends of the King Solomon Bikers Club?

Yes, I alone was the repository for everything she had told me, and I didn't take that lightly. If Levin felt he had to call Lucille, who knew how she would respond? Maybe she would call the cops, or send Bayla to counseling. Everyone at school was getting tested for this and that, submitting to these new Rorschach tests, getting scored, visiting with a psychologist that Rabbi Joel had brought into the temple, and being sent off to see a counselor. When Biff Waterman practically killed a kid during a football practice (I happened to be there watching, from the sidelines, of course, and thought it was a perfectly legal tackle), the coach talked to his parents, and the next thing we knew Biff was going some place to learn how to control his anger.

Where would they send Bayla, who was, I thought, a lot more dangerous than Biff Waterman and the football team combined? Even if I was going to chicken out, didn't I at minimum owe her some measure of protection by not revealing our plan?

I picked up the phone to call Dr. Levin. Hadn't he taught us that every biblical verse has at least five levels of meaning, five interpretations, from the simple and literal to the symbolic to the utterly hidden and only hinted at, the Kabbalistic, and you had to be forty years old, they said, even to begin to understand it? My predicament felt that way. Halfway through the dialing, I returned the phone to its cradle.

I began to feel dizzy. It passed, but I couldn't eat much the whole next day. That really alarmed my mother. She did her chicken soup thing, and I forced myself to eat a bowlful, but not much else. We both agreed that I might be getting a cold. I actually allowed myself to be tucked in by her. I watched President Kennedy on TV say that segregation was morally wrong and that it was time to act. It was time for me too. Lesley Gore had a new

THE HEBREW TUTOR OF BEL AIR

single out: It's my party, it began, and I'll cry if I want to. I listened to it about twenty times, but I couldn't cry, or sleep either.

Desperate, I lifted the phone up one more time, but then replaced it. If not Dr. Levin, who else to call? Where would Kabbalists hang out in L.A.? Up in the Hollywood Hills? With the Negroes and the Mexicans and the other downtrodden on skid row, which Ed often described? Or maybe out in Venice or Santa Monica where they could sit on the sand and see something only they knew in the patterns of the waves?

When I lifted up the receiver one more time, however, my fingers, apparently following a purer heart than my own, refused to do the dialing. If I failed to earn Levin's trust and confidence and Bayla's parents suddenly grounded her, she would instantly know who had ratted on her, and hate me. Yet maybe her anger and displeasure wouldn't last too long; she was like that. I could plead that I was just trying to figure things out for myself, that I hadn't specifically betrayed her; then maybe I could find a way back into her good graces.

Dream on, Hebrew tutor, I heard myself saying aloud as I paced my tiny bedroom. If I suddenly did become her partner on that bike, would I be any good at all in that new role? What did I know about being a runaway?

No, above all I needed to be what I knew and did best, the Hebrew tutor, the guy who sits in a chair with a book in front of him, an easy quotation at hand, and on a schedule. Riding a powerful motorcycle, illegally, without a license. . . . Would Bayla also have stolen Carlos's bike? I hadn't even thought to ask. I certainly wasn't the type to be wanted by the law as well.

Please, Bayla, wherever you are today, you understand, don't you, why I had to do this?

I thought about that camping out conversation we'd had, and I knew the only snakes that I could handle were those that that lived in my mind, that Aaron and Moses had created, from their staffs, and thrown in front of Pharaoh. I was terrified of the rattlers and copperheads that lived year-round in the L.A. foothills. They lurked precisely in those canyons and arroyos that she had proposed we bike through on the very first day.

No, I was the Hebrew tutor, not the Hebrew biker—not yet—and I had to find a way for Bayla to stay put. Yes, far more for my sake, but then might not my gutlessness save her, too, from herself? How do you say *self-denial* in Hebrew? How do you say *lying-to-yourself* in Aramaic? Come and listen: What do the rabbis say is the punishment for committing the moral misdemeanor of being a little chickenshit? What are the punishments, in the Talmud? What levels of compensation are to be offered to the offended?

I had to sort this out. I couldn't just secretly pack my bag and show up in Bel Air without a word to any adult. Maybe that was Bayla Adler's way, but it couldn't be mine. That seemed right and clear, and since little else did after my last conversation with Bayla, I picked up the phone to call Michael Levin, and this time I went through with it.

I told him, in a rush, only that I had something important to discuss with him, and that it involved Bayla. I didn't want to confess any more.

I heard him breathe deeply but evenly, as if gathering himself, like a doctor who works with people for whom there might be no good outcomes, only some less bad than others.

Norman?

I imagined the tight, light skin of his brow furrowing, the glint of his glasses as he looked around his study. I visualized where his phone reposed on the table, with its doily all yellowy beneath a sixty-watt lamp with a green-and-black-striped shade. I knew it well. As his star student, I had sat there often.

Dr. Levin? There's not a lot of time.

She's quite something, that Bayla, isn't she?

Yes, she is, sir. Shall I come to your house, Dr. Levin?

No, no, no, he said. I'm glad you called. Let me check my calendar. I'll come Sunday, shall we say? Will that be all right?

But you don't drive.

I'll pick you up, he repeated.

Yes.

Arrangements will be made.

You'll pick me up here? At my house?

Isn't that where you live? Sunday. It'll give me an opportunity to visit your dear parents as well.

All my warning signals began to flicker on, my switches flung into alarm mode. Neither Levin nor *any* of my teachers had ever come to our house. They always met us at school, for parents' night or awards night. Never here. Friends never came here either, neither mine, nor my parents'. The house simply was too small, too musty, too much like the Hadassah thrift shop downtown, where Esther occasionally volunteered. Not good at all for a meeting, and my parents' would be there too. Esther, anyway. She always was, and then it would get . . . way beyond embarrassing. That's the way it was.

Is there a problem, Norman?

Isn't it a lot of trouble for you to come way over here? I'd prefer to go to your place, like always.

Norman?

Yes.

Who's in trouble, Bayla or you?

It's just that—

Not another word. Sha. Quiet. I'll arrange for a car. Until Sunday evening then. Have a restful Sabbath.

CHAPTER EIGHTEEN

I had an English lit class on Friday, but I couldn't stop thinking about the mistake I'd made, that I had agreed to Dr. Levin's coming to our house, and I completely forgot to go to class. This had never happened to me before. The world's timing never made less sense to me.

When Dr. Levin had met my parents last, it was at a school awards ceremony. Esther had gotten Ed to put on his best suit, but even in their fanciest clothes, I remembered, with my mother's little black hat tilted on the side of her head just so and my having given Ed the evil eye, he said, until he agreed to polish his shoes, my embarrassment had been acute. Even the scholarship award I received—a book about great Zionist ideas—seemed tainted by a rip on the title page. I could not let Dr. Levin in to our second-hand life.

I barely remember that week except that Bayla called once to ask if I thought she should burn her bat mitzvah dress or let Lucille return it to Rodeo Drive for a refund. She exacted a verbal pledge from me once again. I crossed my fingers, like the child I was, and said: We'll go, we'll go.

On Sunday morning, with Dr. Levin having said he would arrive by six that evening, all I was thinking was that, if the visit could not be prevented, how then, at minimum, could I keep him from actually entering the house?

Then I had an idea. I drove up to the University of Judaism and headed for Dr. Levin's office. I would talk to him up there and be done with it so there would be no need for him to come into our house. However, he was not in, and the librarian told me he had cancelled his classes. I drove over to his apartment building, and pushed on Dr. Levin's bell until it might break, but no one answered. I was so frustrated and troubled, but not knowing where else to turn, I went back to the University and I sat nearly paralyzed in the library for several hours.

At four forty-five I left. I drove erratically down Olympic Boulevard and the intervening streets, I reviewed my patchwork of anxious strategies. I almost drove into a utility pole two blocks from home; that would have been a kind of solution.

I entered breathlessly, dropped my books on the chair, and heard my mother happily whistling something from *Oklahoma,* one of her favorite musicals that often accompanied her cooking. The house was filled up with that aromatic, onions-simmering-in-butter smell, which I usually liked, but to my nostrils that afternoon it was heavy, peasant-smelling, and cloying, and there wasn't a window open. Esther's purse and neatly folded black jacket were not on the chair by the door, which would have indicated that she had somewhere to go after she fed me dinner. No, that absence and the leisurely singing meant there were no meetings of the sisterhood, no bingo at the temple. She was going to be home all night.

We exchanged our usual greetings, including her briefing that Ed was in Nevada "on a job" and would not return this night.

He's not in Nevada, I said, because I knew from her tone that she was covering as usual.

Fine. He's just . . . away.

I gave her my perfunctory hug of manly husband-substitute reassurance. I was never more grateful for my father's three-day-two-night gambling jaunts. Or whatever they were. Or whoever he was. Who cared, as long as he was away and out of the zone of my embarrassment. How I wished Esther too had some addiction, some place she absolutely had to be every night, beginning with this one.

I went into the bathroom, washed my face in cold water, and threw some on the back of my neck. On the toilet tank I found the newspaper, opened up to the entertainment section, and, theatrically holding it up in front of me, entered the kitchen.

There's lots of good stuff playing tonight. Some really great movies here. *Lawrence of Arabia* is still up on Hollywood Boulevard. I'm happy to drive you, and I can pick you up afterward, too, if you want.

You want to go?

No, I couldn't. I've got a lot of . . . last-minute stuff to do . . . to, you know, prepare for Bayla's lesson.

Oh, that bat mitzvah is getting very close. Fine. Then we'll have a cozy evening here, together.

I'm pretty busy, Mom. Sweat began to appear on my forehead.

Is it your cold coming back?

No, Mom. I feel just fine.

The career of my childhood had trained me to be an evader, a junior prevaricator. I was not skilled in the art of outright lying, which I was then approaching. I should have just kept my mouth shut and run off with Bayla Adler. A clean, simple break, just the way she had said we should do it. A change of underwear, and goodbye! Let the grown-ups all worry. Let their hair turn white in grief. If running away doesn't accomplish at least that, Bayla had said, then maybe it's not worth doing it. But no, not me. Not Norman, not Nehemiah, the Hebrew tutor of Bel Air.

Norman, my mother was speaking as she followed me about the house with the wooden spaghetti spoon in her hand, like a conductor with a baton chasing down the player who is sounding a discordant note. What is with you, son? You want me to go to *Lawrence of Arabia* and sit alone? Some invitation. Since when can't I be in my own house? Since when do I ever get in your way?

I stepped over to the picture window and looked out toward the street where Dr. Levin would be arriving all too soon.

Aha!

Aha yourself, I said. Sometimes repetition derailed Bayla's relentless demanding; maybe it would work with my mother too.

That girl, Bayla, is coming over tonight. Preparing your lesson, of course. Now I get it, and you want some . . . privacy. Is that it? Why didn't you just say so? I'm a woman, in case you hadn't noticed. You don't have to go sneaking around.

You don't understand.

The both of you keep your feet on the floor, as the rabbi says, and I have no objection.

I don't want the goddamn advice of the rabbi about what to do and what not to do in my bedroom.

Norman!

Well, I mean it. Anyway, you don't understand. You don't understand at all.

No? All right then.

Bayla Adler is not coming over here. You think I would *ever* invite Bayla Adler to this place?

Esther sat down heavily in Ed's chair then, as if what I had said had blasted her into it. It was the big La-Z-Boy that she almost never sat in even when he was away. It was as if the chair, somehow, in its comfort and availability, might mysteriously be a kind of beacon, drawing Ed back to us from whatever ill-lit, card-table-and-folding-chair-strewn gambling hall he happened to be hanging out in. The La-Z-Boy tipped back slightly, and as the footrest rose, Esther settled her hands, which still held the cooking spoon, on her aproned lap. A tomato-red noodle began to slip down the handle.

I'm sorry. It's just awkward.

If you want me to go to the movies, I'll go, Norman.

You don't have to go to the movies.

I said I would go. I won't ask questions.

You live here as much as I do. Stay.

A friend is coming over? Biff? Another friend?

No.

There's plenty of spaghetti, and the salad is nice too. A beautiful red tomato. Have him stay for dinner. I'd love to make dinner for your friends. You know, have I ever? I know what's going through that head of yours. You don't have to say it. I know.

Standing now even closer to the window, my cheek nearly pressed against the glass, I gave her a stare. Suddenly a big Buick came into view, but then, thankfully, kept going down the street.

All right then. So you know.

People don't come to visit a couch and chairs, and a table. They come to visit you, your character, not your furniture, Norman. So we don't have the most expensive items. So we don't have . . .

And here she broke off, and we looked around the room together at the sagging green couch, the old Muntz TV with its rabbit ears covered in tin foil, the plywood box overflowing with years-old copies of *Life* and *Look* and the *B'nai B'rith Messenger* and the *Hollywood Reporter,* which Biff's mother always passed along, a week old, to Esther at the sisterhood meetings. Then there was the dining room table, with its ancient elephant's feet, the misused lazy Susan, and the bowl with all those scratch sheets. All the hand-me-downs and the dust we seemed to live in were suddenly klieg-lit.

I know, I know, I said.

You know so much. Do what you want. But her gaze said, Do what *I, your mother,* wants. Do what I deserve, for a change.

Since I could not, and would not, I looked away.

A half minute, maybe a minute passed in that deepening shame of silence while I continued to survey the street, wishing I had asked Dr. Levin what make of car he would be arriving in so I might identify it immediately and run out to him while he was still parking. But I hadn't, and maybe, since he was not much of a driver himself, he couldn't have told me anyway.

For how many years had I been fooling myself that she did not already know my sad little tactics? Oh, she knew, and I knew she knew. So I ransacked my inventiveness for some new angle, some new lie the both of us might accept, if only to get through the next hours together.

Then Esther did something she had never done before, and it took me completely by surprise. Maybe she wasn't exactly aiming, maybe her anger and frustration and general despair had just spontaneously created a force that, not of her own will, launched the thing in my direction. Yet whatever the physics or karma of it, she leaped up from the La-Z-Boy and the next thing I was aware of, the spaghetti spoon was flying at me. The utensil seemed to glimmer mysteriously for an instant in the light like a kind of domestic UFO as it somersaulted my way across the living room. It missed my head by six inches, ricocheted off the wall behind, and then dropped down behind the TV.

Together we turned, as if our necks were invisibly attached to the same set of gears, to see the tomato sauce, in three or four blotches and a spray of lumpish red dots, stain and slowly drip down the wall.

There! she cried. Mr. Smart Guy! You want something to be ashamed of? There, now you have it. Share *that* dinner with your important guests!

As I had walked out on her so many times, now she left me. Through the dining room, down the short hall, and to her bed. The musty silence that often blanketed the inside of our house rolled in yet again.

I knew what would happen in the next interval. It always did. I let go of the heavy drape I found clutched in my hand, and took up a position roughly midway down the hall to her room, where, like a sentry, I listened to her sobbing. Although she muffled them, sounds and then fragments of words broke through the barrier of her kleenexed hand that I knew covered her mouth: Why are you doing this to me, God? *Gevalt!* Why me? And then the sobbing resumed, but fairly soon it somehow narrowed into an exhausted sigh.

I stepped down the hall nearer to her room. I inclined myself toward her and quietly listened, like a birdwatcher who is fairly certain he's made an identification by sound alone but still fears he might be wrong. I then said, very quietly, that I was sorry, and I listened for perhaps another minute.

Do you want some 7-Up? Some seltzer?

No. I'll be fine in a few minutes. Then I'll go out.

Mom. I'm really not ashamed of you.

Have a nice time. I can walk home too.

No. I'm . . . just a little embarrassed, now and then.

Kids are like that. I'll take a little nap, Normie, and then I'll go. You're a good boy. Leave on the light, please.

As I stood outside my mother's room and listened to her sighs, I thought oddly of Burt Lancaster in *Run Silent, Run Deep,* the World War II submarine movie I had recently seen. Perhaps it was the long, narrow hallway where I always stood, embattled in dim light, that had triggered the memory of how physically at ease Burt was even in the confines of the submarine. There he dodged Jap destroyers and leaped from crisis to crisis with a kind of exuberant agility that seemed to mirror a confident moral courage within; he was almost always victorious. How I longed to be like him, to save the boat and to fulfill the mission—what was my mission?—even as I tightened the compartment door on my mother's weeping.

When I heard the low murmur of a car engine out in front of the house, I left the hall, grabbed my light denim jacket, and, like Burt bounding from deck to deck, I flew out to the porch and down the steps and the walk. There the biggest limousine I had ever seen in my life pulled up to the curb, and its back door swung ominously open.

CHAPTER NINETEEN

Well, this is a surprise, Nehemiah, said Dr. Levin from the spacious back seat. As I glanced in, I could see his legs were stretched luxuriously out, and there was even a small seat-high table in front of him with a pitcher of water and two glasses.

We certainly did not expect valet service.

Valet service is when someone takes your keys and parks your car, Dr. Levin. And you are parked already.

In the cone of yellow light that fell from the limo's ceiling I could see that my teacher was not alone. Beside him sat another man who slowly bent forward in my direction. Right away I noticed he was losing his hair, but in that handsome, tanned premature sort of way, as if he'd lost it not through some sudden calamity or even the normal processes of time, but by having had good, long vacations in faraway places where the sun had shined on him too long and too bright. Two patches of darker hair, streaked gray, were slicked down on the sides of his head above the ears, like little wings.

Nehemiah, said Dr. Levin, may I introduce David Adler, Bayla's father. I don't believe the two of you have met.

I was not really shocked. Alarmed, yes, but also somehow in the presence of the inevitable. After all, I was a person who at any moment was expecting to be caught, and who more appropriate to do the job than Bayla's father? Still, I was surprised, because I expected a tall man, reflective of everything I'd heard about him,

ALLAN APPEL

a giant in the nursing-home industry, a major entrepreneur. But the man who now swung his torso around in the seat to invite me inside was short, and I believe I even spotted elevator shoes.

Except for his compactness and the nervous energy that made him fidget, I didn't see much of Bayla in David Adler. Not her alabaster skin or her small nose or the intensity of her eyes. But when he reached out and shook my hand, as I hesitated at the door, the strength of the grip definitely reminded me of his daughter's power.

Why are you here, sir?

He gets to the point fast, doesn't he? Dr. Levin said, as if taking a kind of personal pride in my directness.

Why, indeed. Look, Norman, David Adler said. I still hesitated to enter, so he slid out of the limousine and stood beside me. I wanted to meet you finally after all this time that you've been teaching Bayla, and your parents, of course, and to express to them my appreciation for all you're doing for Bayla. And also to marvel at how they made such a boy as you.

You could have called.

And a sense of humor too, Michael Levin said. But his tone had modulated now, and in it was implicit criticism. I felt I had disappointed and wanted badly to recoup his approval.

My parents are very grateful for the opportunity you and your wife have given me, Mr. Adler, I said, returning to Junior Cong mode. They, and I, of course, appreciate what you're doing for me.

And where are your parents? Mr. Adler asked.

Busy.

If they're busy, said Levin, we can be very brief. Some things, however, must be said in person, and your parents should know.

Know what?

Why, the matter we were to discuss. *You* called *me*, Norman. You remember? The trip you and Bayla are going to take.

I didn't say anything about a trip.

Maybe you didn't, said David Adler, but Bayla is my daughter.

136

When Michael told me of your call, I knew it was about a little journey. Right? Only a matter of time. She runs off with boys like other girls go shopping.

I see, I said, but I really didn't.

Look, I have no idea of your itinerary. I would like to know it, of course. What you plan to do, where you'll be going. When. Not only for her safety but for yours as well. You're both under eighteen, I don't have to remind you. If you think of it as a school trip, with a parental permission slip required, all will be well. You understand, Norman?

Then they began to move up the walk to the house, with me between them.

Please, I said, stepping ahead of them and placing my hand on Mr. Adler's shoulder, I'm not sure I do understand, sir. Anyway, my father's away, out on business tonight, busy like I said, and my mother's not feeling very well.

That's too bad, said David Adler. He halted. Then he looked up and scanned the sky, pausing for what seemed like several long seconds. Returning his gaze to earth and to me, he said, And what kind of business is your father in, Norman?

Oh, business, I answered. He's downtown, on business. Sometimes he's out of town.

And your mother?

My mother's not in business. She's sick, not feeling well. That's her business tonight.

I'm sorry to hear that. Then he and Dr. Levin exchanged a curious glance. We're not the police, we don't break doors down.

Thank you, Mr. Adler.

Can we take a little walk, Plummer?

I don't know why, but I liked the way David Adler called me by my last name. I wasn't really very fond of it and rarely used it. Kids did, of course. Kids called me Plummer all the time, but in their mouths it was supposed to sound cool. I was used to it enough, and the follow-up quips about wrenches and toilets—all so stupid. Something about Mr. Adler's *Plummer* however, made me feel that he knew something about me I didn't, or that he was trying to treat me as, if not an equal, then a kind of partner. He was, after all, a businessman. His accent was similar to Lucille's, Eastern European but thicker. Above all, he was sizing me up—he was a man who could read others, and give signals and commands with the nod of his head. I saw that in precisely this fashion he inclined his head toward Dr. Levin, who acknowledged David Adler's wishes, and promptly slid back into the limousine.

Adler had apparently also already made a determination about me. For he put his arm through mine, and was soon walking briskly, with me in tow, down the sidewalk, away from our house, south toward Saturn Street.

Ah, my boy, my boy, he said, as his arm shifted so that it now circled my shoulders. At first I wasn't sure if by this gesture I were being embraced or somehow detained, or both; all I knew was at this instant David Adler was trying to take charge.

Ed had never taken such a man-to-man walk with me—I think I probably would have been shocked had he tried. Not that I hadn't been craving it, but I still would have fled from my own father had he made the attempt. Bayla's dad uncannily seemed to know this, my great need and also my revulsion. Although at first I felt myself easing away from his arm because it was not my father's, that abruptly altered when he said, Come, Plummer. You will permit me to call you Norman as well? We should get to know each other. I have something to say to you, brass tacks.

There was a scent of English Leather as once again I felt the pressure of his hand at the small of my back, pushing me along; it was as if he were afraid that if he were not applying sustained pressure I might flee into some neighbor's house.

I've got a proposition to make you.

It was his arm and not Ed's, and then precisely because he was not Ed, or maybe, after all, because I was Ed the gambler's son, I did not flee. I stayed in the game, I relented, I listened.

Plummer, I hear only good things about you. From Michael, of course, and also from my wife. But the most marvelous thing of all, Plummer, is Bayla. She says you are a genius. That you know everything.

She exaggerates. If I was so good, Bayla would know a lot more by now.

I'm not talking about genius in Hebrew, Plummer. Not that I don't respect the language of God and the prophets, but I'm talking about even more important knowledge that you have.

Knowledge of what?

Of people is I think what she means. Knowledge of fellow human beings. Of how to be with them. Put them at ease, listen. You think this is not a gift? In our business I see a lot of people who think they have it, salespeople, who just keep moving their gums and think a client is put at ease. But who can talk and really be listening at the same time? Not everybody has it, but you do, this depth you have for one so young, if you get my drift.

I told him I didn't.

This is what it means to have a gift, Plummer. It's so much part of you, you don't notice. A talent. You listen, like a plug you connect to a person—I know this in the short time we are talking. Now—and he paused long enough for me to notice at least one plane in the distance descending into our basin—shall I tell you a few things about Bayla you maybe don't know?

Sure.

We were walking quite fast now, as if he had accelerated to keep pace with a still unexpressed urgency. With Bayla, he said, always expect the opposite and you will not be disappointed. You understand.

I shook my head.

Of course you do, Plummer. That is why she likes you so much. You let her alone to be herself. You don't press her. She swims, and then she comes to you in her own good time. And this is just the beginning.

Of what?

Plummer, you shouldn't be jealous, but you're not the first boy. Not the first, Plummer, but I hope you will be the last.

I really don't understand you now at all, Mr. Adler.

Of course you do. She should have been named *Tzipporah.* You know what that means.

I did, of course.

All her life like a sparrow jumping from branch to branch. But she is now sixteen years old. She is far too beautiful to keep sowing oats. Now it is time she starts plain sewing, Plummer, if you catch my spelling joke. That's why that Mexican boy had to be let go. He was going too far with her. Taking liberties. I think you too saw this by the pool.

I'm just the Hebrew tutor, Mr. Adler.

Exactly what I mean! he exclaimed, as if someone else besides us were on that sidewalk to hear. Not only insight but such modesty in a seventeen-year-old Hebrew scholar such as yourself. This is a million-dollar package.

Please, Mr. Adler, I said, stopping at the corner below Saturn, toward the bottom of our hill.

Relax, son. I'm coming to it, coming to my proposal, he said. If you don't mind, let's walk a little farther.

We continued south, from Saturn, past Airdrome, and down to Eighteenth Street, where in general I hesitated to travel because the neighborhood became rougher. However, walking here, in the presence of Bayla's father, I felt safe. I knew he had been through a lot in Europe. I knew from Bayla he had been in a concentration camp, more than one, and had somehow gotten out and fought with the partisans and carried a gun. I noticed that nothing we passed, not a raucous party full of pulsating music, not the sudden snapping that might have been fireworks or even a gun, none of this startled David Adler. As if he were deaf, or inured to it all, he seemed hardly to notice. Beneath his arm, which now gave me another squeeze, I felt a powerful comfort, as if we were part of an invulnerable duo.

Norman, he said, the long and the short of it is, I'd like you to marry Bayla.

I stopped walking.

Marry Bayla? Mr. Adler! That *is* crazy.

Norman, her mother and I have had a discussion, and we agree that it's best for her. You love her, we know.

For the smallest instant, as I studied his face, I waited for the dubious, ironic smile to appear, evidence that the this-is-a-joke moment was about to occur. He didn't smile.

Norman, he said, I'm not asking you sign a contract, exactly. I'm not saying, let's cross the i's and let's dot the t's, or commit to a ceremony tonight. All I'm saying is, think on it. Think hard.

But I'm seventeen, Mr. Adler, and Bayla's sixteen.

When I married my first wife, Bayla's mother, may she rest in peace, I was not much older than you. We had a lovely marriage that only cancer broke apart. Age has nothing to do with the matter.

I was silent, and he was silent, and I don't know how much time passed as we stood there. Then nearby, a tall black man in roomy, sharply ironed trousers and white shirt, accompanied by a woman, emerged from the driveway walking slowly and talking quietly. When they saw us, they stopped.

You lost? asked the man.

Not at all. I hope we didn't disturb you.

Nope.

And it could have ended there, but some idea lit up Mr. Adler, and as the black couple smiled briefly and cut across the grass, he seemed to overcome some hesitation and called after them, You look like a very nice young couple. Tell me, he said, do *you* love each other?

The couple halted immediately, the man turned, and the smile of sociability disappeared from his face like the closing of a camera shutter.

I don't know why I should have been surprised that the man who had just asked me to marry his daughter should ask total strangers if they loved each other, but I was.

Who wants to know?

Only compliments are intended.

What I'd like to intend is that you mind your own business!

Please, Mr. Adler said to the man, in a voice as steady and calm as his tone was with me. I withdraw the question if I upset you.

But you *already* upset me. And now I'm getting ready to upset you, you little—

Of course we love each other, interjected the woman.

Thank you, madame, said Mr. Adler.

But her partner was still angry.

And whom do *you* love? the woman asked Bayla's father.

I love my wife, of course, he said. And this handsome young man loves my daughter.

Then we all love someone, said the woman. And that settles it.

That's it, then, said Mr. Adler. Love. Love somebody. End of story. Case closed.

Case closed, scoffed the man, but the woman had him in tow and she was mollifying him even as they got into their convertible, which was parked on the street beside us. She slid over right beside him, like a real girlfriend, in the middle of the seat.

I love her, I love her, the black man called, now, as they pulled away. His left hand was on the steering wheel, and his right was punching the air in a kind of wave to us, a good riddance. I love her! he cried as the couple laughed, and their voices trailed off into the darkness up the street.

Do you want to know how I know you and Bayla are a match, not just a fly-by-night kind of couple? You called us. This means you want to protect her, to take care of her. Isn't this so?

Mr. Adler, I didn't call *you*. And I am in no position to marry your daughter.

Position you don't have to give a thought to. Or money. Ever again.

He put his hands behind his back and continued to walk now in a slower, more side-to-side motion. And, with a small smile, he indicated that I should follow his promenade. American-born people just don't walk this way. It was not a swagger, this new walk, but perhaps a distant cousin to it, as if some deal between us had been brokered. But as far as I was concerned, nothing was settled. In fact, everything was about as unsettled as it could get.

We turned on Eighteenth and were moving toward Fairfax, where the hum of the San Diego Freeway came around the corner, white noise shifting an octave. Everything was strange, even the way the clouds, when I looked up from the sidewalk, seemed balanced on the outer edges of the leaves, if I angled my view just so through the trees, and the incline of Fairfax running down to Venice Boulevard too seemed suddenly far steeper than I could remember. Everything was shifting under the weight of Mr. Adler's determination—assumption—that I marry his daughter.

Arranged marriage, he said. This is, of course, very old-fashioned. Then again, so is a man's daughter marrying a penniless man who is a credit to his people and the world by devoting himself to Torah.

I am not so devoted to Torah, Mr. Adler, as you think. I want to go to college.

So, go. Bayla will follow you. A wife goes with a husband. She'll learn from you. We don't kid ourselves. Bayla is no student, so you, Norman Plummer, will be Bayla's college. And she will be your wife so you don't have to have crazy sex with strangers in dormitories who you share with football players and get diseases from. Who wants that kind of life? What I offer is an all-around good arrangement! Soup to nuts. When you're done with college, you'll do what you want, together. Maybe you will join me and Lucille in the business. Any aspect, it's yours. I advise that you study a little accounting.

Jesus, Mr. Adler.

Lucille says that is one of your few faults, this *Jesus* that you say when you are startled.

Please, sir.

Dave. Please, you must think of me as and call me Dave. By the way, speaking of marriage contracts, *ketubot*, Lucille and I have a little collection of illustrated contracts, about fifteen in all from all around the world. The oldest from Yemen, 1605. You and Bayla will have a contract, the most beautiful ever written. Already Lucille is lining up a calligrapher.

I don't believe this.

No? Wait until you hear about the dowry. That will make a believer. Norman, besides college tuition, which it will be our privilege to pay, there will be a job when you return, like I said, and your living in New York, or wherever you two want to go, in whatever style pops into your heads.

A dowry?

Are you beginning to like old-fashioned, Norman?

Mr. Adler.

Dave.

Oh boy.

Look, Norman. Five hundred thousand? A million is all right too. You want to buy your parents a better house? That can be arranged. Your father's gambling debts, they too can disappear, over night.

What do you know about my father's debts?

If I said the wrong thing, I am very, very sorry. But, of course, I prepare for every meeting. I talked to Michael, Dr. Levin. You must know that with Bayla come the endless possibilities. Thank God we are doing very well. Have I offended?

No, I lied.

I am not a frivolous man, nor an idle talker, not with a daughter like Bayla and the responsibilities I carry. A huge window is opening up for you tonight. Look out the window is all I ask.

You've thrown too much at me.

Of course, of course, my boy. I admire the way you feel you must protect your parents. But how better to protect them and to take care of them forever than through this? Frankly, if you don't want from me even a dime for yourselves, you and Bayla, or for your parents, that's fine too. I respect a person who has principles, and if you have in your head the idea that we are somehow "buying" you, forget this notion. I would not be here if I didn't know, the way I know the sun is going to rise tomorrow, that you love my Bayla. Yes, and you would love her, I know, even if she were a poor girl. Am I right, Norman Plummer?

Yes, I love Bayla Adler.

Of course I loved her and wanted to protect her. I wanted to protect her also from this man, who happened also to love her who also was her father. Wasn't there a father, I wondered, in the entire world, who acted like a father? On the other hand, the man was offering us a fortune, and the world.

We now turned toward home. As was often the case with Mr. Adler's daughter, I felt as if I had wandered into a play, with no idea what my lines were, or should be. Saturn Street lay up ahead, and Mr. Adler's arm fell across my shoulders again. Had someone really just said to her father, *Yes, I love Bayla*? And was that someone actually me?

Norman, Norman, he went on, all this that I have said to you does not come lightly, or without responsibility, of course. Without someone of your caliber in Bayla's life, we worry terribly what will become of her. You will be careful with her. You will not let her ride off the edge of canyons, or smoke marijuana until she becomes a junkie. If she studies a little Talmud along the way, so much the better; that would not be bad either, but we are not fools. Nor were we born yesterday. Or rather, we were born yesterday, and are quite proud of it and see its strengths. By the way, she needs you now, today, not next week, next month, or next year.

I thought you said I should think on it. Look through the wide, wide window, you said. You don't have to sign on the dotted line right now. Just think on it, you said.

A fine memory, of course. Absolutely, as you say. So think. Just make your thinking fast, O.K.? Very fast.

Please, Mr. Adler.

Dave.

You hired me to be her tutor, not to marry her.

There is always pressure in life, Norman. This atmosphere that we breathe presses down on us. But you want to breathe, don't you? The point is that you and I reach an understanding before you take your little trip.

All right, I said, as the whole jigsaw of the night somehow tried to sort itself into place for me.

We walked another half block in silence. In Los Angeles, of course, there is no such thing as absolute silence; the din from the freeway had abated somewhat, to be replaced by two planes gliding over the tops of the Baldwin Hills with an approaching rumble.

Into this mix, Mr. Adler suddenly began to hum a Yiddish melody: *ya-duh dai dai, dai, ya-duh dai dai dai.*

I found his singing strangely moving—as if through it he were transporting himself out of L.A. and back to Europe, to when he had been young, perhaps my age, to a time before all the horrors and losses began to mount, which perhaps now were making him come up with this hysterical scheme for me to marry his daughter. As confused and uncomfortable and even slightly overwhelmed as I was, I also began to feel protective of the Adlers, both Dave and Bayla.

In retrospect this is not surprising, because angry and protective can be held together in mind and in hand with a great deal of steadiness, if you practice, and I had. At such a game I had been a juggler much of my life. I found myself, as we walked, adding Dave's ball to those of Ed and Esther and, of course, Bayla. To keep four in the air was really not that complicated. Up they went, all the balls spinning and sailing happily, and I could protect them all, keep them all from falling, Bayla's most especially. After all, I was the Hebrew tutor of Bel Air. I began to hum along with him.

Occasionally he articulated a bar or phrase louder than others and sent it in my direction. *Ya dai-di-dai-di-dai-di-dai, dai-did-i-dum, ay-di-dai-di-dum.* He nodded and I nodded, like a regular convention of nodders, and as he resumed his *dai dai dai, di dai dai, did um di da,* I began to be enveloped in the oddest daydream, or, as it was quite dark by then, a waking night dream, as we traversed the final stretch back to my little house.

Members of the King Solomon Bikers Club, try to see this dream through my eyes. In it I see Bayla in her wedding dress. It is a diaphanous dress, and beneath it she is wearing a small white bikini, the kind she wore so many times by the pool. It is an image as central to my life as that box of cotton skullcaps or the lazy Susan or the box of twenty-four quarts of oil for the Hudson, or the big Yamaha Road Star that I will tell you about shortly.

In any event, she is both dressed and undressed for the ceremony, which was clearly being conducted by Dr. Levin. With his *yarmulkah* seeming to me a kind of extraterrestrial Hebrew disc, so shining white it seems he has somehow come under a spell of miraculous new physical abilities, for he is carrying the *chupa*, the wedding canopy, all by himself, magically keeping it aloft and balanced by only one of its four poles.

We are where?—beside the pool! Of course. How could I have not known at the first gleam of the vision that this would be its primary stage? Here come Dave and Lucille processing out from one side of the deck to their designated spot under the canopy. She is carrying a large shining platter of Oreos and several glasses of milk, whose liquid is the color of the moon.

From the other direction, also on time but not nearly as good at keeping together in that formal wedding walk, are Ed and Esther. The two sets of parents acknowledge each other with a little bow. Ed is wearing one of his special Santa Anita jobs, a suit of brown, with baggy pants and thin stripes, practically a zoot suit, a throwback even by his standards, and in a design similar to ones I'd seen Benjy wearing; for all I know he's borrowed it from the newspaper dealer.

Esther has on her pretty black pillbox hat, tilted to that angle she favors. She's got on white gloves, and I notice a new twist: there's a delicate black veil that she wears halfway down the front of her hat. It's woven with a mysterious pattern of fine black dots, in a sad Francisco Goya sort of way, an odd fashion choice to be sporting at her son's wedding.

They all approach Bayla and me, and, oh yes, there's Carlos come to our wedding too, but he's barefoot and in a tux and standing behind a table covered with a starched white cloth. Obviously he's going to be doing the bartending tonight.

Let me see. Yes, indeed. There's Biff Waterman, my best Junior Cong pal, making an appearance as my ring bearer. He's giving me the ring now, which I tuck away with a deft gesture, like the fingers of a bar mitzvah boy practiced at receiving slender white envelopes bearing Israel bonds and deftly sliding them into the vest pocket.

I'm wearing my bar mitzvah suit, in fact, which I have stuffed myself into for this marital occasion. I can hardly breathe and I know I look ridiculous. The pants go down barely to my ankles, and the jacket is so snug I almost have no room for any movement of arms, skinny as they may be; still, the occasion calls for it. I am in effect a marionette.

However, no one else seems to notice. They all treat me as if I'm wearing a stylish new suit and everyone admires Bayla, my bride, as if she were wearing a normal wedding dress, not this gauzy apparition in a soft-core pornographer's dream. Everything in *my* fantasy is normal as normal can be.

I shatter the ceremonial glass, wrapped in its napkin, on the deck of the pool, and memories of the destruction of temples, the stench of crematoria, and all bad things are thus efficiently rendered present and then immediately dispensed with. This is my favorite custom, capturing as it does Jews' special knack for living past time and present time all at once.

Immediately afterwards Levin adjusts his disc, then motions Bayla and me to step forward, whereupon I take the ring from Biff Waterman and commence to address Bayla in the classic marital formula: *Haray at mekudeshet lee b-ta-ba-at zote.* Behold you are set aside, just for me, as in the word *kadosh,* holy, through the agency of this ring.

Just as I place the golden band on Bayla's finger, she says, *Mekudeshet* derives from the Hebrew root *kadosh,* as in *kadosh, kadosh, kadosh,* holy, holy, holy is God, as we say in the central *Amida* prayer, the standing meditation of the daily liturgy.

Dave and Lucille and my parents and Dr. Levin are suddenly all nodding and beaming, and even Carlos down by the bar has heard her marvelous disquisition on Hebrew grammar and mimes a high five. Yo, bro. Way to go, Hebrew tutor! Way to go, girl!

Then, as we take each other's hands, Bayla and I decorously and most carefully make our way up, onto, and along the diving board together. First she takes a step, and then I. We make it to the end, where I place my hands around her Scarlett O'Hara waist, and we cry out, in Hebrew, *achat, shtayim, shalosh,* one, two, three, and, holding hands, we consummate the marriage by jumping into the pool.

CHAPTER TWENTY

Well, what'll it be, Norman?

Huh?

I blinked, and all Dave Adler's *dai-dai-ditty-dumming*, his klezmeresque humming, along with my dream, ceased. Dave Adler and I were suddenly in front of the Nefussis' house. These were our neighbors, Greek Jews, originally from Salonika, whose lives I observed through my bedroom window. Several times ambulances were called to the Nefussis' because George Nefussi, the dad, had overdosed on sleeping pills. Esther reported to me that George survived the Nazis, which few other Greek men in the camps did. Decades later, despite his attractive, long-suffering wife and his twin daughters, who played Elvis Presley songs loudly on the guitar, and despite everything Greek or Jewish, George appeared to be trying to join his old friends in death.

We were almost home, and David Adler repeated, What'll it be, Norman?

Excuse me?

Am I talking to my future son-in-law or not?

At that phrase, *son-in-law,* all my cognitive systems stalled. That word and the kid that I was seemed simply to hail from two different, unbridgeable worlds. I felt bone-deep confusion, and fearful hesitancy forming up within me at once and looking for an outlet. I was certain I was about to throw up. When I opened my mouth to gag, however, nothing came out.

Ah, said Mr. Adler, I see you're being very thoughtful. I don't blame you. My respect only grows. You don't have to decide now, tonight, as I say, standing on one foot, this minute. I'm an insistent man, yes, but not an impossible one.

What about the bat mitzvah? I managed to blurt out.

That? Oh, yes, then after that, after the high holidays—what are we talking, the end of September? Fine. *When* is not as important as *if.* If you accept our arrangement, then you will love and protect Bayla on this trip and you can take your sweet time about tying the knot. On the other hand, why not do it when you get back from your little holiday? First a marriage, then a bat mitzvah—she'll have more time to practice.

You can't be serious, Mr. Adler.

Dave. No? It will be a double joy. Let the mothers work out the details. Lucille and who? Remind me, please.

Esther.

Esther, yes, he said. A lovely name. A queen who saved her people. I would like to meet her.

She's sick. Remember?

Maybe she's made a bit of a recovery since we arrived, during the time we have walked?

I doubt it. When she's sick, Mr. Adler, she stays that way for a while.

Until she gets better.

That's right.

The human body is an amazing creation. God was not messing around when he did this. He put his best into it. Another night, then, Norman?

Another night.

We lingered by the Nefussis' driveway. I thought I saw one of the twins, Cassandra, framed in the window, her big head of curly hair, in profile, hovering above a bucket of ice cream out of which she was scooping herself one spoonful after another. She was five or so years younger than Bayla, still a child compared to Bayla's child-woman, but I had always liked her flaunting Americanisms and the way she refused to freak out when George overdosed on his sleeping pills. The mother and Cassandra's twin, Carmen, whose hair was straight, were the ones who always accompanied George out on the stretcher across their lawn. Cassandra stayed in the kitchen, where she was tonight, and ate.

She gave me a little wave as we passed, and I waved back. It gave me enough courage to stop again, to place my arm on David Adler's, and to say, Is this all some kind of test, Mr. Adler? Bayla is always testing me, putting me on. Trying to shock me to see how I respond. Is that what you're doing too?

I have one daughter, who I value more than life itself. With her I don't play such games. For tests, I can recommend a good doctor.

All right, Mr. Adler.

Dave, please! All right. What then?

Dave. I'm very flattered. Deeply flattered, I said again—and I saw all my Junior Cong pals rise from their uncomfortable old theater seats, place their thumbs at the tips of their noses, wag their fingers, and, in unison, as if in a responsive reading send me, across time and space, a huge noisy raspberry—but there's one little thing that occurs to me, Mr. Adler, Dave, that I haven't asked of you about Bayla.

Yes, Norman? Nothing is off the table. The sky's the limit.

Does *she* want to marry me?

She will.

But I don't think she loves me, Mr. Adler. Intrigued a little, yes. Amazingly enough, even respectful of me. That too. But in love? No way, sir.

Love shmove. You just keep her from driving off a cliff. You act as her good angel, and that's enough. Love will come. To love, you first have to stay alive. That's number one. To keep your head from being cracked open. You marry, you take care of each other, you get these Hollywood ideas out of your brain, and then you wake up one morning, all tangled in silk sheets, like the movie stars, and her arm is across you in a bed comfortable like the Garden of Eden. Presto, she loves you, and then more love grows.

I really liked what he had just said, and I found myself thinking hard about it as I checked to see if Cassandra were still looking at us from her window.

Yes, Dave Adler was trying to guess my cards, so to speak, and figuring if he needed to up the ante. Time goes on, and you learn to ride motorcycles, and you study some Jewish law, and life takes you where it will, and you learn what you are at heart. I realized, even then, that in my deepest heart I was the son of a Jewish gambler, and I knew what Dave Adler was up to. No, he was not bluffing, not bluffing at all. He was trying to close the deal, and I was sorely tempted.

I kept thinking about Dave's simple formula as I looked now to see if Esther were at our picture window. Love could grow on you, I supposed, like a pair of jeans finally fits but only after a year or two of wash and wear. But that's not what Bayla Adler wanted from a boy or a lover. Love growing on you was for old people. Maybe that was it, then. Maybe, despite my age, I was the old guy in Bayla's life. That's probably what Dave Adler saw in me too, and he hoped my old-guy-in-young-body love would somehow cast a healing spell over his crazy daughter. Or at least get her down from ninety miles an hour to somewhere closer to the speed limit.

No, just as I knew the first temple in Jerusalem was destroyed by the Babylonians in 586 and then Bar Kochba, whom some Jews thought was the messiah himself, had revolted against the Romans during 132, and the second temple was destroyed again by the Romans in 70, I knew for a historical fact Bayla Adler did not love her Hebrew tutor in the civil rights freedom summer of 1963. Yet this was not a tragedy for which I should say lamentations; this was perhaps an opportunity. So I said to her father: Mr. Adler, I can't possibly commit. Not tonight. Not yet.

So the day after is all right too, or the day after that. Are you thinking on it as I asked you to is the point.

I definitely am thinking on it.

Good then. We're in agreement. More or less. I just need to hear from you that you have considered, while we sit and have a schnapps in my house, another night, that you have considered and you are on the verge of accepting. You will then, as far as we are concerned, be engaged. Right? Then off you go on your little trip and sow your oats together, if you get my meanings. Otherwise, Norman, you don't really think I can let you go joyriding with Bayla?

No?

That's right. Until I hear from you, she'll be under lock and key, my boy. I assure you. Grounded like an airplane in a driving storm. Like the girls in medieval stories where the knight goes off riding to the Holy Land and on his way kills as many Jews as he can find—meanwhile at home she has on her chastity belt tight as Fort Knox.

You wouldn't.

A metaphor. A comparison, Norman. You never read about King Arthur and his knights?

My head made a kind of jerking motion, a gesture somewhere between a no, an expression of complete bewilderment, and maybe a seizure. I felt as if we now were circling around each other on the sidewalk in front of the house. The limo remained there, the driver shaded behind his window and Dr. Levin behind his; if he saw us standing there, he was not opening the door.

Mr. Adler planted his feet on the lawn between limo and picture window and placed his hands, at ease, behind his back. He was a pinnacle of self-confidence and solidity. Look, son, I'm giving you a gift of major size, he said. Please don't look a gift horse all over the mouth.

Love shmove?

Exactly. You become Bayla's Sir Norman. A Jewish knight, the first of his kind, and become rich and secure doing so. Why you don't leap on this, I do not know.

The door to the limo opened then, and to my utter astonishment, following Dr. Levin, my mother slid out.

She straightened her thin green dress, the one she wore when she played bingo, and introduced herself, extending her hand to shake David Adler's.

What a remarkable boy you have.

Yes.

She seemed to be glowing brightly.

I'm so glad to see you feeling better, Mrs. Plummer.

I never felt better in my life!

No longer will we keep you as Norman says you were feeling a little ill. Michael has spoken to you, and you feel better. He's a regular aspirin, our cousin.

Mr. Adler, we're really honored.

Levin stood aside, and after Dave slid in, my teacher followed. The window went up halfway and stopped. David Adler looked up toward the sky again. What a beautiful evening this is.

He gave a flick of his hand—goodbye or hello, or was there a fly buzzing about?—the window rose, and the limo pulled out and then away. Esther and I watched it glide toward Saturn, cruise to a stop, and take the right turn out of sight. To each other we didn't say a word.

I didn't even hold the screen door open for her as she trailed behind me. All I seemed to see was how the mesh was torn from the frame, and how, on first view as we entered, the wallpaper was stained above the ugly fake marble mantle.

What's the point of this stupid fireplace, I shouted after we were both in the living room, if we never can make a fire here!

I bolted for my room, and, like a little kid, slammed the door. Don't even dream of coming in here. Don't touch the doorknob!

Oh, Normie. What is so terrible?

You were supposed to stay in your bedroom and be sick. None of this is right.

Her voice dropped a tone. You're not thinking clearly. I can make you spaghetti, or salmon croquettes. You need to eat something.

Salmon! Haven't you just sold me to the highest bidder? Agreed to give me away in marriage to the nursing-home king? So you don't have to keep feeding me. And, anyway, your croquettes are too salty, and afterwards my mouth smells of onion for hours. I just fake that I like them to make you feel good.

She was silent, and then moved away from my door, but then I sensed her return.

I have not given you to anybody or anything, Norman. I'm just so proud that they even think that way about you. About your potential. That is all.

Really?

Yes, really.

What were you doing in the car?

Talking.

Levin didn't have you sign some document in the car?

Nobody does that any more.

She was right. I was so angry I couldn't think straight.

Let me in there, Norman.

My potential as what?

Norman, you have to marry someone. Eventually.

Oh, Jesus. I was set up. Trapped, sandbagged. Adler walks me all over the neighborhood while Dr. Levin sweet-talks you.

Sweet-talks? He told me about your brilliance in school is all. I listen like any proud mother would, and I gave him a seltzer.

He was here? In the house?

Where else would he get a seltzer? Am I a carhop like you that I should run it out to him on roller skates? What is so terrible, Norman?

Nothing, nothing. And everything. That's what you talked about?

Oh, Normie, we had a lovely drive—

Wait, you drove around too?

Well, he asked if I had ever ridden in a limousine and, of course, I hadn't. We shouldn't wait until we are dead for the pleasure, he said. So funny. So we did. Wait till I tell your father.

Jesus!

Norman, I've never told you this, but when I was young, very young, maybe eighteen, I loved a boy. In Canada. Then I met your father.

We all make mistakes.

That is no way to talk. Bite your tongue.

You're the one who's telling me it's o.k. with you if I marry Bayla Adler, and I should bite my tongue? Bayla Adler basically thinks I'm a Hebrew-school jerk. She doesn't love me; she doesn't want to marry me. She—and her parents—play games. I don't want to marry her or anyone. Love? What do you or Dad or Bayla know about it? It's a word everybody throws around like salt on food. Nobody understands. Nobody. Go away. Leave me alone.

No, she said and rattled the doorknob. You stop giving me orders. You stop being ashamed. Stop telling me, your mother, when I'm sick and when I'm to stay in bed, and who I can talk to and who I can ride in cars with. Since when is that your business? I happened to have had a very nice, extremely civilized, intelligent conversation with Dr. Levin. I don't think he considers me the ignoramus you take me for.

I turned off the light and threw myself on the bed.

Norman?

I listened to my own heavy breathing for what seemed a long time. Yes?

If anyone in the world has a right to say you should marry this person, or that person, it's the body that bore you.

And?

All I'm saying is that one day you drive off to Bel Air to tutor this girl. Three-and-a-half months later they want you to marry her. Either that's an amazing success story or—

Will you please shut up?

Is there something you need to tell your mother that you're hiding? You have always been a truthful boy.

I had never felt so angry. No, it was more than anger—it was a white-hot surge of violence filling me up. I wanted to hurt someone.

I leaped off the bed. With my back, I began to push against the door. I heard its cheap plywood panel begin to creak. I pushed again, and it groaned. Esther yelled for me to stop, but I refused. I kept pushing, and as I did I imagined the panel separating from the frame and it, along with me falling after it, like some absurd Tom or Jerry or Roadrunner, flattening her.

Just stop it! she shrieked. How can this be the same person they want to marry their daughter? You're scaring me, Norman. I don't recognize you, Dr. Jekyll and Mr. Hyde. They leave, and suddenly you turn into a monster.

I was always a monster.

Norman, please. I didn't mean that any more than you meant all your harsh words. Sticks and stones, Norman. You remember. You are not a monster, you are a miracle of a child. I will cut my tongue out if I ever say that again. It's just all the excitement from tonight. Won't you come out, Norman, and I'll make some tea— we'll sit and discuss everything, like normal people?

There's nothing to discuss.

No?

It's my life, and I want you to step back out of it, way back, starting now.

All right, dear. Just as you say.

I was always amazed how her good will could return, how her tone meant she still cared about me, all this despite the nastiness I had been sending her way.

She was soon in the midst of chopping those infernal onions for yet another batch of her cure-all croquettes. It was not as if she actually believed food could correct all the ways we kept failing each other. Rather, if you're too wrought up to think clearly or to sleep or to read, and if you have not yet discovered the palliative effects of riding fast down a long, endless road, completely by yourself in the ripping wind, then chopping is often good therapy, although Esther would not have used that word.

After I had yelled through the bedroom door, still securely on its hinges, for the fifth time that I was not hungry, Esther relented. The frying pan was replaced by a tea pot, and when I heard its whistle, I emerged, washed my face, and joined my mother in the breakfast nook.

If someone, such as Cassandra Nefussi, had peered into our kitchen that night, we would have appeared normal. Who could have guessed that Esther was telling me about a boy she had loved once in Canada? Someone who was brilliant and wrote poetry about the beauty of the orange trees of Zion, as seen from the working-class ghetto of Toronto? How they were thinking of running off together, the poet and my mother, to Palestine. His skin was white, almost alabaster, she said, practically no beard, and they all thought he was an angel. But the pallor turned out to be not seraphic but tubercular. His family was too poor to send him to the sanitarium, and Esther's parents said they couldn't help either, no matter how much she begged. Esther's recollections, usually pretty scanty, were in this instance highly detailed. She had worked in a cardboard box factory and he, on roller skates, fetched items from the Montgomery Ward warehouse, and they saved enough to book one passage on a steamer to the Holy Land. They held hands at cultural evenings at the Jewish Center. They were working on the second fare when the boy suddenly did not have the lung power to keep skating at the warehouse. He rapidly declined. Her parents prohibited her from going to his funeral. My mother, after that, decided to leave Canada forever at the first chance she got. That chance would be Ed Plummer.

By the time we got to the end of her tale, she had not mentioned Bayla Adler once (she uncannily knew it was part of the terms of our unarticulated truce), yet still, by the time the tea was cold, and we as always made up and she kissed me on the cheek, and simply said, Think on it, again—David Adler's phrase—I knew it was not on the young love of her life that she wanted me to ponder, but on Bayla Adler. Amazing. Me, a Hebrew-school nerd, a history wonk with skinny arms, had really been proposed to by the nursing-home king, Bayla Adler's father, and my own mother was seconding it. I was completely confused.

It was by now close to midnight, and Esther's lids were beginning to fall as we continued to sit at the table. Her lower jaw dropped away slightly from the upper, so that a little wheezy sound began to emerge from the *o* formed by her lips, as if she were trying to blow up a beach ball.

Ma, I said. Now you really need to go to bed. One, two, three. Get up. Go.

She didn't seem to hear me, so I carefully removed the cup of tea from the surround of her hands and placed it, along with the saucers and spoons, silently in the sink. Her hands remained eerily cupped, and her snoring remained loud. I took her by the arm and walked her slowly down the hall to her bedroom, where I eased her onto the mattress. As she fell asleep again, she said, not to me, it seemed, What a wonderful son I have. I'm so sorry.

CHAPTER TWENTY-ONE

I too should have been ready to drop, but I wasn't. I felt the opposite, as if I'd just awoken from a strange but refreshingly deep sleep. I went down the hall, into the living room, and pulled the drapes shut at the picture window. Almost no one, with perhaps the exception of the Nefussi girls, in high spirits and to play tricks on us, ever came up to the window and looked in. However, I often thought the world was nevertheless always there and peering in. I knew, of course, that simply by pulling the thick, heavy drapes, with their floral pattern, shut, I couldn't really keep out whatever it was bothering me. I was seventeen, yes, but, as I think on it, I quite literally rarely acted my age—more often than not I lived in the imagination and fears of a far younger child. No wonder I felt the need to act old.

I walked back down the hall, stepped into the bathroom, and clicked on the light. The mop-headed kid with black glasses and a white T-shirt, who blinked and stared back at me—who was that? It was hard to believe this was someone to whom words like *love* or *marriage* or *half a million dollars* pertained. Who were they talking about? I said, touching my finger to the mirror. Not you!

I walked back out into the living room, sat down in Ed's La-Z-Boy, and kicked back. I continued to feel very clear-headed and calm but in a stunned sort of way. What was all this talk of love? I hated myself for saying that I loved Bayla Adler. Did my parents love each other? Did Dave and Lucille Adler love each other?

What did Michael Levin love? All the solitary nights he spent in his small apartment, with its smell of Old Spice and old bindings? Love? Please. I may as well have said I *frzykltpd* her, for all the meaning the word conveyed. Frankly, if it conveyed meaning at all, it seemed to range from negative to toxic. Banish the word is what I say. Between Bayla and me the word had rarely, if ever, come up. That, to me, was a credit to the honesty of our relationship. Bayla was too busy with all of life—angling to outsmart and demonize Lucille, using Carlos, negotiating everything in the world with her dad—to narrow herself down to anything as obviously self-limiting as loving a single person. And certainly not the likes of me.

If *I do love her* had flown out of my mouth but a few hours ago, as I now remembered it had, it was as if another source had projected it, a weird dybbuk drunk on the elixir of my fantasies or the salesman's magic Dave Adler had spun. Why wasn't he confident in and proud of such a beautiful, self-willed little rocket of a daughter that she was? Why the need for so much bribing?

On the other hand, another voice within joined the debate— and to mark the new interlocutor's arrival, I pushed the La-Z-Boy another notch back. Isn't it also true, said the voice, that if Bayla ever turned to you and said, Hebrew tutor, Don't fall right over when I tell you this, but I really do love you. I adore you. I can't explain it, but there it is. If she said even a part of that, wouldn't you be a goner? You can't tell me, the voice continued, that in response to that declaration you would do anything other than prostrate yourself before her little white toes with their red nail polish, kiss them one at a time, and say softly, Will you marry me, Bayla?

I mean what else could you possibly want from life?

Who was I kidding? Perhaps a little fling is all she wanted with this pale erudite boy, who was reading too many biblical prophets and war stories, a kid she could prevail on because he had combative, depressed parents he wanted to get away from.

That was one thing. Maybe even in Bayla's mind this desire to rescue someone from being dead already in this life and at a far too young age was a calling, maybe even a noble calling. Maybe she needed such missions.

I didn't know what was between Bayla and me, but it was not that thing that does not alter when it alteration finds, or bends with the remover to remove—who the hell was this remover anyway?—because Bayla was as fast and flighty as a ball being whipped around the infield at Dodger Stadium. Whatever it was, it was not love.

On the other hand, there was that five hundred thousand dollars. I said the words out loud. I repeated them, slowly: Five hundred thousand dollars. Even a million, a cool million just as Dave Adler had said. Five hundred thousand. A million. Wow. Had I just been offered a million to marry the most beautiful and interesting girl I had ever set eyes on? To marry someone who made the kids in the Latin Club and the rabbis' and cantors' daughters, who had studied Mishna with me at the University of Judaism's enrichment program that summer, in their demure, long, long skirts, seem hardly alive at all? Mmmm. To marry a girl I nightly had been fantasizing about since the day I met her nearly four months ago, a girl who . . . was I really so principled about relationships to turn this all down just because of a confusing little thing called love?

Maybe all my hesitations about love were just so much nonsense I had absorbed, but from where? From Junior Cong? From the Jewish tradition that I was always quoting, or rather, parroting. What is love among the Jews anyway? Of course, you're supposed to love the Lord your God with all your soul and all your heart and all your might, and these words that I command you this day had better be in thy heart, or else. And you're supposed to love your neighbor as yourself. Yet where or how does that necessarily apply to your girlfriend? As the Talmudists say, Come and listen. Come and explain.

But none of the various visitors to my brain took the challenge as I sat in the La-Z-Boy in the darkness of our living room that night, and then there was something else: the scent of my father began to rise up from his chair in which I sat, and from the old poetry anthology that I now noticed on the adjacent table, and from his rumpled pack of Lucky Strikes. LSMFT. Lucky Strike Means Fine Tobacco. And then I remembered Ed having said to me once, as if the recollection were arising, like the sweet nicotine and Vitalis scent, from the leather all around me. Despite what your mother might tell you, gambling does have some wisdom to give a person as he moves through life.

Such as what, Ed?

Two rules, kid. One applies to the horses and one to cards. As to horses, you must get out to the track early to watch the horses warming up. Rule One: You never bet on the ones that have bandages wrapped around their legs. When it's race time, the bandages come off, but the injuries remain.

Rule Two: In cards, never go for the kicker on the inside straight. This means that when you think you've got an absolutely winning hand, if you can only draw one more card, even if you've been counting and are ninety percent sure what the others have, beware, for this moment is the most dangerous. Be very cautious at the point of greatest confidence because it's right then that you will lose the rent.

Having observed my father in it for so many years, I thought I knew every move, sound, and scent a La-Z-Boy could generate. But I swear that I felt the chair do something new—it felt as if it were elevating in the darkness and directing me to somewhere that was obvious to everyone but me. The more I thought on it, the angrier I became at David Adler. He had been doing nothing but insulting Ed—in absentia, to be sure, but wasn't I there? Wasn't I the son?—and suddenly I decided on something it had never occurred to me to do before.

It was about one by the time I looked in on my mother, who was by then snoring loudly. I arranged the comforter and pulled the door three-quarters shut. She liked it that way. Out in the driveway I added new oil to the Hudson and took off to consult with my father.

First I had to find him. I knew he wasn't on any job in Nevada or anywhere else. He was broke so he was likely nearby. As the races at Santa Anita were long over, my best guess was that he would be in Gardena, the little gambling enclave south of L.A., where the Chinese played mahjong and the Jews stud; they played even on a Sunday night—no, *particularly* on a Sunday night—to stave off the inevitable coming of Monday.

I myself had been to Gardena with Ed a few years before, on a night when Esther was ushering at the Hollywood Bowl for a Frank Sinatra concert. Ed had promised her he would stay home and supervise my studying. Halfway through our discussion about why the Articles of Confederation had failed, my father got the itch. He said I would be his good luck charm if I joined him, and I did.

When we got there, however, he parked me in the coffee shop for most of the night, in front of an unending plate of glazed doughnuts that the honeys brought me—he always called the waitresses *honey*, no matter their age or condition.

It peeved me, but still, the doughnuts, I recalled as I drove out to find him, had been really good.

Of course my father didn't win that night. Next time, he would, he said to me, but his reassurance hadn't been convincing as we slowly cruised toward home, that long-ago night, with absolutely no eagerness to get there. We poked along on the right side of the road in what Ed called the losers' lane.

Next time you'll sit right by me at the poker table. My mistake. Then I'll win big. Guaranteed.

There was to be no next time. Esther told him the next day with a forcefulness rare in their confrontations, a real face-off, nose to nose, that his excuses—gambling helps discipline the brain, helps with algebra and probability—were completely unfounded, and, what's more, plain stupid. If she ever caught him taking me to the casinos again, teaching me to follow in a gambler's footsteps, instead of those of my doctor uncles, who had bought me the Hudson—aren't you embarrassed?—or in the path of Rabbi Joel, well, there would be not only the bank but also hell to pay.

So, on this night in question, launched by that memory in Ed's chair I felt like some airborne figure in a Chagall painting, flying over the freeways Hudson-style, which is to say at about thirty-nine miles an hour max. Thirty-nine, my fellow outriders. This was, curiously, as you may recall, also the number of lashes mandated in the Torah for public punishment. I was trailing a few plumes of white smoke out the exhaust, but I was in Gardena in twenty-five minutes. I cruised Casino Boulevard looking for my father's car. Just when I was beginning to doubt my hunch but thinking I might enjoy one of those glazed doughnuts anyway, I spotted the car.

CHAPTER TWENTY-TWO

He was at the casino on the boulevard, the Silver Dollar, a ramshackle old motel refitted for slots, with a small poker floor thrown over where the kidney-shaped pool had been. There, in the side lot I found his beat-up Plymouth. I saw only coincidence, not a hint of destiny at the time, that he was parked beside several gleaming motorcycles, all leaning handsomely just so on their kickstands that, in memory, I see now in perfect alignment, like a kind of chorus line, there to greet me.

As I approached Ed at the seven-card-stud table, the woman sitting to his right, who had a large crown of puffed-up hair the color of straw that was kept off her forehead by a beaded headband, slammed her cards down on the table. You got to know when to hold 'em, she declaimed, and when to fold 'em. My foldin' time has come.

God bless, honey, said a man in a worn leather jacket, who was sitting on Ed's left. Now there's nothin' to do but for me to win for the two of us.

I love playing against you folks, said my father, looking up at the woman. I don't mean *against,* I mean *with,* he added with a wink.

Against my ass, with my ass, said the man. Any way, you lose, Abie.

Watch your mouth, honey, said the woman.

But it was all genial, or so I thought. The others around the table—for the most part nondescript men like Ed in rumpled slacks with short-sleeved white shirts that appeared not very well ironed, with the crescent moons of their undershirts showing through at the neck—one after another, tossed down their cards. But not Ed.

I decided to keep out of view behind the cigarette vending machine and observe him, since I'd never actually seen him in gambling action before.

My father and the man in leather kept on raising and bluffing each other, and the silence around the stud table grew deeper in the windowless pit. The man, even seated, I noticed, was big, thick, imposing. Yet Ed, at the center of the table, had a certain kind of presence too. He struck me not as subtle, yet *powerful* is not the word that came to mind. Rather *coiled* like a fire hose, quiet but ready when necessary. In this setting he was a little like Bayla Adler.

After several rounds, Ed faced the biker quietly—I had by now associated the players in leather with the motorcycles out front—and he acted not with the overweening attitude he often deployed at home to describe his poker prowess, or with the insecure comedian's barely concealed yearning to please and impress. Instead, with a slowly unfolding, almost impish confidence, he said, Last chance, mister. I'm going to see you and raise you, and then the rubber hits the road.

There's nothin' you can tell me about rubber hitting the road that I didn't know before you were born, Abie. Show your cards.

Straight to the king, said Ed, and he placed them confidently on the table. And my name's not Abie.

King, countered Ed's antagonist, as he placed one card down on the table, another king, then an ace, each time he peeled the card from his palm with his thumbnail, so that the cards made a flicking sound that reminded me of the *tick-tick-tick* that came up from our wheels as we rode when we used to clothes-pin playing cards to the spokes of our bicycles. *Tick-tick-tick.* When the man finished his little act, he had not the full house that he was threatening, but only two kings and two aces, a modest two pairs.

This is a very sad night for one of us, he said, while his straw-haired girlfriend circled around behind Ed. Everybody at the table, including my father, grew still.

A very, very sad night, and I don't like sad occasions, do you?

Without reaching for the chips, my father said, quietly, I won the hand, so the night for me will not be sad.

You had the better cards, the man said, but I don't know as you won anything. I just don't know.

Ask anybody around the table. There's nothing wrong with this game.

Nobody around the table spoke.

You see, said the man—and it was just like a Western then, or so I remember it now—as he eased back the front of his vest and everyone could see the big sheath attached to his belt, a silver handle sticking out.

Listen, mister, said Ed. If you got any problems, call over the pit boss. Make your complaint official if there's something I did. They got rules here. This is not the Wild West.

No?

The woman, who was by then practically on top of Ed from behind, exchanged some sort of glance with her man, and the atmosphere shifted. She put her hands in my father's hair, and as her partner watched her, she said, You are one smart little Jewboy. I'm feelin' for the horns, honey, she went on, but I guess you remove 'em, leave 'em at home, right, when you go out to play cards?

In retrospect I want to say that I was ready to rush out from behind that cigarette machine, a one-man cavalry force, John Wayne to rescue the beleaguered platoon that was my father. But that's not what happened.

Aw, come on, honey, the woman said to the man. The pit boss won't do anything for you. Look at 'em. They all stick together.

Take half the chips, my father said, if you think I did something wrong. Take them. I mean it.

And the man was about to when the woman removed her hands from my father's hair. She slapped her thigh and a smile broke out on both her and the man's faces.

You didn't do anything wrong, Abie. We were just havin' our fun. You got to have some fun if you lose so much. Shake on it? And, unbelievably, the man extended his hand toward Ed.

My father hesitated, as if calculating what new trick was about to be unleashed, but then he decided to shake. As his hand disappeared inside the biker's big mitt, and I still feared some further humiliation, a collective exhalation seemed to arise out of everyone who'd been clustered at the seven-card-stud table. When the couple turned and walked toward the door through which I had entered only ten minutes before, the woman stopped at the cigarette machine. She put two quarters in. As she picked up her pack, she said, What are *you* staring at?

With a dry mouth, I said, Nothing, absolutely nothing.

I braced for some new threatening gesture from them, but they just shrugged and moved toward the parking-lot door.

Ed, hearing my voice, turned, and our eyes met. I don't think either of us even blinked, each not quite believing in that instant in the reality of the other.

And here's my son, Ed said, to the remaining people at the table, the great Hebrew scholar. You saw this?

I nodded.

Crazy people. They should get a guard here.

Involuntarily I reached into my pocket and felt the teeth of my long black comb as Ed introduced me to his gambling friends. This is Raymond, he said, who almost always gets a heart attack each time he draws for the straight. Say hello to my son, who's going to be a rabbi. Maybe he'll visit you in the hospital. And this is Sarah; my son, the Hebrew genius.

I've heard so much about you.

You have?

Not really, she said, but you're supposed to say that when you meet people's children.

We never talk about our children here, said a thin man with a lariat holding his shirt collar closed.

Why's that?

Bad luck, Sarah answered me. Then she added as we shook hands, Tonight you were good luck. And, Ed, he's good-looking too. Must be the mother.

Ed raised his arms high over his head, twisted his torso from side to side and stretched himself in a poker player's version of the calisthenics we used to do in gym class.

What's what? Whaddaya doing? he asked me from his stretch.

I became aware that I was holding my comb out to my father. We both stared at it, the narrow end with the dense teeth, which I used to keep my duck's tail combed just right. Since Bayla liked to tug at me there, it had become the epicenter of my vanity. Ed's dark hair needed some work since it was shooting out at a half dozen angles, thanks to the biker's ridiculous horn search. Since Ed was, I thought, the very real hero of the moment and at least should be decently groomed, I held it closer to his hand. Ed rejected the comb.

After he collected his chips, he ran his fingers through his hair and said, I should go to the barber your mother uses, six-fifty for a styling, and then send the bill to those Nazis. You hungry?

CHAPTER TWENTY-THREE

I was soon back in the coffee shop with my father, sliding into the booth I remembered, its red upholstery thick and shining.

Your mother will kill me.

She doesn't know I'm here.

Well, then, to what do I owe the pleasure of this great honor?

When a doughnut the size of a tricycle wheel was placed in front of me, and he had added three sugars and a powdering of Cremora to his coffee, I told my father everything.

Uncharacteristically, he sat there in silence, pressing one side of the coffee cup against his upper lip. There are times when we test our parents to see if they are fully the people we have been led to believe they are; for me, this was such a moment.

Please say the right thing, I remember thinking. I liked the way Ed had handled himself with the biker Nazis. True, he hadn't slapped the woman's hand away from his hair or used his vast experience in the martial arts, heretofore hidden from me, to disarm the man. Nevertheless he had not caved; he had acted like a man. That's why when he introduced me to his friends I had not corrected his *Hebrew scholar* claim. He had earned my forgiveness, and more. I think those people really liked him and approved of the way he had gotten through that dicey situation. I was very proud of him in that moment.

Yet that was poker, and this was my life, and I had a momentous decision to make. I was giving him a chance to be a true parent, to act like a genuine grown-up, to offer me sage advice. After all, he too was a businessman. A businessman as failed as Dave Adler was successful, but he had, allegedly—had he not?—a lot more experience in life than his son. Maybe there was something going on that he saw that I didn't see or yet understand. Please redeem yourself, I thought. So, Dad?

So Dad what? he echoed. You want another doughnut?

The problem, of course, with these tests that we give our parents—I have learned since—unlike the ones we took in school, is that the recipient doesn't know when he's being graded. Did he think I was really bluffing? My presence at the casino in the middle of the night should have tipped him that the stakes were very high.

Don't be a dope, Ed then said, with a strange cogitative poker light suddenly flickering across his eyes. You are worth more than five hundred thousand, more than a million too. Ask for a million five and a percentage of the gross in the business.

When I told him that I wasn't interested in the nursing-home business and that I was certain Bayla Adler was too wild a girl ever to be happy with a husband like me, no matter what the price tag, that I was too confused to be in real love even with Bayla, and that I was certain I was being played but wasn't sure the angle, Ed said only, Are you sure you don't want another doughnut?

I did not.

Then he placed his large coffee cup between us like a stack of chips and added, You've never heard of divorce? With that kind of money, you can hire the best lawyers. Most of them are *gonifs*, so you just hire the smartest.

That remark might well have been the high point of the wisdom he offered that night, because then he got started on lawyers, thieves, as he called them. I don't know why, except maybe all his run-ins with them because of his failed businesses made Ed disposed to hate them (How many lawyers are there at the bottom of the sea? Answer: Not enough). Then I think he just completely forgot he was talking to his needy son.

THE HEBREW TUTOR OF BEL AIR

You remember this big blowout your mother and I had, and the next morning, at nine, you better believe I was the first customer at Blumberg's Stationery over on Fairfax. You know where that is? In the legal section there they have a pamphlet and all the forms you need. Find two witnesses not drunk and over twenty-one, and you can write your own divorce for a dollar ninety-five. You don't need lawyers. Did you know that?

How badly was he failing the test again?

I think I may still have the forms out in the garage. When you need them, you'll let me know. In the meantime, you make a tidy profit.

There's more, I patiently went on. Mr. Adler said that he'd pay off the mortgage on our house, plus you wouldn't have to worry about your gambling debts either.

No kidding? He said all that?

Some deal, huh?

You must be one helluva tutor, son.

Oh, that I am.

Go on then. What bad can come of it?

Maybe it was because we were at the Silver Dollar—and the clicking of the chips floated in, as did the wisecracking of the waitresses and the honey-smooth voice of Dino singing *Volare* on the jukebox—that I said to him, Dad, shouldn't you give a little more thought to wagering your son? Your only son.

What wager? Are you kidding!

Then he lit up a Lucky. He took a long drag and then blew the smoke at me. He aimed it over my shoulder in rings he still thought amused me. Then he announced his parental conclusion: I'd say you were a sure bet.

Really?

What other kind of kid would I have but a sure bet! Sure, go on, he said. Run off with the girl. Have a good time.

Marry her?

If you want. What bad could happen, like I say, that you're not young enough to fix?

But it might turn out to be more than some little jaunt. Bayla's sort of crazy, you know, and she thinks I have crazy potential. We could . . . I don't know . . . really run away . . . stay away . . . longer than you think. A lot longer. Maybe you wouldn't see me for a very long time.

He took another drag on the Lucky, this time sucking the smoke way down into his lungs. I thought he'd found a way to circulate it around all his internal organs, lovingly massaging them with smoke, because when it emerged, this time through his two big nostrils, the smoke seemed to announce, like incense from some personal Jewish Vatican, that an authoritative new pronouncement was about to be made.

Look, Norman, you're suddenly growing up, and I'm seeing it maybe for the first time. With new eyes. If the girl's parents know what's going on, and they're offering so much . . . look, for goodness' sake, just go. Take a week, take two, take more. Who's counting? Have a good time. See what happens. You really want to run away and never see us again? I'm not the world's best father. I know that. It would not come as the greatest surprise that you maybe want to say *kaddish* for me *before* I die.

Please, Dad.

No, no, no. That's o.k., Norman. Just do it after I croak. Will you promise me that? That'll increase my odds.

What odds?

Of getting into heaven.

What's heaven to you, Dad? Nothing but a big card table?

With all your Torahs and all your studying, I don't really think you know any more about heaven than I do, son.

Maybe not.

And maybe I should not have cut him off from me as I did then, because this was the first, and only, theological discussion I had ever had with my father, and at the casino no less.

But, Dad, the real problem tonight, for me, is that the very act of getting on the road with Bayla, isn't that like signing some kind of contract with Mr. Adler? Marriage with Bayla and everything I told you. Would I be doing that?

He picked at the doughnut crumbs that had fallen off my plate, popped them into his mouth, and then said: What if you don't touch the girl?

Excuse me?

I mean, you know, you don't screw her, pardon my French.

Please.

Well, some agreements are sealed with a handshake, some with a signature. Like you're saying, sounds like this one is sealed with a fuck.

Jesus, Dad.

I shock my scholar-prince of a son? This is a night of many firsts.

That's it, I declared. I stood up, for he was indeed right—I was shocked. These proceedings had to be ended. Ed was little more than a coarse, uneducated man who had about as much wisdom, to use Esther's phrase about him, as you could squeeze into a thimble. If he wanted to go on masquerading as my father, he was, I supposed, entitled. But I'd had enough. The visit had by no means been a loss. The doughnut had been good.

He called out to one of the honeys to get me a coffee to go so that I'd be awake on the drive home. Then he announced he intended to keep playing until breakfast. He walked me to the Hudson, where we shook hands with a wordlessness and formality that felt like a farewell.

CHAPTER TWENTY-FOUR

The instant I walked in from Gardena, without even taking off my jacket, I called Bayla. Two hours later I was standing by the picture window. An hour before dawn the eastern L.A. sky over the desert can be red as a hibiscus flower and almost as ruffled, at the edges where the streaks of first light appear above the horizon.

I wasn't feeling stuck or angry or ashamed but just tired, bone-tired but with a body almost humming and washed over with a kind of exhausted affection that was beginning to feel like nostalgia. These poorly hung drapes, the old radio and thrift-shop sofa, the La-Z-Boy, and the lazy Susan, all the lazy objects of my life that seemed always to be there, never to move or even to be covered over or to be replaced by the new and improved, all the unnecessary oldness before its time didn't seem to bother me at all this night. Even the State of Israel apron—only in my house would this vibrant new state full of energy, audacity, and guns become something you wiped your hands on—was casually flung across the ironing board, which was always set up in the dining room.

I let the drape fall from my hand and slowly circumambulated the room. I ran my fingers along the edges of my father's green-glass ashtray on the table beside his chair; I picked up and felt the dull tip of the letter opener (*bill killer,* he had named it) that I had made for him in metal shop. Here was his poetry anthology, with its dog-eared page marking Gray's "Elegy in a Country Churchyard."

The tiles beneath the mantel of the never-used fireplace had a faint design of racehorses leaping barriers. I wondered if Ed thought about them—there were no bandages on these legs. I felt as if every cell in my body had its own photographic memory operating at maximum capacity. Everything I scanned or touched or pictured or thought in that hour, every view, breath, and sigh became a snapshot or artifact in an album I was preparing before my departure.

Making all the difference this time and altering the space completely, like an arrow in the target, was my small blue duffel, sitting in the center of the living room all neatly packed and, like me, waiting for Bayla to arrive. In the duffel were toothbrush, underwear, and T-shirts. But how long would we be away? Without waking Esther, like a thief in my own life, I entered her room and took the new pair of jeans she still had on her dresser; she was shortening them for me.

Maybe I *should* have been thinking about it as merely a little vacation from parents or as going to camp, as Ed had suggested. Maybe I should have awakened my mother to say good-bye after all, especially if we ended up staying away far longer. Except I always liked them better when my parents were away from me or asleep. It now suited me and seemed as appropriate as hugs and barely concealed tears that Esther was snoring away in her bedroom, and my father was still waiting for his fourth ace in Gardena.

Because, running away or not, in my mind's explanation to itself, I was still the Hebrew tutor. I'd also packed a copy of the *Tanach,* the Bible, with Bayla's bat mitvah sections marked by ribbons, and one of our workbooks that contained paltry notes for her speech. Yes, I was fooling myself, but there it was. The side pocket of the duffel bulged with *The Rise and Fall of the Third Reich,* whose paragraphs I was using to build up my vocabulary.

At five fifteen in the morning, a month and a day from the bat mitzvah that I knew would not be, Bayla pulled up in front of the house silently flashing the light of her 1300 cc Yamaha Road Star

Silverado. She had on a leather skirt that rode up her thighs, a leather jacket, long white socks up over her calves, and engineer's boots with big silver buckles.

I think I was on that bike, behind her, my bag lashed to hers, before she even raised her visor.

Here, she said, matter-of-fact as always, I only have one helmet. Her hair, which she had been letting grow, flowed then down her neck to her shoulders as she pulled the helmet up and off. My arms circled her waist and I pulled tight. I think I would have been content to go absolutely nowhere with her, just to sit there, the Road Star's engine still on and ticking, the seat vibrating, and Bayla in my arms.

Whoa, she said, I can't breathe. You want me to throw up? Cut it out, Norman!

She worked to undo the clasp of my hands around her middle, but her hair smelled of freshly cut grass and her skin beneath the light of the street lamp was like the vellum of a new Torah scroll. I thought I would cry if I let her go or even looked at her in the eyes, so I stayed there, almost hiding, my head pressed against her back and neck.

Not since I met you, I managed to say to her, have we ever started a session on time until this one.

We haven't started anything, Norman, and we won't until you let me go. What's with you? Your call really surprised me.

You said call any time.

But the middle of the night!

What better time to disappear?

Through the picture window I saw a light go on. I let Bayla go.

Always hold on, but lightly, she began her first lesson. Here, with your fingers inside the belt if you want, or hang on here at the waist. But not here. All right? Nowhere near the boobs. You got that? Or we'll crash for sure. Later I'll teach you to drive, and then we can change places. Until then, you wear the helmet, Hebrew tutor. There's more to lose inside your head than mine.

There's nothing inside my head but you.

Liar.

I eased on the helmet, snug yet still comfortable. The helmet was large and white, like the space travelers described by Werner von Braun in the *Wonderful World of Disney* programs. I was so excited that I would not have been surprised had Bayla identified herself as an astronaut and we shot up then and there, straight for the moon.

The drape in the picture window moved slightly.

Wave toward the house, Bayla, I said as she tucked up the kick-stand and cranked up the accelerator. But with the roar of the engine I don't think she heard me. It's too bad. I know my mother would have liked Bayla to wave to her. I could have waved too, I guess, but what more stupid thing is there in the world to do than wave to your mother as you run away from her? Even the Hebrew tutor of Bel Air had his principles. I lowered the visor, tucked both my hands inside Bayla Adler's leather belt, and we were off.

CHAPTER TWENTY-FIVE

At that hour, only the boxy white delivery trucks of the Adohr Dairy were on the road, leaving water trails dripping from the huge ice blocks they carried. In the relative quiet, the clicking of mechanical switches inside the light signals seemed loud as they swayed from the slowly moving wires overhead.

Since I expected Bayla to be able to defy gravity, that she turned out to be not even a moderate law-breaker while driving came as a real surprise. I marveled at her patience and wondered why we didn't just run those red lights when there wasn't a cop for miles. However, from the very beginning of our getaway, there was something cautious that I sensed had worked its way into her mysterious, impulsive nature. Although we didn't linger, we didn't speed, and, as I said, we stopped at every red, slowed at every yellow, and exceeded no more than thirty or thirty-five when the green signaled us to go. It was more my Hudson style of driving than what I thought would be hers. It crossed my mind to wonder if perhaps she was becoming a little like me already—real couples, according to Esther's *Reader's Digest,* develop similar habits. After all, we'd been a couple already for a few hours. Or maybe it was simply that Bayla and I were both very scared, and deliberation and caution were her way not to be the first to show it.

I wasn't sure Bayla knew that she was being bargained and offered, dealt and dowried, but I certainly wasn't going to be foolish enough to be the one to reveal it. Not yet anyway. As long as neither she nor I mentioned the parents who seemed to have arranged for all of Los Angeles to make way for our great little escape, we might be able to sustain the illusion of real flight. I don't know. I was very confused. Maybe we were driving slowly simply because she was being my tutor, giving me a primer in the fundamentals, the *aleph-bet* of running away.

That was just fine with me. All saddled up in that seat behind Bayla I felt so cool with the wind blowing her hair in my face—I had raised the visor—and my arms around her. All that was missing was an audience. And suddenly they were there too: There were the guys from Junior Cong who had razzed me at the skull-cap box; there, my friends in Latin Club; and the demure, soft-spoken daughters of the rabbis, here now completely astonished and clapping wildly. Here they all were in my imagination, jostling for the best viewing spot along the empty sidewalks of L.A. as if we were our own parade. Applauding enthusiastically, they were just awestruck at who their shy grind of a friend had become: a biker with a fantastic girlfriend all in leather.

We cruised sedately north on Fairfax past Canter's, past the Farmer's Market, which was just beginning to stir with trucks pouring out their redolent cargoes of just-picked melons. Over to the west, the black box of the CBS building was showing a few lights in the windows—maybe the reporters on the graveyard shift were taking a break from their typewriters to watch the sun rise. Who could blame them?

We approached the Self-Realization Fellowship of Paramahansa Yogananda, an outfit that for years I had been wondering about and admiring from my perch on the university-bound bus. I was all for self-realization and all for fellowship, but I had never had the time, or courage, to stop and go in. I was always on my way to Torah or to Talmud or to Jewish history, destinations fine enough, but. . . . Well, because everyone was counting on me so much, it seemed that even to be curious about Paramahansa might be construed a form of disloyalty. Here now two women in saris were arriving, perhaps to meditate. They turned slowly to look at the motorcycle as we passed.

I felt so delighted with this novel sense of freedom that I was experiencing with Bayla on the Yamaha that it grew into delight for all the peoples and the religions of the world who were all struggling so hard, like me, toward self-realization, so I bent slightly from the waist, trying to give those fine ladies a little Hindu or Buddhist *gassho,* or bow of thanks.

Sit still! Bayla yelled as the bike fishtailed almost out of control. You want to get us killed? Don't move. She leaned dramatically opposite our scary tilt until we were righted. That, by the way, was the first and last bow, Buddhist, Jewish, or anything else, I ever offered from the seat of a moving motorcycle.

As we rolled up to Sunset, near Tiny Naylor's, where I could see a few cars already parked, the occupants availing themselves of the twenty-four-hour breakfast menu, I shouted into Bayla's ear, Are you hungry?

Yes, she shouted back, but not for food.

All right. The University of Judaism isn't far from here. My training ground. Right over there. The school where they prepared me to teach you. Should we go there first? And then breakfast?

No. From now on you go to school with me, Hebrew tutor. Ready?

It's hard to describe in memory the roar that bike made then. It erupted like an explosive the precise instant Bayla raised ever so slightly from her seat. I noticed the small ripple of muscle in her right forearm as she gave the accelerator a turn, and we shot instantaneously out from that intersection, leaving Tiny Naylor's and its plates of sunny-side up eggs behind—they were yellow specks growing smaller and smaller as we launched into orbit, just the way the astronaut Gordon Cooper had done in the spring. 162 miles up at 17,000 miles per hour. Only my pilot was Bayla Adler.

In seconds we were cruising down Los Feliz and then entering Ferndell, the gateway to Griffith Park. Did Bayla ever know how to make that machine dance! We dipped and wound around curves, and once or twice took them too wide and skirted the retaining walls of the corkscrew park road. Each time we recovered, we shrieked at having had a far closer view than we ever wanted of the steep hillsides with their car-sized boulders and scrub ponderosas plunging to the arroyo below. On the narrow straightaways we got up to sixty, and sometimes more.

As the city receded below us, the road curved through a section of Ferndell past brownish-green stretches of grass bordering public picnic grounds. Here, long green tables and black grills leaned at odd angles, trailing off into stands of pine trees. As we sped past, these picnic facilities seemed to my eyes transformed into strange, fading monuments to the happy family life of a tribe to which Bayla and I, different as we were, had never truly belonged.

The bike and Bayla felt so warm, vibrating, and comforting, and I was so happy to be simply in motion, going *anywhere,* that it had not occurred to me to ask her where in fact we were headed. Lake Gregory was not north, but east, off to the right. All those times she had told me about Carlos and riding the hills with him, wind blowing through her hair, now I didn't mind. All that with him was then; *now it is with me,* I kept repeating. *Now it is with me,* and that was all the destination I seemed to need.

Incredible! I shouted. Absolutely incredible.

Only just beginning, Hebrew tutor. Hang on tight!

She gunned the engine and as we blasted away, my worries about school and my parents and all my responsibilities to the Jewish community and to my people Israel began to drop away like so much baggage. Whoooie! There it went. Bye-bye! So long, suitcases bulging with anxiety, boxes I thought were lashed onto me so tightly that I'd never be free. They bounced away and broke up as they toppled down behind us, and we raced on through Griffith Park; let someone else stoop to find them and make them their own.

I remembered seeing Brando on his speedy little hog in *The Wild One* as he and his posse in their leather jackets and shades roared through Wrightsville, a town so square, square, square—Brando in that film never smiled once. Then there was us. The few people who were in the park on that morning thought, I am certain, Who are those remarkable young people, so fast, handsome, and free?

After a thrilling zigzagging ascent, we emerged onto a plateau, with all of the smog-girdled City of Angels stretched out before us. There, at the end of the expanse, lay the answer to where Bayla was taking us: the L.A. Observatory was, of course, closed at this early hour, its lot and grounds completely deserted. Bayla cut the engine, and we dismounted.

Crunching gravel underfoot, we approached the building and its huge pendulum beside the immense bronze doors. Its dangling ball was moving invisibly in keeping with the rotation of the Earth. The sunlight gleamed off the blue-painted dome. I've approached Uxmal and Chichen Itza and other temples and pyramids since, but nothing has compared to having been atop Griffith Park with Bayla that morning, and the *tick-tick-tick* of the bike cooling down, making the music for our ceremonial approach.

This is my house, Bayla said that sublime morning. And that's my observatory and my parking lot, Norman. I let the rest of L.A. use them, of course, now and then, if they behave themselves.

That's very nice of you.

I'm a good girl, Hebrew tutor.

Very good. Whoever could doubt that?

Don't forget it.

Then she took my hand as we walked, and began talking about everything under the sun, literally, for our star began fully to appear then, big, huge, and full, almost scary in its immense orangeness, looming up over the Mojave.

Look at that! That would be all we'll need, she then said, mysteriously. It's the perfect decoration for my bat mitzvah.

Up here?

Absolutely.

You're not really thinking of it, are you?

A little, now and then. I do practice, when you're not looking. But it's just not speaking to me. Sorry, Hebrew tutor.

Oh, don't be sorry. I now pronounce you bat mitzvahed already, I said. By the power vested in me by I forget who. We can attend to all the details later. Retroactively. I always knew you could do it. Congratulations.

Oh, no, she said. I don't expect you to let me off the hook so easily.

She said Lucille had cancelled the caterer, florist, and photographer.

She then confessed, as our arms wrapped around each other, that her anger at Lucille and Dave had grown stupendously, and instead of studying anything to do with bat mitzvah or the Jews, Bayla said she'd been reading and rereading *The Fountainhead* and a book of lectures by Ayn Rand, who'd been in town giving a series of speeches at UCLA.

Just do absolutely anything you want to do if it doesn't hurt someone else. I could have told her that myself, Bayla said. I could have written that book.

One day you'll write a better one. But don't you think you hurt them by not going through with it?

She ignored my question and asked, You believe all of what Ayn Rand says, Norman?

If I'm not for myself, who'll be for me? Yeah, I guess I go with that.

Did Ayn Rand say that?

Try Hillel, about two thousand years before Ayn Rand was born. It's hard to find a new idea.

I always liked Hillel, of all the rabbis I've had to put up with. Have I told you about my mother's rabbi? The dead ones are much better.

She repeated Hillel's dictum, turning each word over, slowly, like lozenges, as if she were trying to discover in them something no one had heard, seen, or tasted before.

THE HEBREW TUTOR OF BEL AIR

That was only half of what was on Hillel's mind, Bayla. *If I'm not for myself, who'll be for me?* Yes. But he finished off by adding: *But if I'm only for yourself, then what am I?*

Yeah, so what are you?

You're a *what* is his answer. He doesn't say *who* are you but *what* are you. The answer's there, sort of. In the *what*.

I don't get it.

Yes, you do.

Too deep for me, Hebrew tutor.

No, it's not. You get Hillel. He's inside everyone just waiting to shake your hand and say, Finally we get to know each other. That's my philosophy.

I didn't know you had one.

I didn't either. See what riding that bike has done to me already?

So, look, she said, as she placed her arm thrillingly around my waist and yanked on my belt. Let's say I'll be Ayn Rand and you can be the Hillel guy. Let's play.

I like to quote him. I don't really want to be him.

Then you can be Rand and I'll be the rabbi.

No rabbi ever looked like you, Bayla. How about we just be ourselves. I thought that was the point.

But she had latched onto something—she was, up here, a real student of something—and she wouldn't let go: How come there are no girl rabbis, Hebrew tutor? No Hillel-a.

Couldn't tell you.

Yes, you can.

It's just against the rules. Why do you always talk to me as if I know everything? Most things I know nothing about.

If Ayn Rand were a Jew, I bet she'd be a rabbi. If she wanted to be one, those old guys with beards couldn't hold her back.

Maybe not. You're way beyond me, Bayla.

Don't humor me, Norman. You always said to ask any question and to express any thought. *Any*. Up here, she said, motioning out across the Observatory grounds, things just come to me. Here I feel free. At home Lucille is always spying. But what if she's followed us? Maybe she's even over in those bushes now.

I ran over and made a show of slapping at the bushes, flushing Lucille out. That pleased Bayla so much that she ran toward me and leaped into my arms. Then we kissed and kissed, and I finally set her down.

With that we began to walk toward the edge of the plateau, with its set of public telescopes on cantilevered observation platforms perched over the retaining walls. I don't know what there was about the way she had taken my hand, and then my belt, then dropped it, then did that again, and then found my hand with hers, and held it for a moment so firmly. She walked her hand across the small of my back, her fingers grabbing, this time, at my shirt. With one hand she held onto the metal railing surrounding the telescope and pointed out her favorite patch of the landscape—it was a kind of green gully with two huge boulders at each end guarding it like sentinels.

Will you picnic down there with me one day, Hebrew tutor? She leaned out farther. Well?

Sure, I said, and I held onto her tight as she leaned close to the edge. Why not today?

Not today, Hebrew tutor.

Some day then. Come back in here, Bayla. Come back closer to me.

But she did not. She seemed to be daring me to lean out there with her.

So, she said, swinging slowly back, but briefly, as if on her own circling merry-go-round, tell me: if Ayn Rand wanted to become a rabbi, wouldn't she also have to grow a beard, or at least have enough hair so she could, you know, wrap it around her ears like those little Orthodox boys?

Maybe she could get a wig in one of the stores down on Hollywood. Religious Jewish women wear wigs to cover their hair.

I'd like a lock of your hair one day, Hebrew tutor, and maybe I'll give you one of mine.

THE HEBREW TUTOR OF BEL AIR

I think it was what she said, about locks of our hair exchanged, that made me lunge and pull her in toward me. I hugged her and looked in her eyes and she was all at once a new girlfriend and a little kid asking for permission for something—but what? So I tried to take in the whole of what was happening, even though I couldn't even have been close to naming it. Bayla, the fresh morning sky, the Observatory, the Road Star cooling down half a football field behind us, the new sun climbing up from behind the cumulus clouds, just like the way it appeared in my mother's Zion Cemetery calendar, which was always pinned up in our kitchen, depicting the giving of the commandments at Mount Sinai. It was all there in that instant, my past, present, and future. I sensed enough that I should stop and breathe deeply because something incredible was happening.

What is it, Hebrew tutor?

Just catching my breath.

You're funny, Norman. You're by far the funniest person I've ever run away with.

I felt an angry turn of that worm of jealousy in my gut, but it settled down quickly. I could have felt insulted at being on a tour that she had conducted before with other boys. I could have stayed angry or at least felt less than exceptional, but I didn't. I was emptied out, exhausted with a sense of good riddance for who I had been in the city below. The motorcycle ride up had performed, already, that much of a miracle in my life. Who cared if there had been other boys invited to ride with her? Good for them. Lucky boys. Now it was me. Now it was my turn. There had not been, nor would there ever be, another Bayla for me. So beautiful in that outfit, so tough and yet so tender, so full of raw wisdom and yet so innocent: What could she possibly want of me, and what did that little scrutinizing smile mean? Was I some work in progress for her, and was she happy at how I was progressing thus far?

Clay in the hands of the potter, I think it says, in the Day of Atonement liturgy. A sheep in the hands of the shepherdess. All I wanted to do then was fall on my hands and knees, look up to her, and say, Baa, Baa.

Norman, you do take me seriously, don't you?

Bayla.

Sometimes you think I'm stupid, I know.

Cut it out. Let's just look at the sunrise.

Look at me.

I am, Bayla. Believe me.

You're looking through me. Like everybody else.

Nonsense.

How's this for nonsense? And then she hauled off and hit me. Not hard, but no tender tap either, and right in the stomach.

Jesus, Bayla.

What do you really see?

I see—

I'll make it easier for you. What do you see that's different about me, Norman?

You're just more beautiful than ever, that's all.

I really thought she was going to slug me again, only harder, and she was plenty strong enough to do so. I retreated from her, I feinted, I mock-shadowboxed to try to get us back in the play, in both senses of the word, that I often imagined us in. But she stretched out her arm, and reeled me in again just by saying my name.

Norman.

Honestly, Bayla. I feel like you're giving me some kind of test. I'm failing, and I'd do anything for the right answer.

Go on.

I see you. What's different? Let me see. You're you, you're beautiful and angry, and we've started out on this . . . whatever it is we're doing, and wherever we are going. It's o.k. with me. Even if nothing else happens but this morning, it's o.k. with me. I look at you, and that's what I see. How'd I do?

A for effort, Norman. But how about down here?

We had by now walked around the Observatory twice and had circled back among the viewing scopes at the platforms. I was nervous being there with her again so near to the edge. She threw her arms backwards between the handholds of one and as she pushed her abdomen toward me, the buckle of her leather jacket rose and her belly button emerged. It was a fine specimen, a beautiful button, one that I had noticed many times before by the pool. I knew, however, that if my answer were only that I saw her belly button now, she well might whack me again.

Down here, Norman. Take a good long look.

I proceeded to study Bayla's belly button like a scientist. Here was a small tanned crater rising and falling with her breathing. Of course I also imagined the plains below and the little foothills above. I was a seventeen-year-old boy, and a gorgeous girl was showing me her belly button at dawn at the Griffith Park Observatory. What else should the world expect of me? God help me, I felt my adrenalin rising again, as if I had been preparing for the SAT and then when I entered the room, the proctor spoke in words I couldn't understand and the test booklet was not in English. I decided to try to focus on a tiny pigtail of fine hair at the upper right of the omphalos.

Keep looking, Norman. Take your time.

O.K., well, maybe that obstetrician was so pleased he had helped bring someone as remarkable as you into the world, he just had to leave a kind of signature, a cute little bow as the mark of his handiwork? You know, like signing his work of art? Yes? No?

No, Norman.

What was she after? I shifted my gaze from her stomach to her eyes, and then over her shoulder to the red-tiled rooftops of so many little stuccoed houses like our own and, beyond them, the yellow-green bottle-washer palm trees doing their early morning hulas above L.A., as if to say, Up here, up here, please pay some attention to me.

I really needed some help, and I would have cribbed and cheated if I could, but everywhere I looked, everyone and everything seemed to turn me down.

For Christ's sake, Norman, you certainly miss a lot. I'm pregnant.

CHAPTER TWENTY-SIX

Oh my gosh, I said. Just like that. *Gosh,* like a kid. We've got to get you somewhere.

Why? And by the way, who the hell is *we*, she said very matter-of-factly. I'm not sick, just pregnant, and don't stare at me that way. What's wrong with boys, anyway!

What way? What way am I staring at you?

You don't even know, do you? Here, she said, and she came right up to me, flicked her hip in that way of hers, and extracted a small hand mirror out of her back pocket. Take a good look at yourself.

I looked but still I didn't see. I certainly didn't see much back then.

You look guilty, Norman. Don't worry, it's not yours. Unless you can get pregnant through tutoring. You remember people once believed the Hebrew letters had a kind of life of their own, that they were alive, and could rise from the page?

Where did you hear that?

From you, Norman. That's right. And they could float in the air, you said, and enter a person. Floating *alephs,* wild *bets.* Kabbalah. You remember? I think if anyone could make that happen, I'm looking at him now. So who knows? Maybe you found a way.

Oh sure. You're really pregnant?

No period.

Look, I said, we should go somewhere to talk.

What's wrong with here? And we're already talking.

I don't know.

You don't know much, I guess, after all.

What I did know is that I wanted for some reason to get indoors with her, and very fast. Outdoors was too big, too scary; outdoors was out of control. Indoors you could find a book, a Jewish book, and maybe near it a Yellow Pages, with a list of obstetricians. With those I might *do* something. Take some action. Do something, anything.

Or was it a sense of shame that enveloped me, as she suggested? Bayla didn't seem in any way ashamed. In the junior Jewish film noir that I seemed to be experiencing in that instant, it was a time for a cigarette, a drink, a *brocha,* a blessing, and a seedy hotel room. At such moments a person realizes what a cliché he can be.

That's why, by the way, I love the big bike with the Star of David emblazoned on the gas tank and my Bible in the saddle bag. That can never be a cliché. Ever! That's Judaism always on the move, getting the wind in its hoary old hair. Plus, gentlemen and ladies of the King Solomon search committee, I do need the modest additional income.

Anyway, back then, at that critical moment with Bayla, I was grateful and not a little surprised that she didn't really resist leaving the Observatory with me. A few cars were already driving up—it was no longer Bayla's private park—and there was even one yellow school bus full of camp children. Little kids, not too many years from being babies themselves. Bayla fell into a silence and stared at them as the kids got off the bus and pointed up to the Observatory pendulum.

I remembered a hotel, the Casa D'Oro, that I had gone to once when one of my teachers at the University of Judaism, a visiting professor of Hebrew from Venezuela—see, we Jews are always on the move—had administered my final exam there. It had been after the semester was over the previous year, and the professor had been waiting a few days for his plane back to Caracas. He liked the Casa d'Oro because the place had the feel of early Los Angeles,

he'd said, and was filled with people who spoke Spanish and
minded their own business. So he could speak Spanish to them,
and to me Hebrew, for it was a conversational Hebrew course on
which I was being tested. An oral exam, as I recall, and I had spoken Hebrew to him and done pretty well in that hotel atrium full
of tall coconut palms and prickly Spanish Bayonet and the tran-
quil trickle of water falling on a pond of oversized goldfish.

It was quite close too, up on Franklin, actually visible from the
upper floors of the University of Judaism. Like so much in my life,
even hotels to which I might take pregnant girlfriends on motorcycles, it whirled toward me out of the orbit of the Jews.

And so we went there and parked and with our bags slung over
our shoulders walked into the lobby like long-distance bikers, even
though we had not yet left town. There was a tall eucalyptus in a
cracked terra cotta pot at the entryway surrounded by mulched beds
of yellow hibiscus. The stuccoed façade around the front door was
painted in a kind of blazing apricot, but with some chipping paint
no one had attended to, it seemed, since the old hacienda days of
Rancho Los Angeles. I saw lots more plants visible in the atrium,
just as I had remembered them. And there were the tall floor lamps
with stripes of gold running down the shades.

Since money was no obstacle—it never was with Bayla—and
the desk clerks didn't ask many questions, not even for Bayla's ID,
only mine, for which I gave them my University of Judaism student card, it was easy. In five minutes we were in a room with a
king-sized bed with a full, gauzy, ornate canopy over it like from
the bedroom of Isabella, who had kicked all the Jews out of her
kingdom in 1492. I believe they even gave me a student discount.

We hadn't said much on the short ride over, and now we lay
down on that big bed together, pregnant Bayla Adler and her
Hebrew tutor.

The chenille bedspread was bumpy, the room had a slight cam-
phor odor as if too many mothballs had been left in the drawers
and closets, and above the mirror there was a little raised cartouche

with swords arranged like the mark of Zorro. Bayla and I stared straight up at the ceiling. We coughed nervously, our hands clasped over our bellies, a foot of bedding between us, the whole place oscillating slowly from a somewhat cheesy romantic hideaway into a kind of adolescent crisis center, though with no counselor in sight, and then back again.

Do your parents know?

Well, maybe they suspect. I only missed two periods. It's still pretty early.

Something began to dawn on me, the way Dave Adler had talked. All he was offering. Then I knew she knew.

Oh don't flatter yourself too much, Hebrew tutor. It's got nothing to do with this, she said patting her stomach. Offering me in marriage to boys I get interested in is a sicko game he plays. It works sometimes, doesn't it?

Excuse me?

I mean, you're here, aren't you? He had your number. The idea, the very prospect of marrying me, didn't that give you, you know, permission to be here with me? Would we be doing this otherwise? I don't think you'd be here on your own steam, would you? Too daring for you, right? Without the marriage cover. So why not marry me and have a dozen children? Make it two dozen. My father's a genius when it comes to manipulating people. I'm only just pretty good at it, but I'm learning. Anyway, he likes you very much and thinks, yes, you would be excellent husband material for me. What a joke it all is.

You're right. About that.

Let's be clear. I think you're pretty terrific, but nobody's taken the bait, or me. It's exciting though, isn't it? The question is, will you?

Oh, stop it.

She took my hand then and placed it on her stomach and held it there. I wanted to be the tutor, the teacher, the older, wiser, under-control one, but I couldn't hold it in any longer. I felt anger rising in me—at her, at her family, at how they had figured how much money would buy me, and at, yes, me, for being the perfect sucker. But this particular situation was just the surface layer of it. A lifetime's worth of anger welled up in me then. I wanted to cry, I think, but tears didn't happen. Instead, a kind of universal rage, disappointment, and shame seemed suddenly to fill me up and expel everything else of who I was.

I wrapped my arms around my knees, and without looking her way, I said, How many boys, Bayla?

You disappoint, Norman. But o.k. I don't have a problem. I'll tell you. With you, and not counting Carlos, just three that my dad has proposed marriage to on my behalf, with varying degrees of seriousness, although you, I think, are by far his best prospect.

Shut up, Bayla!

Oh, don't be afraid to listen, Hebrew tutor. You know you want to. Carlos he drove away, not very open-minded still in this day and age, even though Carlos showed him papers—that I helped him find, by the way—that he had Jewish relatives going back to the Inquisition. You'd think that would impress my dad. But no. I don't care how many of your relatives were burned at the stake five hundred years ago—you're the pool boy and you will not marry my daughter. Got it?

I worked on him, and he calmed down. But shortly after you started coming to the house, I knew it was over. That's why I hated you so much in the beginning. And then one day, Dad just told Carlos to get the hell out.

Because he started thinking of me?

Let's put it this way: your arrival was not just a coincidence. When I . . . well, when he guessed that Carlos and I . . .when Lucille spied on us one afternoon and saw us . . . she reported to him. Well, that's why you've been offered the world, and then some. Am I right, Hebrew tutor? Dowry and all.

You think I'm this great big joke, don't you?

I'm not laughing, Norman.

Who's the father, Bayla? Is it Carlos?

To the best of my calculations. However, I could be wrong. I've actually never been pregnant before. Have you?

Jesus, Bayla.

Jesus yourself. It's not the end of the world. Carlos is a jerk, and you always make mistakes with jerks. You, on the other hand, are a very serious boy that no one could ever make a mistake with. I always thought you'd be a good nurse. You'll help me, right?

To do what?

Now relax, she said. You don't see me getting up a sweat, do you?

And she was relaxed, remarkably so. She actually seemed to be enjoying herself at the Casa d'Oro with her Hebrew tutor. She reclined on the bed, pregnant and alluring, and eased me back down beside her.

I'm a rich girl, she said. No coat hangers in alleys for me, if it comes to that. Maybe because of you my body is adjusting to Judaism by causing me to skip periods. Not to worry. When the time comes, if it comes, my abortion will be a gold-plated Rodeo Drive affair. Maybe I can even get Lucille to make up a guest list. I'm just kidding, Norman. Unless of course, you want to marry me.

I no longer knew how to understand Bayla, and I told her that her joking was dishonest and infuriating. I told her that she was the most mysterious, unfathomable human being I had ever met.

Oh, she said, very casually, you're right about that. Why in the world would you accept such a situation? That's too much to ask.

Even of a Hebrew tutor.

Even of a Hebrew tutor, she slowly repeated.

Then we lapsed into one of those silences again that is worse than shouting. I was plenty familiar with these from home. A raft and then another raft of thoughts, all unexpressed, drift past you, like survivors from a shipwreck shrieking for help, shouting to be heard. But they're all muffled or even voiceless, and everything was quiet in that hotel room at Casa d'Oro until one of us, finding it intolerable, spoke again.

Here, she said, you want to feel? I don't sense anything alive or growing in there yet. Do you?

CHAPTER TWENTY-SEVEN

She took my hand, as I lay there on my back, and placed it on her abdomen. I didn't remove it. Beneath my palm I felt her belly button.

Does Judaism have anything to say about abortion?

Oh, Bayla. Judaism says, Don't be so dumb as to get into this kind of mess.

Then I guess Judaism's irrelevant for me.

Where's Carlos?

Like I said, Carlos is gone. Carlos has a wife and two children.

I was dumbfounded, and if my mouth didn't hang open then, it was only because I was lying on my back and grateful for the gravity that had kept it closed despite jealousy, anger, and callow dismay.

Norman, my sheltered little boy. Look, she then said, sitting up on the bed, let's play. Let's make believe for a second. I could have lots of children. I mean, I *could*. I'm terrifically healthy. We could be one of those big Orthodox Jewish families my parents are always talking about. Replace all the dead Jews. We could have twenty kids, and each of them could have a Hebrew tutor. The nursing-home business is prospering. The dead and dying will support the living.

Is that your idea of a marriage proposal to me?

Isn't that what I'm supposed to be doing out here, Norman? But it was really just a thought that came to me spontaneously. Thoughts and images do occur to me now and then, you know.

Stop it, Bayla.

You can call it whatever you want.

I can't tell if you're putting me on—what, if any of this, you really mean.

I can't tell either.

Jesus, Bayla.

There is just too much Jesus in our talk.

I really don't want to talk about abortion any more, I said. It upsets me.

It upsets me too.

And I really don't want to talk about marrying either. That's even more upsetting.

Fine with me, she said.

So what do we talk about?

How about sex? Look at me. I'm here again for you, abortion or no abortion, marriage or no marriage.

This is all so crazy.

Well, I don't know how a man can make up his mind one way or another if he wants to marry his pregnant friend if he hasn't slept with her. So I'm available, Hebrew tutor.

Unbelievable.

What you see is what you get, Norman. And then she let me see, shimmying out of her leather skirt and her underwear and her jacket, kicking off the boots, so she only had on her white socks, rising up to her calves.

I averted my eyes just like, I remembered, one of the really religious men at temple always did when the girls from Junior Cong rushed giggling and pretty out into the hall after services. That was me all right, and I hated myself for being him then, and I looked at the floor of the room at Casa d'Oro and started counting flowers on the tiles and wanted to cry. But Bayla wouldn't let me. When I felt her hand under my chin, turning my face toward her, I looked.

Go on, Norman. Study me, if you want, like a page of text, letter by letter, vowel by vowel. Don't be afraid. It's what we're here to give to each other.

Bayla. How could she have guessed that that's how I had always admired her?

I've never enjoyed being tutored, she said then, as much as I enjoyed being tutored by you. Just us, Hebrew tutor. Just us, she said, in that way of hers, naked, stripped of pretense, of romance. Just matter-of-fact. Lying on her side now with only her white socks and black bangs, with her legs demurely together like a model on a studio divan—a picture from A.P. art history, from the French painter Edouard Manet, came to me. What else would you expect of me at such a moment?

Kiss me, Hebrew tutor. It won't hurt you. You're not breaking any laws. Plus, haven't I just told you that I'm pregnant, the greatest contraceptive of them all?

Yes, I thought. Yes, you jerk. Do this. And then the brakes hissed: Wasn't there something very wrong here? It couldn't possibly be right, or the correct thing to do, if it were happening to *me,* could it? Where *was* Carlos? Could he right now be climbing up the fire escape to break in through that window and kill us both in a frenzy of jealousy? And, furthermore, shouldn't it be dark? Or shouldn't Bayla and I be in the back of a convertible, or behind a curtain at a school dance? Never mind that I had avoided every school dance. Bayla was completely confusing, contrary to expectation. I thought I had been missing so much, and then along came Bayla, but instead of catching me up, she was always launching me so disconcertingly far ahead of my natural development, skipping all these steps so that I landed in panic.

Yet she was also undeniably beautiful, fascinating, and so rich, and I was the son of a poor gambler, trying to turn a little preternatural Jewish erudition into a real life, and her perfume smelled so green and her touch was so good. What the hell was I supposed to do?

CHAPTER TWENTY-EIGHT

Did we make love there in the Casa d'Oro behind the long, rippling cotton curtains with their designs of sunflowers and sombreros tailing off toward the ceiling? And, if so, how was it for you, Hebrew tutor? And was the sleep that then washed over us post-coital or just dead tired exhaustion, we having been so exercised in flight from our homes and our lives? And if we made love and, afterwards, shuffling off the coil of consciousness so that we dreamed, did we then enter each other's dreams, spinning images of motorcycles and marriage and what life might be like if we grew together into each other's bodies, habits, and hearts for ten, twenty, thirty, forty years, then unimaginable durations of union? Did we see or feel all that? Any of it? Who's asking? Who's going to tell now? Those are all the wrong questions, and the curtain of discretion now descends on this scene.

Except to say that Bayla did come out of the bathroom later wrapped in one of Casa's thick terrycloth robes, her hair turbaned in a white towel. Looking every bit a high priestess, she stood at the foot of the bed, where I still lay like the clapper of a well rung bell, and said, What's the blessing you say after *that*, Hebrew tutor?

With happy deliberation, I stood up on the bed, slow and naked, and I began to bounce with the badge of my Jewishness flopping about ridiculously. Up I leaped and down I dropped with all the trampolining that a mattress could take, while I recited the *She-hechi-yanu,* the blessing that marks holidays, new moons, and, yes, first times, first times on a motorcycle, first times with a pregnant girl in a hotel room. . . . I still really like to hear that blessing. Let us all recite together: Blessed art thou oh Lord our God, king of the universe, who has kept us alive, who has brought us through for yet another twenty-four hours of life, who has kept us, in our private lives, from killing ourselves or others, and, in the public sphere, who has kept the Russians from nuking us and us from nuking the Russians, who has kept the blacks from rising up, as they sorely deserve to do, and killing the whites, and bless He who has enabled us to arrive at this day.

How's that? I said to her.

And Bayla, my first congregation, answered in a quiet voice, yet to me it was louder than the echoing roar of an engine around a canyon curve: Way to go, Norman. Amen!

We stayed in that room all day and all night. I would have been happy to remain for days more, without moving except to go down for food and a newspaper and to check on the bike. Yet even if you're living in an imagined hideout, pleased about yet also guilty of having committed some kind of beautiful misdemeanor of love, still you can't stay hunkered down forever. People are thinking about you, the worrying begins, photographs of you are nervously passed from hand to hand, or are taped to telephone poles and bulletin boards, and it all starts to ripple your way. What was our next move going to be?

Do you mind if I make an observation, Bayla said the next morning, since we've been living together, so to speak, like man and wife? You're so very still and quiet it's almost spooky, Norman. You definitely have this capacity to just sit, sit, and stare out the window. Are you seeing something out there that I'm missing?

Just the air shaft, Bayla. But with you here, it's a very beautiful air shaft.

I could put a sign around your neck—*Inertia*—and carry you into school as a science fair project. I might even win.

She of course was right. Sitting at a school desk, reading on my bed surrounded by books, staring out the picture window with the parents, and spinning the lazy Susan while at my homework labors, such were the snapshots I saw of me through Bayla's eyes. If I weren't so engaged in them, what was my life, and who was I?

As you've noticed, Bayla said, I am your opposite. I am stir-crazy right now, Norman, and I need to get the hell out of here.

I felt my odds with Bayla, which had seemed so incredibly high just an hour before, suddenly begin to plummet. I'll go anywhere you want to go, Bayla Adler.

You may live to regret those words.

You talked about Mexico or the Grand Canyon or going up toward San Francisco. That's fine with me. Look at what almost happened in Cuba last year. We could be particles in a mushroom cloud any day now. I don't need to know where we're going. I'm with you. Let's just go.

Absolutely, but the itinerary's changed a little. We have an errand to run first.

She went back into the bathroom and came out in the shortest time fully dressed and carrying a black bag I had not seen before; it hung heavily by a wide strap over her shoulder.

I guess I would like you to tell me where we are going after all.

Why don't I just keep it a surprise until we get there.

An hour later, the Casa d'Oro's bill having been paid by Bayla with three new twenties she'd extracted from the black bag and both of us wearing a pair of stylish sunglasses that we had picked up in the pharmacy next to the hotel, we entered the Rexall Drug Store at the corner of Santa Monica and San Vicente boulevards. Did we look like models or like thieves? We found a roomy booth, and each of us ordered a chocolate malted. The place was fairly deserted and after the waitress brought over the two tall, frosted glasses, she had a smoke at the end of the counter and ignored us, which was just as well.

Why, you may ask, have we come here, Norman?

I may and I will.

You see that office across the street, where we parked the bike?

Over the stream of traffic that separated us from it, I glanced at the sparkling Road Star. It was parked at a jaunty angle beside the small professional building in question. The building was a low structure with a flat roof, shiny, black-tiled façade, glass-brick windows I couldn't see through, and a beige door up from a short, balustraded stoop.

We are about to do something, Bayla said over her malted, which has never been done before. She spoke with a casualness that, had they been awarding them, deserved the Nobel Prize for nonchalance. She took a big slurp on her straw and added, What I mean is, I am going to do it, but it will go much better, my chances of success will be far greater, if you are my helper, or—what's the word?—my accomplice.

Accomplice?

Across the street there is the office of Dr. Morris Klapfman, who gave Lucille her nose job. He's my errand. What time is it, Hebrew tutor?

I checked my watch. It was ten forty-five.

I've been researching this guy for months. He's in his office every day from eleven to two. Like clockwork. So he'll be there in fifteen minutes, Norman. He's got a staff of four. He's one of the only doctors who does the procedure in his office. It's all set up. Anesthesia, the whole thing. No hospital, no bad food, no bed pans. After a few hours, I'll just walk out. Then we'll drive to the Grand Canyon and do all those things we talked about. I might be a little groggy, but I think by now you can handle the bike.

Yes, I can drive the bike, but what in the world are you talking about? You're pregnant and you've got an appointment to get your nose fixed? Is there a connection between your nose and being pregnant that I'm missing here? Oh, and by the way, there's absolutely nothing wrong with your nose.

Yes, there is, Norman.

Then that strange light came into her eye, and she moved forward in the booth. She pushed the malteds to the side and drew my hands toward hers across the table. This is what she told me, and I remember it as if she spoke it yesterday:

You remember the twenty thousand they are giving me for the bat mitzvah, Hebrew tutor?

I nodded.

Well, I've got it with me in the bag that's under the table. Right here. Then, as if proof were needed, she tapped my shin with her boot and moved my leg so that it inclined against all those sheaves of bagged dollars. I'm going to go in there, with the big bucks, and pay Dr. Morris Klapfman, who clipped Lucille's nose. By the way, he is *the* major nose-job guy for the Jewish girls in Los Angeles. I am going to ask him to do mine, but it's not what you think.

I'm really missing something here, Bayla.

Yes, you are, Hebrew tutor. You're the first and only person I've ever told this to, except, of course, for Dr. Klapfman. I call him Morris, and I know he can do it.

Do what, Bayla? What?

He's going to take this nose of mine and give me a reverse nose job. Instead of a ceremony for my bat mitzvah, I'm going to get a real Jewish nose. That's what I want.

Bayla was right. I am normally a very quiet person. Too quiet perhaps, as she said, but this declaration of hers flung me into an even deeper trough of aphasia.

You're smiling, she said. And you know why? Because you know it's the best idea for a bat mitzvah that you've ever heard in your entire life.

It is?

Yes, and you inspired it, Hebrew tutor. Like it or not, you're my accomplice already, sort of.

Explain this phrase, *sort of.*

Thanks to your example, I'm prouder of being Jewish now than ever. Sort of. Really, Norman, if it weren't for you, I couldn't have put my finger on how sick I am of being around my stepmother and all these girls at school who leave on Friday with a perfectly good nose and come back on Monday looking like Rudolph the Red-Nosed Reindeer. Something really special to do on the Sabbath, isn't it? They lie about it, and then giggle, and their friends ooh-aah about their new snouts, but not me, not ever. They don't have the slightest idea how shameful it all is. If I have to keep seeing that, without doing something in response, I won't go back to school. Are you taking this in, Hebrew tutor?

Inside that fairly silent Rexall, a number of alarms were sounding within me: There's nothing wrong with your nose. I love your nose, Bayla. Everybody loves your nose. Leave it alone, please!

Remember what I said about taking me seriously? The point is that I don't love my nose. It's my nose, no one else's, and I want to change it. I want a Jewish nose.

None of this is making sense to me, none of it!

I'm like you, Norman. I'm not going to sing well or perform well or do any of that stuff in the synagogue, no matter what you teach me. Sorry. If I ever do have a bat mitzvah—and don't bet on it any time soon—I won't have anything profound to say in a speech either, and I refuse to patch one together with other people's words and fancy quotations. What's the point of that? It's them, not me. Anyway, I don't understand what they're all trying to say.

You understand Hillel.

No, I don't. Not really.

Then make a speech based on all the questions you have. Just ask questions—it's very Jewish.

Nice try, Norman, but no prize. You know it, and you've known it for a long time, that I can't master Hebrew, or anything else. It's not adding up, and I refuse to sound like a fool. That's it.

What's it?

Just like I told you. For the bat mitzvah, *my* bat mitzvah, instead of what all the other girls do, which is get a nose job by which they *hide* being Jews and then have this ceremony proclaiming they are and this ridiculous party afterwards, I am going to get a *real* Jewish nose. And that will be my bat mitzvah. A gift to the Jewish community, and to myself.

I thought we were going to run away, Bayla.

Yes, but *after* the reverse nose job.

I just stared at her and then I reached over and touched her admittedly small and perfectly fine nose with my finger: two small nostrils, a healthy septum, a nose that called no attention to itself and did the job of breathing, filtering, and facial designing that God intended. An excellent nose just as it was. She responded to my gesture and my incomprehension by carefully removing from the bag beneath the table a large envelope. She opened it and withdrew a photograph of a woman she identified as Sarah Bernhardt, the nineteenth-century actress. Bernhardt's nose was circled, by Bayla presumably, in yellow Magic Marker.

That's the one, Bayla said. I want a nose just like hers.

And you've discussed this with whatshisname, Dr. Klapfman?

Morris. Now, listen, Norman. Lucille goes to him every three months to tuck this or to hide that, and like I said, they're on the telephone all the time. I admit I've broken into their conversations. I think she might be having an affair with him. Who knows, but, yes, yes, we've talked, he knows me. He jokes with me like an old uncle. So I've talked to him, in a general way, about nose jobs. He does more than noses by the way, and that's why I know he is our guy. He's a plastic surgeon. He can do anything. He's been to the house, too. He's tight with my parents, something with their business, although why a hundred-year-old would want to get a nose job I can't say. Can you?

Got me.

Anyway, every time he sees my nose, he comes up and tweaks it and jokes, Too bad, no new customer here. Little does he know. Right?

Bayla.

Norman, he's going to give me a real Jewish nose, and when it's over you're going to say that blessing over it. The *She-hechi-yanu* for the first ever Reverse Jewish Nose Job.

I am?

Yes, Norman. I have the right blessing, don't I? Bingo! This is a real contribution to the Jewish people. A unique contribution. Where's *your* pride, creativity, and real Jewish spirit?

Was she putting me on again? She always was, but this time, when I was almost praying the idea was a joke, I realized it was not. No, she had a real plan; she had already launched it; we were already in the middle of it. If I pointed out how much she seemed to be doing it to spite Lucille, would that really get me anywhere, this time, when she was so passionate?

I knew I had not heard all of it yet. The voice inside my head began to sound suspiciously like my father's. She was not showing all her cards. Wait, Ed was cautioning. Patience. Check out the odds. If you just keep from saying something she will find insulting or obnoxious, if you restrain yourself from behaving toward her like a chiding tutor, that'll get you some advantage, and her real angle will emerge.

Wow, Bayla.

Exactly, she said. You know how you're always telling me how great JFK is, how inspiring?

What's the president got to do with your nose?

Ask not what the Jews can do for you. Ask what you can do for the Jews. Your words. And you thought you were making a joke, you thought I wasn't listening. You just don't know how deep your influence runs, Hebrew tutor.

Bayla, we're running away, sort of. You're pregnant, sort of, and now you want an operation on your nose, sort of, because JFK has inspired you?

Not sort of, Norman. A real reverse Jewish nose job. And it's you who have inspired me.

Oh boy.

Mind your tone with me.

Bayla, I said, reverting suddenly, despite her warning and my lame resolution, to full tutorial mode, let's think about this thoroughly before we leave this booth.

O.K., she said, equaling my raise with one of her own, I'm getting my nose fixed in a way that honors the Jewish people. That's what I'm doing, and what's wrong with it? What's to think about? And don't roll your eyes like that. The looking through me thing, the Bayla is wild, Bayla is crazy thing. You know exactly.

Nobody said you were crazy—you just act like it occasionally. Like now. I've never heard of anybody getting a reverse nose job. Nobody, nobody in the history of the Jews or in the history of noses.

All the more reason to do it, Norman.

We are not messing with your perfectly fine nose.

It's not fine.

This *is* crazy.

Stop saying that or I'm walking right out of here and I'll do it by myself. To hell with you. Maybe I don't need you at all.

Well, if you've got an appointment with the nose guy and you've got the money, yes, why *do* you need me?

In case he refuses.

Well, if he refuses, he refuses.

Oh?

I mean you can't force the guy to give you a reverse Jewish nose job.

Oh?

Then she looked about the Rexall to make sure no one was watching us. Down the aisle, the idle waitress was puffing on another smoke. She caught Bayla's eye, misunderstood that we might want to order something more, and took a step in our direction. Bayla shook her head, definitely no. When the waitress halted, and gave a what's-with-you-dumb-kids-do-you-want-me-to-call-a-truant-officer look, Bayla gave her back a little dismissive wave and then, to me, she whispered, Come over here, to my side.

Dutifully I slid out my side of the booth and into hers. She certainly smelled good and looked good and I was happy to be right beside her again, just like on the bike.

You're staring at my nose, Norman.

It's a compliment. I can't help it. I'm also sending you a non-verbal message.

Kiss it if you want, Norman.

I'd love to.

But you'll be kissing it goodbye.

The kiss was interrupted because Bayla suddenly pulled back, bent down, and raised the black bag to the table. Slowly, dramatically, she folded back a white sweater that lay on top, revealing wads of rubber-banded hundred-dollar bills.

There's certainly more than enough to pay for the malteds.

Hebrew tutor, she said, with a flicker of a smile, look back down there again. Yes, there, below the money.

I saw it then, the long, shiny, black muzzle, dare I say, nosing out from among the bills at the bottom of the sack.

Is that what I think it is?

Yes, yes, she said, covering it up with the same alacrity with which she'd revealed it. But Morris is really a sweet man. He likes me. It won't come to that. I'm sure we won't have to use the gun.

We?

You can't expect me to hold the gun on him while he's operating on me!

No, I guess that wouldn't be reasonable.

Norman, she said, as matter-of-factly as if she were giving road directions, when it comes time to administer the anesthetic, that's when I pass the weapon on to you. Right before I go under. You make sure he finishes the operation right and doesn't call the cops. That's all you have to do: hold the gun on him to make sure he gives me a beautiful Jewish nose.

What's a Hebrew tutor for?

You took the words right out of my mouth. So, it's decided?

CHAPTER TWENTY-NINE

I took a long sip of my malted. A very long sip. I stopped with the sweet chocolate flow not quite risen to the top of the straw, for I had just had an idea of the delaying kind I was so adept at: As long as we stayed put, as long as we didn't leave this booth, we wouldn't have to pull a gun on Los Angeles's most famous Jewish nose surgeon, Dr. Morris Klapfman. Since we both agreed that the malteds were terrific and we didn't want to leave a drop, there I was slurping away with infinite slowness. I'd make the malted last if not forever, then, drop by delicious drop, for a few hours, and in the meantime I'd think of something.

Didn't your mother ever teach you not to play with your food, Norman?

Didn't yours teach *you* not to play with guns? I slurped.

First of all, I am not playing. Second, my mother—my real mother—actually knew guns pretty well and was a very good shot. So I've heard. She was in the partisans with my dad. That's where they met. And this old thing somehow became hers. A German Luger, I think. Dad usually keeps it in his safe. But I stole it because it was really my mother's, and so it's rightly mine now. But don't worry, Norman. It's practically an antique. It probably won't even work if we're forced to pull the trigger on him.

There goes that *we* again.

For goodness' sake, Norman. It's a prop. A teaching device, like the stuff you brought to tutor me. Anyway, Morris is a serious, religious person, like whatshisname . . . Michael Levin. As soon as we explain the idea behind it—the pride, the new way to celebrate being Jewish—he'll go right along with it, I'm sure.

Oh, absolutely.

You're such a chicken, Norman. Ayn Rand would be ashamed of you.

The rabbis would be ashamed of you.

No, they wouldn't.

Rabbis don't pull guns.

Some do. And if they don't, well, maybe they should. Maybe after I get my nose fixed up, I will become a rabbi who carries a gun. There are a lot more Eichmanns around, Dave says, that need shooting. Even here in L.A.

Really?

He says most are in South America; Paraguay is the worst. But, yes, here, among us too. All the money Dave sends to Israel, he always writes a note: Please, Prime Minister, use my contributions to round up more Nazis. No more trials, he says. Just find them and shoot them. The more you capture and shoot, the more money I send. That's what I can do. I love my father, and he'll love this. I'm not afraid.

You've got big plans. A lot to do.

You're beginning to get it. But the nose comes first. The nose is very important to me.

She paused then, as the sunlight began to shine brightly through the window of the drugstore, pooling, it seemed, in our booth. She put her sunglasses back on and slouched down, keeping a steady stare on me; at least I thought she was staring because, behind the dark glasses, who could see her eyes? I wanted to lean over and remove them in order to see down into all the wild canyons of Bayla Adler's intentions, deep inside her eyes. Here were her words, but were they true emissaries of the soul? To this day, whenever I see a person wearing sunglasses, I know their soul is likely on vacation somewhere. How I wish I had removed those shades then, but I didn't dare.

The more I felt stared at by Bayla from behind her glasses, the more under her gun, so to speak, the more I continued to pause over every drop of my malted. And then there was this: Bayla appeared exactly the way she had on what seemed like that long-ago afternoon in April, that first day of tutoring, at the boardroom table up in Bel Air. She was drawing that silence of resolve around herself like a cape I could reach out and actually touch. I felt that if she did love me and need me it was only the way a missile loves and needs its countdown. Move me to do otherwise, she seemed to be challenging me. An expression of unspoken, impermeable resolve.

What in the world could I say or do to head this off?

Finish up your malted, Norman. We'll be late for my appointment.

The only appointment you have is with a big disaster.

I instantly regretted what I had said. My words were like flies that had escaped from some nasty part of my interior, and I wanted to reach out, capture them in my hands, as I had done to many an insect when I was a murderous little kid, and crush them to death. Sometimes I think that if God were truly just, really a guide for human conduct, part of the deal would be that every person be permitted to choose one sentence, one phrase, one moment—well, maybe a couple—to reel back inside and erase from the official record of life forever. Calling what Bayla was about to do a disaster would be *my* first choice.

If I can't count on you in this, she finally whispered as she quietly stood up, more composed, if such was possible, than before, how could I even consider being married to you? Partnership is the basis of a good marriage, all the sex-ed manuals say, and where's the partnership here?

This is a very dangerous game you are playing when you walk into a doctor's office with a loaded gun.

Who says it's loaded? I have the bullets right here, in my bra.

The police don't care where you store your bullets. They will consider the gun, you, us as fully loaded. We will go to jail.

And what's wrong with that? You're the one who has been telling me to look out at the world. What's happening out there, Norman? People are going to jail for what they believe. All those Negroes—

You want to go to jail on behalf of the Negroes? Let's do it, I said. Let's go join the Congress of Racial Equality. There's another demonstration out at UCLA next week. Let's drive out there on the bike. Let's do it, Bayla. Let's go right now to Birmingham and have Martin Luther King, Jr., conduct your bat mitzvah! Yes! Do *that* as your bat mitzvah substitute, and I'll lead the way. I'll read the Torah with you. We'll give Dr. King an *aliyah* and slip him all the money you have to bail people out of the Birmingham jail. But I do not want to go to prison for a nose job—

Reverse, Norman! Reverse Jewish nose job! You can say it.

Bayla, I said, placing my arm over her shoulders and easing her back down into the booth. We need to talk about this some more.

I want to do it, Norman. She crossed her arms over her chest and rose from her seat again. There is nothing to talk about.

Oh yes there is.

I too had no idea what there was left to talk about. That didn't keep me from trying to prolong things. The malted was gone, and all I could do now was hope words would emerge from my mouth, and that their sounds would drag some meaning, some sense, some cargo of very serious caution behind them that would influence Bayla to abandon her plan.

To my surprise, she didn't bolt, and, what's more, she suddenly ceased resisting. She stayed seated and, for the first time, actually seemed to pause in her headlong pursuit of an altered nose. I was beginning really to feel in the middle of a poker hand, in which I was truly a player; in the business of bluffing, I did have some experience as well as some pretty good DNA. I felt a ripple of relief in the Rexall as we both slumped down in the booth, shoulder to shoulder, legs entwined, and fended off yet a new solicitation by the waitress. Advantage, Hebrew tutor.

O.K., Bayla finally said after a long interval, what is it you want to discuss now, Norman, because I have thought it through already, all the details. Look, she then said, as she removed from inside her shirt, presumably from the cozy fossa it shared with the two bullets, a small piece of paper, which she now unfolded.

Two other surgeons, she announced, pointing with evident pride at the names, addresses, and phone numbers written on the sheet. This one's in San Diego. The last week of school a new girl came to class with such bloodshot eyes that I knew instantly. She gave me the reference, but I think compared to Morris he's a butcher. The second guy's in Tijuana.

Mexico?

That's where Tijuana usually is. Would you feel more comfortable going down there instead? A place where we're not known? Would that allow you to be a little more cooperative? On the bike we could be there in two hours. I'm not a lunatic, Norman. I am capable of compromise.

In Tijuana I bet you could cop two or three operations for the price of one with Dr. Klapfman. Why stop with your nose?

Very funny.

Who gave you the reference in Tijuana?

What difference does that make who gave it to me!

And then I said the next thing I'd like to reel back inside me and obliterate. Was it Carlos?

Yes, she answered. So what if it was?

I don't know what happened then. More thoughtless words fell out of me in a torrent, as if they had been secretly lining up again and getting ready to march out, dumb participants suddenly becoming vocal in a fool's parade. It was a shock to hear myself rage on: So why don't you go to Mexico with Carlos? What do you need me for! Baby by Carlos. Nose job by Carlos too.

That's it! Done! And she hoisted up the black bag and slapped it on the table with enough force to make the empty malted milk glasses jump. You know a lot, but you're still just a jealous, creepy boy. You don't know what friendship is about! And you're also a coward. You're right. I don't need you. I don't need you at all!

Then she walked away from me, down the long aisle of the Rexall, past the cash register, giving the staring waitress a defiant glare, and then out the door into the hazy late morning light.

Her abandonment of me seemed to stop time, and in the arrested interval I imagined her crossing the street without me and entering Dr. Klapfman's office.

He was, after all, a doctor. A Jewish doctor who had taken the Hippocratic oath to do no harm. He would never do this operation for Bayla.

No sooner had the thought entered my mind than I hated myself for having it. Cockeyed as it was, the reverse nose job was pure Bayla—impulsive, impractical, daring, inspired. I hated myself for the failure I had scripted for her even in my imagination. No, I wasn't worthy of Bayla Adler.

Yet beneath all my equivocating I also realized something else lurked that might help, if I could only tap into and draw courage from it: I simply didn't want to leave Bayla Adler. Not then, not ever. And in writing this today, perhaps I haven't.

I knew it then precisely as Bayla walked away from me. Prevent this, I heard myself thinking. Above all don't lose her. What was the alternative? Never to ride with her on the motorcycle again? Never to have my arms around her waist, hanging on tight as we took a deep curve in the park? Instead to ride the Fairfax bus to Hebrew classes at the University of Judaism on into eternity? What about the University of Everything Else? To resume my scholar's grind, to worry that my right arm, the bearer of my book-laden briefcase, might be getting longer than the left? To never again vow that if the Russians threaten to nuke us or we them, Bayla and I would meet at Casa d'Oro, in that very room, and be doing it when the thermal wave strikes? To return to a Bayla-less life seemed worse than boring and sad—it would be joyless and without any wonder. Would I threaten to shoot the nose man, Dr. Morris Klapfman, in order to avoid such an outcome? I thought I just might.

CHAPTER THIRTY

I caught up with her at the red light on the near corner. Fortunately it was one of those interminable traffic lights where you look up, then look up again and wonder if you are the only pedestrian in the City of the Angels and the state of California and if the entire signaling system has forgotten you exist. And it was good, exactly what I wanted: a never-ending malted, a never-changing signal, any time-attenuating magic would do. *Baruch atah Adonai,* thank you, Lord God of signals red, yellow, and green, and for our ability to organize time, even if thereby we only fool ourselves.

Bayla didn't even turn her head to acknowledge that I had caught up. In its endless stream, the traffic continued to race by us on Santa Monica. She kept her eyes forward like a soldier on her mission. I decided that I would interpret her silence not as ongoing reproach but as forgiveness. She was forgiving her callow tutor for what he had both said and thought.

So I stood there, my head bowed in its way, like heavy laundry from the line, as if offering my neck to God to chop off. Oh, those childish games we make of prayer. Still, I was praying again, then, in my fashion, as I stood beside Bayla. And, for the record, I'd like to point out that one of Judaism's most endearing lessons is that the verb *to pray* is reflexive, and it means *to judge,* so that prayer isn't asking for anything from anybody, but is instead a process of self-judgment.

It's all part of the wild ride of life, as I've come to understand it, and the God of Abraham, Isaac, Jacob, Sarah, Rachel, Leah, and all the rest provides only the open road. The bike, the speed, the wanderlust, the guts—that's up to each of us.

Was I practicing this lesson at that long-ago time? I'm afraid not. I was praying for the light to be broken and the cars never to let up, or for Bayla to get some sense.

Then, without quite knowing what possessed me, I moved my fingers across the exquisite small of her back, just as she had taught me. When she reciprocated, that was a kind of prayer answered. As if this were not thrilling enough, I then felt her hand stealing under my shirt, flattening against my skin, then rising from under my collar to my neck, my aching neck, and her strong fingers began to knead the tension away.

Jeez, Norman, you are sweating like a pig, and we haven't even done anything yet.

There's going to be a lot more sweat where that came from, I think.

You'll change your T-shirt and feel a lot better.

The light finally turned green—surgical green, I thought—and we crossed the street, our hips touching, our arms entwined, to Dr. Morris Klapfman's office and to our fate.

As we stepped up onto the far curb in front of the medical building, where the mica chips in the black tiles of the façade sparkled like tiny explosions, will it surprise you to hear that I saw one final opportunity for delay, and that I seized it? The motorcycle. That big Yamaha was just leaning there, of course, just where we had parked it, the front wheel turned toward us. Bayla, in her deliberate way, was moving right on past it toward the office door. Not me. With my eyes fixed on the bike, I halted and held Bayla there beside me. She was in the instant like a kid trying to pull away, beginning to have a tantrum, but I was stronger, or there was something powerful about that bike that somehow gave me sufficient strength to overcome Bayla's pulling. I just wouldn't let her go in.

I have always admired the handsome way a motorcycle looks when at rest—a concentrated power, like I saw in Ed when I watched him play cards at the Silver Dollar—especially when it's parked at a nifty angle, and never more so than that bike on that distant morning. This was what I thought it was saying to me: Hey, whatever else is going on in your life, don't forget that I'm your incredibly swift friend. This big seat I have welcomes you, and zero to sixty in under ten seconds will soon feel like you are riding on air and about to elevate toward the sun, moon, and stars. So thank God He created the lights of both the sky and of the bikes. Hey, whatever is ailing you, whatever grieves you—come on, have faith, throw your leg over. Your trouble will all fall away when we're on the open road pushing eighty. Blessed art thou, oh Lord our God, who has created acceleration in the universe.

I'm sorry, Bayla, I said, in my imagination, but this is for your own good. Then I swept her up and heaved her onto the seat of the bike.

There was a roar and a rush of adrenaline, wind, and power, and the sweet burn of gasoline, and somehow a corridor opened up in this daydream I was having, and it ran straight from that parking lot of Klapfman's office out west to the Coast Highway. Within minutes Bayla and I were moving south. She flailed a bit at first, but keeping her safely in front of me with one hand while controlling the powerful thrust of the Road Star with the other—no problem whatsoever. We raced south, the windy Pacific breaking waves to the west, the terraced and gated housing developments in Mission Villejo to the east, flaunting at us their tangerine-colored walls and rectangular blue pools, a quiet domestic life we would never have together. We passed Camp Pendleton and the United States Marine Corps. Ninety, a hundred miles an hour, wow, and I'm humming, *From the Halls of Montezu—u—ma to the shores of Tripoli, we will fight our country's ba—a- tles on the air and land and sea.* There was not an authority figure in sight. Soon enough we crossed the border, also without incident, and gunned it a

Mexican coast down through Ensenada, then onto the Pan American Highway. I didn't have to hold Bayla in place any longer. But it was even better than that. At the next long straightaway, she turned, lifted up her face, murmured something to me that, in the rushing wind, sounded positively biblical, and then she began to kiss me. She sent her tongue into my mouth, exploring as if she were spelunking. I held them all in place—Bayla; the Hebrew words she uttered between nibbles, bites, and little gasps for air; bike; speed; tongue—and the world was absolutely perfect.

Then, and this is the beauty part, just when this sense of at-one-ment felt as if it could go on and on as long as I kept us steady on the road, and Bayla had surrendered herself to whatever it was I'd wrought, at precisely this moment, when I felt God not as anything external, but as a completely internal sense, an immanence and peace in everything—the rush of wind, the reassuring hum of engine, the traces of gasoline in the racing air, in all of this—when we were on a deserted strip of highway, a bike with a silent engine came floating toward us from behind.

I knew she was a huge one, a giant hog, immense, but completely muffled. And then there it was, pulling alongside not aggressively, in fact, but almost graciously. The bike was blindingly polished, silver spokes and golden rims, and handlebars of an unearthly chrome the likes of which neither of us had ever seen before. I couldn't even look directly at the bike, or at its rider. But there they were, unmistakably, wheel to wheel, rim to rim, spoke to spoke with us on the straightaway, going an easy ninety. The rider, best I could make out, was a man of middle age, with a red bandanna, wrap-around shades, and muscled arms bulging out of a sleeveless, leather vest. There was also a white scarf, like the Dalai Lama's very own holy neckwear, trailing behind him in perfect flutter.

The bike, I noticed, had a large *aleph* painted on the gas tank, and the man nodded, as he slowly began to accelerate by us. Be cool, brother and sister, he said to us. I kept my fingers at the controls—just in case we needed to make a quick getaway—but

Bayla was suddenly relaxed and gave the strange rider a little wave. Something had just happened. I tried to keep up, but no way could I get any more speed. The rider looked over his shoulder, a final wave from him, a beneficent rippling snap of that scarf, and he raced on, disappearing at the horizon point in a rush of speed that could not be matched by motorcycles of the Earth.

The absence of proof is, of course, no proof; yet today I believe that was the Lord taking a form I might then comprehend. To this day when I get on a bike, His look, His style, even His facial expression—one of brotherly and sisterly inclusivity—as He bade us good-bye forms the model I strive to emulate.

But Bayla did not allow me to pause very long in real time by the parked bike on that long-ago late morning. She had another destiny to pursue, and she soon enough got pissed off and yanked me away from witnessing any more of the divine ride we had just taken together. She did not even heed the Please Ring sign on Dr. Klapfman's four-paneled beige door. She simply turned the knob, pushed her sunglasses up high on the short bridge of her nose, in a gesture that may have been both unconscious and symbolic, and let us in.

CHAPTER THIRTY-ONE

Dr. Morris Klapfman had quite an unusual schnoz himself, and I could certainly see why he had found his way into the nose trans-formation business. Without filling out any paperwork, we were whisked immediately into one of his examining rooms. I took it to mean that Bayla, a daughter of privilege, was receiving the kind of special treatment elite clients such as Lucille Adler always got when they graced a doctor's premises.

I liked Klapfman immediately, which was too bad, for if Bayla's persuasiveness foundered, I would have to try to hold a gun on him. Smelling of soap, and in a standard white medical smock unbuttoned and flowing, he closed the door behind him and began rubbing his hands with a rapid eagerness as if either he needed a final touch of drying, or he couldn't wait to get his hands on the next customer.

Dr. Klapfman introduced himself to me with a quick, uncon-scious bow and pronounced Hungarian accent, and asked Bayla how her parents were. His head was large and longish with a face almost equine, framed by thin, wild hair that was slicked down a little too much for good style toward the front of his dome. All this would have made him seem nerdy if it weren't for his hyper-alert-ness—eyes that seemed to take in everything, and the nose too, as if with a life quite its own, sniffing the air for motes of information.

The prominence of the nose was offset by his crescent-shaped nos-trils, smooth and carefully groomed, and their roseate hairlessness fascinated me. His forehead was broad, outsized as well, but that was a good sign, as Ed had taught me the larger the forehead, the larger the number of brain cells inside. Dr. Klapfman would need every one of them for the job Bayla was about to charge him with.

As the doctor made small talk, quite nervously, I thought, Bayla sat on the examining room table, sidesaddle, the lucky tissue paper crinkling slightly beneath her little bottom. Because of the bright neon bulbs in the ceiling above, we both were still wearing our recently bought sunglasses. The black bag containing the money and the firepower was right beside her, with her arm draped across it. Although there was a spare chair in the corner, beneath an extravagantly detailed otolaryngological cross section of the human head, I, by plan, stood right beside Bayla, just in case, she had whispered to me as we entered, you have to threaten to shoot.

As Bayla reminded Dr. Klapfman of their previous conversations, his face seemed to grow even longer, inch by skeptical inch. Already I feared her magic was not getting off to a very quick start.

But, Bayla, I thought this was a joke between us. Ha ha!

I would never joke about something like that. Would I, Norman?

Never. Never.

Have I mentioned that Klapfman was also tall, and lanky in that way of someone who could have been a basketball player good on defense had he chosen sports instead of surgery? His hands at the ends of gangly arms—I began to take my mental measurements—would easily be able to knock down a gun brandished at him in the small confines of the examining room. But we weren't there yet and wouldn't be, if I could help it.

However, when the doctor realized Bayla was quite serious, he appealed to me.

Surely you see this is ridiculous, even if it could be done. By the way, young man, you look familiar.

He's my Hebrew tutor.

Ah, yes, I've seen you up at the house.

Now he's my fiancé.

I see. Really?

Bayla lifted up her sunglasses for a moment and aimed at me her ray-gun eyes.

Really, I said.

Well, Klapfman responded, after a long, professional clearing of his throat, congratulations are in order, I suppose. Yet it's very strange your mother didn't mention this *naches,* this joy, to come.

We planned on surprising her, said Bayla.

It's going to be a really big surprise, I added.

Bayla lifted up those sunglasses again. As if to emphasize our solidarity to the good doctor, I lifted up mine.

Klapfman had still not gotten his bearings, and who could blame the poor man?

You, young man, as her fiancé, he said, you can't possibly let this beautiful girl with her beautiful, God-given nose, go through with such nonsense. Can you? There's always, always danger involved in an untried procedure. Plus, aha, aha! Bayla, you are not married, not yet, you are a minor, so I cannot do this without parental permission! Shall I ring them up?

And, hem of gown flying, he was halfway to the door before he finished his sentence.

Please don't leave the room, Dr. Klapfman, Bayla said quietly.

No?

No. My parents will love and approve the operation because it's for the Jewish people, like I explained.

I don't think the Jewish people care one way or another about your nose, Bayla. Do you want me to lose my license? This is the state of California. There are laws, oaths, procedures. This is *mishegas,* children, what you propose. Let us understand each other.

Dr. Klapfman, Bayla said, remaining as calm as if she were merely there to get her nails done. Will this help us understand each other?

Then she pulled out one of the banded packs of hundred-dollar bills and waved it slowly in front of him like a metronome.

What is this? Put that away! It is not a question of money.

That's too bad, she answered, because we have quite a bit of it in here, don't we, Norman?

Quite a bit, I confirmed. I felt myself beginning to sweat.

I know you can perform the operation, Dr. Klapfman. Lucille says you are a genius when it comes to graft.

Not *graft*, child. *Grafting*. But . . . I . . . really . . . Bayla, it is absurd to insert a bump in the nose. Where did you get such ideas?

Were you lying to me when we discussed it?

Such discussions I don't remember, Bayla. Please. Sometimes I talk too much, make little jokes, especially with the pretty girls. That I actually would say I could do this for your nose . . . Was I drinking? No, it is impossible!

You weren't drinking, and what you said was *sculpt*. You said that human flesh was like clay in your hands. You could sculpt anything, is what you said.

There is a serious misunderstanding here.

None whatsoever.

Then you are simply lying, my dear.

Do I lie, Norman?

My experience with Bayla, Dr. Klapfman, is that she doesn't lie. I also think you should do what she says.

I refuse to do this thing.

You prefer to be coerced? Bayla said, again, almost casually, but she also began to search deeper in the bag.

Excuse me? said the doctor. What is this *coerced*?

Even though I knew all too well what she was rummaging for, that Bayla now appeared ready to go through with her plan was as surprising to me as it was to Klapfman.

A girl's bag is always so crowded, she said. O.K. Right. Here it is.

Bayla slowly withdrew the gun and handed it to me, by the barrel. Norman's going to shoot you if you don't begin the procedure right away.

The doctor seemed suddenly to lean away from us, as if pushed by an invisible wind. He took another step toward the shut door, but there was none swifter than Bayla when she wanted to be. She was off the examining table in a bound, had circled behind, and was barricading the only way out before Dr. Klapfman's long arm could grasp the handle.

Please step aside, Bayla.

Please keep your promise, Dr. Klapfman.

There is no promise. You're crazy!

No, we're not, Dr. Klapfman. We're just eager to get my nose fixed here and now. Think about it. There could be articles about you in the Jewish press, and way beyond. It'll be good for business and your reputation.

I do not need more clients, Miss Bayla Adler! My schedule is very full. My life is very nice, until you two walk in. *Gevalt!*

Look, Doctor, you want me to sign a waiver? I know all about them. That's what my father has people sign all the time. I'm happy to do that if you just break out the anesthesia and the instruments and give me the Jewish nose I want and deserve for my bat mitzvah.

My God!

It'll be the greatest bat mitzvah present anyone ever received.

I also take care of eyes and ears, and I can't believe what mine are seeing and hearing now. Stop this, children! This is a crazy experiment, and a shame for such a pretty face.

Norman?

Yes. It'll be much easier, Dr. Klapfman, on all of us, if you just do what she says. That's been my experience with Bayla.

And it is not an experiment, Bayla said. To quote you, it would simply be a tried and true procedure, only in reverse.

I said no such thing.

You did.

I did not. Are you taking any drugs, Bayla?

Just the anesthetic I am waiting for you to administer.

I refuse.

In that case, I must call on my assistant. Norman?

Actually, Bayla, I said as my heart began to sound loudly at my temple, less, in retrospect, out of fear for myself, but because Klapfman was beginning to look ashen. Sweat was pouring down his long face as if he were a horse who'd raced more miles than he ever trained for. I feared the doctor, who was considerably older than our parents, might have a heart attack and die right there. That would not be good for him, nor for me, nor for Bayla's operation. At least that was, if I can recall, the baroque argument that I pursued.

Actually, Bayla, I just don't think it's wise to shoot Dr. Klapfman.

God of mercy!

But, Norman, he won't operate!

Bayla, I agreed to hold the gun on him when he operated. *If* he operated. But if he's refusing to operate, I don't think I'm obliged to shoot him or to keep aiming at him. There's got to be another way.

Finally some sense! Bayla, you are a lovely Jewish girl. You don't need such a procedure. Marry this obviously intelligent young man, this tutor of yours. I had an aunt once in Budapest who married her tutor. Turned out to be a lovely couple. Have children. Raise a Jewish family. Your nose will not get in your way. If, later, when you're older, you want to discuss this, then come to me. No charge.

Instantly I knew that Klapfman had set us back. Bayla hated to be denied. She hated to be lectured, or told she was too young for this or couldn't yet understand that. Once I'd heard Lucille tell her that she could only understand something later, after she became a mother herself; and her reaction had been to fling two chairs at Lucille down the length of the boardroom table. She found most of what passed for wisdom in the adult world either laziness of mind or bias masquerading in clichés and nostrums, and it was all just plain infuriatingly stupid to her. This was one of Bayla's finest traits.

No wonder I allowed myself to be her accomplice.

Now she motioned me over to her where she barricaded the door, and I obliged. She took the gun from me as if I were a misbehaving boy who had gotten hold of a toy that was intended for another.

You, she said, to me, have a seat. And Dr. Klapfman, you get yourself up on that table.

Bayla.

Now! Let me play doctor.

CHAPTER THIRTY-TWO

So the doctor hoisted himself up on his own examining table.

Lie down, Doctor, and she waved the gun at him. Stretch out, please.

It'll be better for your blood pressure, Doctor, I offered from my chair.

Norman, I expected better from you.

Before I could answer, the doctor pushed up into a sitting position and cried, What is this? You walk in here, the two of you in your leather this and that and with your sunglasses on and your swagger and your weapon and you order people about like . . . like those two criminals from before you were born. Like Clyde Barrow and Bonnie Parker.

Who? she said.

You're like a Jewish Bonnie and Clyde. You're ridiculous. I'm a doctor. I am not a bank that you should threaten to hold me up. *Gott im himmel!* What do you want of me!

You know what we want. Lie down, doctor.

As he slid back onto the examining table—for what else would a sane man do confronting Bayla Adler's Luger?—she was practically stroking his nose with the barrel of the gun. From my perch I saw poor Klapfman's darting eyes, Bayla's back, and the gray-black sheen of the weapon.

Bayla, sweet child, isn't that gun from . . . the war?

Yes, it is. I know what you're thinking. But think on this, Dr. Klapfman, what if it does work, if it does go off?

Bayla, my darling, let me call your sweet mother and father.

Sweet mother?

No? Oh, God! I see I've said the wrong thing.

She's not my mother! Bayla screamed.

Children, please, how long can this go on? I am a busy man. My assistant out there will soon knock on the door. I'm a man in demand. If I don't respond, they will call the police. Perhaps they have begun to dial already. Things bad will happen. If I can help you at home in any way, Bayla, tell me how and tell me now.

Operate, Doctor. Just operate.

This I can't do.

Don't shoot him, Bayla.

I'm frustrated, Norman. I'm very frustrated.

I have an idea, I said, and, for a change, I actually did. What if the doctor promises that although he can't give you the reverse nose job you want, still he agrees to discontinue the basic nose job for all Jewish girls who come seeking them? What do you say to that?

Excuse me?

He will sign a paper, a contract, that he promises you, Bayla Adler, that as *his* bat mitzvah gift to you, and all of Israel, Jewish noses in Los Angeles will be allowed to remain Jewish noses. No more operations performed on these premises. What do you say, Doctor?

Well . . . I've never heard of such a—

Of course you haven't. I've just thought of it! But it's simple: a moratorium on all nose operations for Jewish girls. You'll do this for Bayla, whom you love. Whom I love.

You're giving up too soon, Hebrew tutor. We've got the gun.

Who's giving up? I'm simply . . . adjusting to a changing situation. Plus he's nervous about the operation. I can see that. You see that too. He's never done it before. He'd have to improvise. I don't want to see you being a guinea pig, or getting hurt or scarred, or worse, Bayla. What do you say, Doctor?

I say you're ridiculous, the both of you.

May I point out that you're lying on your own examining room table. A very beautiful girl who is passionate about her Jewish heritage and wants to express it through her nose, among other ways, is aiming a gun at you because you are being recalcitrant, or, worse, going back on a promise you made her and are now denying. Who's ridiculous?

I made no promises.

I think that what we're asking of you—if no operation, then a moratorium on this practice embarrassing to the faith—is simply . . . And here I sought to find just the right word, because as I spoke to Klapfman I was detecting ever so slight a shift in Bayla as she had lowered the Luger an inch or two and instead of aiming at the doctor's nose, it was pointed now to a spot midway between his belly button and his groin. I chose to take this as a sign of possible flexibility in her, and I didn't want to squander it through wrong vocabulary. Bayla may not have been much of a student, but she was superbly sensitive to diction, at least, it seemed, to mine.

What Bayla is doing, Doctor, is nothing short of praiseworthy. Consider it. There must be a better way to earn a living than messing with noses.

You could restrict your practice to ears, for example, Bayla said.

How do I know that one day you won't run in here with a machine gun and threaten me about ears?

Jewish ears are not an issue, Dr. Klapfman, I said. Never have been, never will be. A non-starter of a controversy, I assure you.

I'm still really disappointed about my nose, Bayla said. I've been dreaming about the operation. I've been planning on this, Norman, ever since we met.

Really?

Since that first day you walked in. I said to myself then, Yes, here is the boy. He's quite a Hebrew tutor, isn't he, Dr. Klapfman?

Yes, yes.

So do we have a deal, Doctor?

I'm thinking on it.

Bayla?

I'm thinking too.

Please! Can you put that gun down while this thinking is occurring?

The thing is, Doctor, I hate what you've done to Lucille. Her face is like a tray with a service of crystal on it. How can you do that kind of thing to her?

It is her face, child. How do you know there is not more unhappiness without the procedures?

I can't stand to look at her anymore. I want to walk in there with the nose on me that she got rid of from herself using money from old Jews going into her nursing homes. I want to see the expression on her sharp little face when I walk in, and—

Bayla, I interrupted. He's not going to do it. He's not going to perform the reverse nose job.

Let's go then, Norman.

Yes, go. Please go.

There are other doctors who will do it. Remember?

What others? said the doctor.

Others, Bayla said to him, moving the gun like a baton about the room. In Mexico, other places.

Butchers, said Klapfman. You could get a serious infection or bleed to death.

Then sign this, I said to Klapfman, having pulled out from my back pocket one of my *machbarot*, the thin writing notebooks I had been using these many months to teach Bayla Hebrew. As other people carried handkerchiefs, I always had one of these rolled and stuffed in the back pocket of my jeans, beside my comb. Never had a Hebrew workbook been of greater service. On the first sheet, I wrote the cease-and-desist-nose-jobs contract.

After scanning it, the doctor asked, What about non-Jews?

On them you can do what you want.

Go on, sign it, Doctor: a moratorium on nose operations for the Jewish girls. Bayla, will that do it for you? Will you put down the gun if he signs?

I'm still thinking, she said to me, and I could see that she really was.

I wouldn't want anything to happen to your face, Bayla. I told her. I love your face the way it is.

You're afraid, aren't you, Hebrew tutor, if I get myself a Jewish nose?

Meaning what?

The thing is, Norman, I don't think you love the people of Israel as much as I do now, she said, with a wave of the gun toward a place on the far wall of the room, across from the nose chart, where a window might have been, had there been windows in the examining room. I don't think you're going to be a rabbi at all, or a teacher like Michael Levin, or any of those people out there when you grow up. I think you're going to travel as far away from the Jews as you can get. I think you like me, Norman, precisely because I'm so different, including my nose, from all the Jewish girls you have ever known. I'm the future for you, Norman, and you like it just the way it is. You wouldn't want to see me wake up from the operation and look like your past. If he made me look like Sarah Bernhardt, would you still love me and want to marry me?

It was difficult for me to take all this in. So odd, so unexpected. It had never occurred to me to think about any of this, which is not to say that it didn't have merit. Bayla had this eruptive ability, one moment to sound like the peeved and petty sixteen-year-old spoiled rich girl she was, and then in the next instant to expose and accuse me and the whole world like a prophet.

All that sounds like an episode from *The Twilight Zone,* I said, and now's not the time for it. Will you please let Dr. Klapfman sign what we've discussed, and then we'll sign too. We'll have a real contract, and we can get back on the bike and ride. How about it?

Can we trust him, Norman? He could be operating as soon as we leave.

I assure you, said Klapfman, as his large head rolled forward into his hands as if it were suddenly too heavy to be held by the normal anatomical means. There will be no more operations, of any kind, today.

But what about tomorrow and the day after?

Doctor? I said.

Yes, yes, I'm thinking. I'm considering. Put away your paper. What do you know about the law? An agreement signed under duress is no agreement at all. May I look at the gun, Bayla?

We could take you with us, you know, Dr. Klapfman. Norman and I could strap you across the Road Star and take you as a hostage to Mexico. You won't have to worry about licenses and laws down there.

The doctor, who had risen from his examining table and was standing with his head bowed and his hands cupped in front of his groin—it was hard to tell if the posture was for prayer or for protection—began to mutter some words in Yiddish but otherwise remained very still. Slowly, however, his manner changed and he raised his hand and he touched the gun with a gesture I can only describe as affectionate, even benedictional.

Your mother's?

Bayla nodded.

Some wordless current ran between them. I began to wonder if Klapfman had perhaps been in the partisans with Bayla's mother. Maybe he had loved her too, once, long ago during the war. Maybe the young medical student had lost out to the young nursing-home king. Maybe Bayla knew of this. So many maybes. But there was some connection, some karma at play in that room as surely and as solidly as there was a table there, and a chair. How crazy I was then, crazy and in a such a swoon of wonderful, heedless love that we both could have ended up doing serious jail time. Now, as if in slow motion, and to my mounting surprise and profound relief, Bayla handed Dr. Klapfman the gun.

Promise you won't call the cops? she said to him.

Of course not.

Or my parents? You promise?

No, darling girl.

What?

I mean, yes, I promise, and, no, I won't call them. Go. Go. Go. Get the hell out of here and may you never do anything like this again. Jewish children! No charges will be pressed. Just leave, leave.

And we did.

CHAPTER THIRTY-THREE

Outside the sun shone on us like a spotlight, and the bike was there too, solid and reliable friend that it always was.

You did pretty well in there, Hebrew tutor.

I did, didn't I?

We mounted up, she in front and then I behind, my arms around her.

Thinking on your feet. Inventive. Getting something for me.

I know when to throw in the cards and when not to, Bayla. That I know. So where to now?

Let's just ride.

How to explain all this to you, dear readers? We rode for another day, not down the coast as I had thought, but north up past San Simeon, on the Coast Highway toward Half Moon Bay. We had lunch on an old fishing pier and drove into what would later become wine country around Santa Ynez and San Luis Obispo. Yes, we were running away, but we also knew we would return, she to her life and I to mine, although to different versions of each forever changed by what we had done, and we weren't finished yet. We knew this so deeply, it never even occurred to us to ruin what we were doing by admitting it; we even studied a little Hebrew in motel rooms by the sea.

The motorcycle hummed beneath us for two more days, and then early on the next morning we pulled up in front of my house. It was just before dawn, the time I still like to arrive or depart for a good long ride, a prayer service, or preferably both. The street was hushed, the drapes of the picture window still.

Don't worry, she said, I won't go in.

I wouldn't mind if you did. You'd be the first person I wouldn't mind coming in. Come in if you want to, Bayla.

It's too late, Norman. I mean, too early.

Without uttering many more words than those—that is, nothing of that stuff about life and love, Kierkegaard, Kafka, and Sartre that we'd go on to b.s. about ad nauseum in college—we had decided: we really were far too young to get married. I was going away to college soon, and I knew it was going to be to a school as far away from L.A. as possible, which meant far away from Bayla too. The only further studying she wanted to do, she said, was by riding a bike around the world. I told her that I knew she would do it. She said she just might have a bat mitzvah, too. She'd figure out what to say, where and when, but, she wouldn't take any money for it. Not a nickel from anyone. I told her that I'd return from wherever I was, no matter the distance or circumstances, to be with her, if she wanted. And if we found we still loved each other—whatever that meant—we'd see.

We decided an awful lot out there as we leaned against the bike in that early morning hour. It was August 16, 1963—the Russians hadn't nuked us yet, JFK had promised more support for Israel, and the Dodgers, still being led by Koufax's incredible arm and Frank Howard's power, were now definitely on their way to a championship season. As the night dew still glistened on the lawn and on the path up to the porch, the snails peeked out of their delicate brown shells and tested the air with their antennae.

We also decided that if there were another Cuban missile crisis or anything like that in the next months, we would definitely find each other, marry, ride off, and have children together as fast as we could. We'd travel to Australia and New Zealand, where the biking is terrific, I know now, and we might survive.

We also vowed that if the whole world escaped destruction and we along with it for twenty years more, we would meet then at dawn at the Griffith Park Observatory. She would ride up on her bike and I would ride up on mine. We would do this no matter what paths we had taken in life. It would be exactly like the O. Henry short story we had both read in school, "After Twenty Years." It would be like that, only on motorcycles. So we decided.

There was one more kiss beside the Road Star while the dew sparkled, the engine idled, and our hearts—well, mine anyway—filled up with a longing that has never been satisfied. That is the source, I think, of why I always become restless and then need to ride; the source of why I am a searching man, most at home, most in the spirit, when I'm leaving here and going there, but not yet arrived, not ever arrived.

Bayla drew my face close to hers so my lips were touching her incomparable nose. Then she whispered to me. What she said I will never reveal—except to say that it was in a Hebrew without error. Then she rode away.

CHAPTER THIRTY-FOUR

Ed and Esther accepted with remarkable grace the near complete silence that was my response when they asked about what had happened during the four days we were away. They really did know, by remembering their own big moments from their own childhoods, I'm sure, that whatever I shared with them of my adventure would be taken away from me; so after a few sardonic remarks, my parents ceased their nudging.

Bayla's words to me, her whisperings, her scent, the sound of the gunned engine, the peal of the tires, her audacious laugh—all the memories were indeed like an emotional savings account on which I might build, or at least depend, in the months and years to come. They were therefore worth far more than money, and these riches of recollection, which my parents let alone to grow, only increased for me in value and have continued so all my life since.

Amazingly, on the Monday after our return, Lucille called. Bayla's bat mitzvah had not been cancelled, she said, only delayed somewhat. That's the word she used: *somewhat.* Without a reference to the time we had been away together or what had happened between her stepdaughter and me, she asked me to resume the tutoring.

Learning for learning's sake, shall we call it?

When I asked her if Bayla really wanted to resume, she replied, I would not be calling you, Nehemiah, if it were otherwise. She was more formal than I could recall her ever being before; she was certainly not the Lucille of the gift of the green bathing suit, the revealing dresses, and the huge tips. Maybe Bayla had kept a vow of silence on our days together, just as I had, or maybe Lucille knew everything. I didn't care. I was so happy to return to Bel Air that I could have cried.

The Hudson, however, didn't seem to share my ardor. Or maybe what it was expressing was resentment for a new preoccupation—not just untamed girls like Bayla, but motorcycles. I leave it to you to decide if an engine can become jealous, but the Hudson made sounds I had not heard before. Unsure of itself, self-conscious, it seemed reluctant, living from sputter to sputter without a clean, continuous burn. A third of the way up to Bel Air, the Hudson simply broke down. The spot it chose was on Santa Monica Boulevard, not more than two blocks from Dr. Morris Klapfman's office.

No amount of new oil worked, and after two attempts I was lucky to get the car over to the side of the road. I waited another ten minutes, turned the key, but still, no ignition, not even a click. When I lifted the hood, I found the engine spattered with oil and other hemorrhaging fluids.

I located a phone booth at the corner and thought of calling the Adlers to apologize for not being able to get up there. Yet I hesitated to pull open the folding door of the booth. If I didn't call and instead prayed as hard as I could, offering multiple *brochas,* maybe some mechanical miracle could be wrought on the Hudson to make it function now just one more time, please, I seemed to be saying, just one more ignition to carry me up to see Bayla.

The Hudson's radiator let off a plume of steam, and I realized how ridiculous my request was. If I called a cab instead, appealed to a more earthly power, even if I managed to get up to Bel Air with time left to tutor, which was highly unlikely, how would I return home? I guess I could call for another cab to take me back—what was twenty or thirty dollars to me and my still bursting wallet?

THE HEBREW TUTOR OF BEL AIR

Or, if Lucille were there, maybe she'd insist on driving me home. She had already said many times that she wanted to meet my parents; wouldn't I be giving her that opportunity? I could definitely see how they might sit among the dust balls of our living room, ask me to run out on some errand, and then discuss for an hour what their children had been up to.

Or maybe Lucille had been outright lying to me. Maybe she wanted to get me up there alone, to get even with her stepdaughter. Maybe Bayla would not be home—if Bayla were really going to resume tutoring, wouldn't she have called me herself? Bayla hadn't at all sounded as if she were ready to pick up where we had left off. Bayla sounded like she was closing a whole chapter, and that was all right, because so was I. Wasn't that what our trip had been all about?

The more I sampled these various plotlines, the more I realized that the Hudson was doing me a favor in breaking down. I do believe a machine, especially the marvelous internal combustion engine, does have a touch of a soul, by the way. You can't explain some things theologically—you just feel the truth of it beneath you. So when the cab dispatcher I had called picked up, I told him, Thank you, but my problem was suddenly solved.

Where do you want one to go? he insisted.

Nowhere, I told him. I'm not going anywhere, and I hung up.

I opened the booth's door and carefully stepped out. I leaned against the fender of the Hudson. It was really hot, but I forced myself to stay pressed against the metal. I raised my eyes to the elegant palm trees swaying slightly in the distance as if directing the traffic along the San Diego Freeway going north, and the city became almost silent to me but also brighter, and full of a sense of the future I would not alter by going up to tutor that day.

CHAPTER THIRTY-FIVE

A horse named Newman (close enough to Norman) had finally come through for Ed, big time. Ed was at home when I returned; it was very unusual for him to be enjoying his winning this way, but there he was. I could see his left pants pocket bulging with his money roll while he watered the grass and the small bed of yellow and pink snapdragons beneath the picture window, which he took particular pride in. Ed looked up to greet me when the tow truck brought me home from the garage where I had left the Hudson.

Newman was a thoroughbred with an uncertain start but a lightning finish, Ed said, as if we'd been discussing it together already for a half hour, and without as much as asking me what in the world I was doing in the cab of a tow truck. In short he was plain excited that there was going to be lots of money for us for a change. I knew instantly that "lots" would last a few weeks, maybe a month, at most. When he finally asked about the car and I told him the engine was shot, Ed said, We'll get you another one. And not another jalopy. Whenever you need it. Not a problem.

In the following days, the weather dramatically cooled and it felt like summer's real end was in sight. There were no more calls from Bel Air. School would resume, my last year, in two weeks, and shortly after that the high holidays, and all the pattern of my life, familiar, but also now forever changed.

Esther said it would be only polite and professional for me to try to call the Adlers. Since no resistance arose in me, surprisingly,

I picked up the phone and called, but no one answered at Bayla's mansion. Had I misdialed? I called again, and by the time I hung up this time, an aroma of onions simmering in butter had filled up the house, and I heard my mother humming away, likely something from *Oklahoma*. She reminded me how much she liked Joel McCrea's voice. He is a fine actor, she said, completely unappreciated. His time will come, she said. That was Esther's view of history, I think, that for everyone, a time would come. She aimed her remarks out the window above the sink where she worked, out where she was looking toward the Nefussis' window. I took the words personally, a comment on Bayla and me. Our time would come.

I didn't call the Adlers again, nor did they contact me, and a week passed during which the most astonishing happening was that Ed stayed home every night. On August 28, we watched the news together. We heard Martin Luther King, Jr., give his I Have a Dream speech in front of the Lincoln Memorial in Washington. We were all silent when it was over. And it was the only time I ever saw my father cry.

After dinner Ed went back to his chair and his paper and I to my thoughts. My sense of oppression had lifted, and I felt like thanking God both for Bayla Adler and now MLK. Maybe I'd become a rabbi after all, like Abraham Joshua Heschel, just so I could lock arms with Reverend King and march with him. Maybe I'd forget all the Jewish stuff, go to law school, and work in the South. Who knew.

What I did know was that I was going to leave this place fairly soon, so I did a Joel McCrea imitation along with Esther to amuse her and Ed. I parted the drapes and peered out at the quiet street. Carmen Nefussi and her father were pruning their rose bushes, and Ed said the Nefussis had told him earlier that they were selling their house. Maybe it was in part from the exuberance of his win, but Ed went on that we would never leave our house, that although more and more white families were moving out, Ed had decided that he had no problems with Negroes and that we were going to stay.

We stay and we help out the guy who needs it most; that's what Jews do, right, Norman?

Right, Dad. Very right.

I was proud of him for saying this that night, even though I knew that following any fleeing whites would never be an option because we barely could afford this house, let alone a more expensive one like up where Rabbi Joel and Esther's sisterhood friends lived. Still, all the blackjack and the poker weekends and the horses were once again O.K. with me, and were suddenly, inextricably, linked with my father's values. A defender of the common man, an acknowledged underdog himself, my father, Ed.

It was all, of course, too good to last. Ed was fond of saying that the wheel of fortune is not only always turning, it is also being run by a carnival operator with no teeth and bad breath who sometimes falls asleep or wanders off to have a corn dog. Under those circumstances, you just never know.

That night, I began to feel not like the young man I had just become, thanks to Bayla Adler, but like a little kid, between the ages of maybe seven and ten, when, as Ed never ceased reminding me, kids are perfect because they are old enough to go to the track with you but still young enough not to talk back.

I went up to him, sitting there behind his paper, and wanted to give him something. I felt strangely full of a tenderness I didn't understand because it came to me so infrequently, and it was wrapped in this childishness that no longer seemed right for me to own. I decided to play a trick on my father in order to show that I loved him, to be, for him, seven years old once again.

As I got on my knees behind his *L.A. Times,* getting ready to surprise and probably irritate him with a silly face emerging from behind the edge of his paper, I saw it: at the bottom, a small article, which he had apparently missed, or he would have announced the news to me: Nursing Home Operators Indicted.

Sure enough, David and Lucille Adler, I read, were among those cited. The charges included excessive billing, submitting forms for those who had already died, and other schemes to skim money from the reimbursement agencies. More than seven million dollars was unaccounted for.

What are you doing there? Ed said, his irritation growing.

Peek-a-boo, I answered.

In the following weeks the indictments grew and became major news that lasted for months. There was no resumption of tutoring, and although my mother scanned the Jewish papers, there was no indication that Bayla Adler's bat mitzvah was back on.

Ed took what might have been the position of a public relations firm the Adlers hired, that a lavish affair would be unseemly with all those old people suffering from bed sores that could have been prevented.

She will never have a bat mitzvah, I told them. Not here, not ever.

The whole thing was ugly, bad for the elderly, bad for L.A., bad for the Jews. Good only for the anti-Semites, Ed said.

As we followed the story, I imagined a knock at our door, and a detective, like Jack Webb from *Dragnet,* standing there demanding to see the records of my tutoring, the contents of my mother's *knippel,* and the receipts from our jaunt. Furthermore, what, if anything, could I tell him of the surgical practice of one Dr. Morris Klapfman?

That knock on our door never came.

CHAPTER THIRTY-SIX

Shortly before Hanukkah and the winter break, in mid-December of '63, Michael Levin announced that he would stop teaching at the University of Judaism. Although his name never appeared officially linked to the Adlers in the scandal, everyone knew he was Lucille's uncle. I insisted that he was innocent until proven guilty, and no one was going to prove saintly Michael Levin guilty. What I wanted to remember was his praying in the hallway, my subbing for him, his caring face, his cologne, and how he had loved hearing about Bayla and me studying by the pool.

Eventually, I heard, Levin got a job teaching at the first Hebrew Academy in Ventura. But then not long after Lucille and her husband divorced, my mother said Levin got sick with cancer and went to live with his sister in Tarzana. As for Carlos and Bayla, once or twice, as the years went on, I thought I saw them in surfing movies on late night TV, but I'm not sure. Once, as I was driving along Sunset out toward UCLA, a motorcycle sped by. Both driver and passenger were in leather, and the woman's hair was streaming behind her, and I thought I heard Bayla's voice call my name. Yet who can be sure, especially a person like me who often imagined what he didn't live? I heard that Carlos became a chiropractor, but I'm not sure of that either.

My father died of cancer—a tumor, he said after the doctor's visit, exactly the size and shape of a poker chip. I rode bikes all through college, and beyond. I've had six motorcycles. Currently

I'm riding a Harley, Special Edition. I divorced twice, both times amicably—and I should add, from wives who refused to ride with me. I went through many periods when my yearning to meet up with Bayla again was difficult to contain. I certainly was at the Observatory on that morning two decades after I last saw her. I stared at the pendulum, daring it to act contrary to gravity, and I put a quarter in a telescope and scanned my home city through the smoggy haze. I waited for two hours and forty minutes after the appointed time.

I was of course disappointed but not completely surprised either. My mother wrote that she'd heard Bayla had emigrated to Israel, that she lived on a kibbutz, and insisted on doing guard duty even though only men, back then, were allowed. She said that Bayla had become a crack shot in the Israeli army. I thought of vacationing in Israel, renting a bike, tracking Bayla down, and riding up to her at her guard post, or wherever. I'd keep my visor down for the surprise, but maybe she would shoot me before I could lift it. I heard from someone else from Junior Cong, who claimed to have stayed in touch with Bayla, that she'd become very Orthodox and had eight kids. Of all this, I just can't be sure.

Do I still want to see her again? Of course, but finally I've entered a calm place: last wife gone, kids out in the world, enough pension to live on if I keep it modest. You know, semiretired. But I don't like to be idle. So I'm really interested in being your spiritual leader. You know, according to Kabbalah, there are the white letters, invisible in the white space in the prayer book, and the black. We read the black, but the white space is the goal—it's the white space, where language fails, that's really exciting. That's where God resides—that's where we go when we fire up the engines and ride. Amen.

It won't surprise you to hear, in conclusion, that I haven't been in a temple, a traditional temple, that is, for many years, but as I say, for me Hebrew prayer and the sound of the bike out on the open road, that's all the temple I need. So, King Solomon Bikers

Club, if you want a conventional rabbi, I'm not your guy. You've got my story now, my application, and a lot more, I'm certain, than you ever expected. Salary requirements you asked about? Hey, even a labor of love deserves a minimum wage. Check out Sanhedrin 12:54. But I tell you honestly, I feel, having written this, that whatever your decision, I've been paid already, amply and in full.

P.S. At my mother's funeral—which, by the way, I conducted myself, in Hebrew—as I was saying how she was wonderful to Ed in his final illness, and how she had always loved following the lives of the Hollywood stars, but that he, my dad, was really her one true star and she'd hitched her wagon to him, or some such, I became choked with tears. I couldn't continue. I was remembering, and I think this is my greatest regret, how many times it would have been so easy to bring my mother to see Paulette Goddard's mansion, Bayla's house in Bel Air, but I never did.

ENJOY MORE BY ALLAN APPEL

CLUB REVELATION

ISBN 978-1-56689-118-9 | $14.95

In his hilarious follow-up to *High Holiday Sutra*, Allan Appel takes another irreverent view of religious manners, this time examining what faith and marriage mean today. In *Club Revelation*, three interfaith Jewish/Christian couples unwittingly rent the ground floor of their brownstone to a charming, young Southern evangelist. Serving up his own blend of Christian cuisine, he opens a restaurant in the space, hoping to convert the Jews of the Upper West Side. His scheme threatens to destroy the harmony of the building when one of his six landlords finds comfort—and much more—in the preacher's conversion-by-gastronomy methods.

HIGH HOLIDAY SUTRA

ISBN 978-1-56689-065-6 | $13.95

Selected for the Barnes & Noble
Discover Great New Writers Program

"Hilarious . . . In this deft satire, Allan Appel plays devil's advocate, wryly prodding readers to ponder the validity of borrowing from other religions to fill the gaps in one's own."

—*New York Times Book Review*

COFFEE HOUSE PRESS

THE COFFEE HOUSES of seventeenth-century England were places of fellowship where ideas could be freely exchanged. In the cafés of Paris in the early years of the twentieth century, the surrealist, cubist, and dada art movements began. The coffee houses of 1950s America provided refuge and tremendous literary energy. Today, coffee house culture abounds at corner shops and online.

Coffee House Press continues these rich traditions. We envision all our authors and all our readers—be they in their living room chairs, at the beach, or in their beds—joining us around an ever-expandable table, drinking coffee and telling tales. And in the process of this exchange of stories by writers who speak from many communities and cultures, the American mosaic becomes reinvented, and reinvigorated.

We invite you to join us in our effort to welcome new readers to our table, and to the tales told in the pages of Coffee House Press books.

Please visit www.coffeehousepress.org for more information.

COLOPHON

The Hebrew Tutor of Bel Air was designed at Coffee House Press, in the historic
Grain Belt Brewery's Bottling House near downtown Minneapolis.
The text is set in Garamond.

FUNDER ACKNOWLEDGMENTS

Coffee House Press is an independent nonprofit literary publisher. Our books are made
possible through the generous support of grants and gifts from many foundations, corporate giving programs, state and federal support, and through donations from individuals
who believe in the transformational power of literature. Coffee House receives major general operating support from the McKnight Foundation, the Bush Foundation, from Target,
and from the Minnesota State Arts Board, through an appropriation by the Minnesota
State Legislature and from the National Endowment for the Arts. Coffee House also
receives support from: three anonymous donors; the Elmer L. and Eleanor J. Andersen
Foundation; Bill Berkson; the James L. and Nancy J. Bildner Foundation; the Patrick and
Aimee Butler Family Foundation; the Buuck Family Foundation; the law firm of
Fredrikson & Byron, P.A.; Jennifer Haugh; Anselm Hollo and Jane Dalrymple-Hollo;
Jeffrey Hom; Stephen and Isabel Keating; Robert and Margaret Kinney; the Kenneth Koch
Literary Estate; Allan & Cinda Kornblum; Seymour Kornblum and Gerry Lauter;
the Lenfestey Family Foundation; Ethan J. Litman; Mary McDermid; Rebecca Rand; the
law firm of Schwegman, Lundberg, Woessner, P.A.; Charles Steffey and Suzannah Martin;
John Sjoberg; Jeffrey Sugerman; Stu Wilson and Mel Barker; the Archie D. & Bertha H.
Walker Foundation; the Woessner Freeman Family Foundation; the Wood-Rill
Foundation; and many other generous individual donors.

NATIONAL
ENDOWMENT
FOR THE ARTS

*This activity is made possible
in part by a grant from the
Minnesota State Arts Board,
through an appropriation by the
Minnesota State Legislature
and a grant from the National
Endowment for the Arts.* MINNESOTA
STATE ARTS BOARD

TARGET.

To you and our many readers across the country,
we send our thanks for your continuing support.

Good books are brewing at coffeehousepress.org